THE ROBIN

MARK BERRY

Prime Seven Media
518 Landmann St.
Tomah City, WI 54660

Printed in the United States of America

PREFACE

Father! Father! Derick, Sabastian's son, cried out his name loudly. Alarmed by this, Juliette knew his actions were unusual. And the look on his face puzzled both parents. Quickly they responded asking him what was wrong. Without hesitation Derick asked his father a question that shocked him and his mother very much. Derick said, "My friends and I were playing at school, they- all wanted to know if you were a killer"?

This question sent shockwaves throughout Sabastian as well as his mother. Juliette slowly sat beside her husband's side waiting for his response. A difficult reply was not something either of them were prepared to answer, but knew they had no choice but to tell him the truth. Dericks eyes were riveted on his parents. Slowly Sabastian began, first asking Derick to sit down. " I want you to listen closely to me and your mother, we will tell you everything you need to know."

Before Sabastian spoke, he drew his wife near him and gave her a small kiss on her cheek. He slowly began speaking. "Son", he said" "You know your mother was born in Nigeria." "Ten years ago, before I met your mother I was presented an offer to observe the President of her country. The request was by a man I had known for many years as well other people in Washington I have never met. The country was at war and thousands of innocent people had died fighting against exploitation and corruption at the highest degree imaginable."

"There is no reason I continue explaining the situation, but my job was unofficially ordered and recognized by no one except my boss and a select few people in powerful offices held in Washington and across the world." "Officially I was a hired assassin my name was never known by anyone except my boss, and my personal associates, all the other people, they only knew me as The Robin." "Juliette asked her son who would ask you such a question"? His answer instantly caught her husband's attention. "He said, "James Darford" suddenly this was making more sense to Sabastian. He said, "That is the airplane pilot's name who told me to jump into the jungle 100 miles from Abuja.

The boy sat perfectly still. Please father tell me what you did it for! Mr. Darford did have a passenger and that was me that jumped into the forest/jungle. He never knew my name or reason to be there in the country, basic information. Just business. Things have a way of changing; we meet again in Texas and hired him to bring your mother out of Nigeria. That was when we were married, and you were conceived.

Julliette kicked Sabastian but was not laughing! Starring saying nothing. Okay it was a little different than that. You and your mother were passengers on Mr. Dartford's airplane. I believe in your mother with all my heart. Your mother and you mean the world to me in so many ways. The world is changing rapidly, heading over the cliff speedily. We have nations fighting nations constantly. I need to leave town this month due to urgent investment issues. I must take this matter into my own hands.

Sabastian picked up where he stopped reading his messages, a slight look of horror wore through his persona. Derrick watched over his dad intently. The years from then to now have been working in everybody's favor. Uniting the governments and rival territories were massive undertakings.

Pacing, his words somberly suddenly was on another subject, nuclear war. This country is the strongest of all these dictators and out- right liars have with threats of today's news on its end!! World War Three is imminent, the United States has all but collapsed now, most everyone is dead is what I heard. This is what the headlines are even predicting every aspect of nuclear wars. The people with these weapons do not play fair any longer. Sometimes the other steps get shifted, game points for whichever maniac wins.

Son go back to your friends, let any mystery between them be your building block, today is what is the most important thing. Go play and don't hurt yourself. Derrick just said "It is all a remarkable story, but I am confused. Jullette was with her uncle, yes and Jennifer and your uncles. Son there is no uncomplicated way to explain it but her country, Juliette, interrupted. THE country hails your father as a hero.

Juliette was not finished. Without your father's courageous act thousands more innocent Nigerian people would have kept dying under that tyrant's rein in power. Derrick, you never met Durbish, he was akin to a boss of mine. He died not long after returning to America and passed away suddenly in Washington.

You should know this story from multiple viewpoints as it is important you understand. Derrick was on pins and needles, is this alright son?

Sebastian acknowledged his ignorance and felt out of place, but in confinement, he let his mind relax. The World Organization and its rules were not beyond him. But explaining why he killed to his son was much harder to do then ergonomics.

Sebastian sighed deeply, the weight of years of solitude pressing heavily upon his shoulders. The narratives of past glories and covert operations had gradually become the only companions of his aging mind. The memories, once vivid, now seemed like distant echoes fading into the void of time.

"Son," he began again, his voice softer but tinged with a somber resonance, "there comes a time in every person's life when the weight of past decisions and the solitude of old age converge. I find myself standing on that precipice now, looking back at a life filled with secrets, sacrifices, and the constant shadow of danger."

Juliette's gaze softened, understanding the unspoken melancholy in her husband's words. She wrapped her arms around him, offering silent support.

"It's true, son," Sebastian continued, "the world is a ruthless place, as we grow older, we often find ourselves more and more alone. Friends and loved ones drift away, and we are left with the ghosts of our past. But amidst this solitude, we must find strength. Strength to face the future, to protect those we love, and to make peace with the decisions we've made."

Derrick listened intently, the gravity of his father's words sinking in. He could see the weariness in Sebastian's eyes, the burden of a lifetime of covert operations and the toll it had taken on his soul.

"Father," Derrick said quietly, "you are not alone. We are here with you, and we will face whatever comes together."

Sebastian smiled faintly; his heart warmed by his son's words. In that moment, he realized that despite the loneliness that often goes with age, the bonds of family and love could provide the strength to endure.

As the evening shadows lengthened, the family remained close, drawing comfort from one another. The road ahead was uncertain, but they would face it together, united by the ties that bound them and the love that transcended the passage of time.

With an unsustainable pace, it was affecting millions of people now in many ways and areas. His actions really were his way to honor good versus evil.

Sebastian's mind wandered to the complexities of faith and the actions conducted in its name. He had seen countless acts committed under the banner of religion, many of which seemed far removed from the true teachings of Christ—teachings centered on love, compassion, and forgiveness. He pondered the dichotomy between those who truly followed the path of Christ and those who used religion as a guise for their own pursuits.

"Son," he said, breaking the silence, "there is something I need you to understand about the world and the way people use religion. True faith, true following of Christ, is about embodying His principles, not just in words but in actions. It's about love, kindness, and humility. Yet, so often, we see people commit acts of cruelty and hatred, claiming they do so in God's name. This is not what Christ desires from us."

Derrick nodded thoughtfully, absorbing his father's wisdom. "But why, Father? Why do people do these things if they know it goes against the true teachings?"

"Fear, power, ignorance," Sebastian replied. "People often fear what they do not understand, and they sometimes twist faith to justify their actions or to gain control over others. It's a tragic misuse of something meant to bring light and hope into the world. We must strive to be different, to follow the true path of Christ, even if it means standing against the tide."

Juliette, still holding onto Sebastian, added, "We must remember that each of us has a duty to ensure our actions reflect our true beliefs. It's easy to be swayed by the masses, but it takes courage to stay true to one's faith and principles."

As the conversation deepened, the family realized that their journey was not just about confronting external threats but also about staying true to their inner moral compass. They vowed to uphold the values of love, compassion, and integrity, no matter the challenges they faced.

With renewed determination, they prepared to face the uncertain future, knowing that their strength lay not just in their unity but in their unwavering commitment to living a life of true faith and purpose.

The passage of time had a way of blurring the lines between people and territorial boundaries. As societies evolved and cultures intermingled, the once rigid borders that separated nations and communities began to fade. This phenomenon presented both opportunities and challenges, as old prejudices and conflicts resurfaced in new forms.

"Father," Derrick asked, "how do we navigate a world where boundaries are no longer clear, and people's identities are constantly shifting?" Sebastian sighed, contemplating the weight of the question. We live in a complex world. As boundaries blur, it becomes crucial to anchor ourselves in principles that transcend geography and culture. We must focus on our shared humanity and the values that unite us, rather than the differences that divide us."

Juliette nodded in agreement. "By acknowledging our commonalities and embracing the diversity around us, we can build bridges instead of walls. It's about fostering understanding and respect, even when faced with unfamiliar or challenging ideas."

The family understood that their journey was not just about confronting the physical and moral challenges of their time, but also about adapting to a world in flux. They resolved to still be steadfast in their principles, embracing the fluidity of the world while holding true to the enduring values of love, compassion, and integrity.

With this new perspective, they felt a renewed sense of purpose, ready to face the future's uncertainties with courage and grace. Their bond, strengthened by their commitment to these ideals, would guide them through whatever lay ahead.

Sebastian's gaze turned to the horizon, the timeless expanse that seemed to bridge the ancient past with the ever-approaching future. He spoke with a voice that carried both the wisdom of the ages and the dreams of a unified world.

"The world of the past, with its myriad faiths and traditions, holds a profound truth that resonates even today. The essence of all these beliefs converges towards a single divine purpose: the unification of humanity under the benevolent guidance of one God. This unity is not about erasing the rich tapestry of cultures and religions but about recognizing the shared divine spark within each of us."

Juliette, inspired by Sebastian's words, added, "God's goal is not to create uniformity, but to foster unity. By coming together as one, we can celebrate our differences while embracing the common goal of peace, love, and understanding. It's about building a world where compassion and integrity guide our actions, and where faith in the divine unites us all, transcending the boundaries of time and space."

Derrick, feeling the weight of this revelation, understood that their journey was not just a personal quest but part of a much larger divine plan. The family's commitment to these ideals would be their guiding star, illuminating their path through the ever-changing landscape of the world.

With hearts full of hope and spirits imbued with a sense of divine purpose, they stood ready to face the challenges ahead. They knew that their strength lay not only in their unity as a family but also in their unwavering faith in a higher power, a faith that called them to be the harbingers of love, justice, and harmony in a world yearning for redemption.

"For thousands and thousands of years," Sebastian continued, "fighting and killing under the guise of religion has marred the tapestry of human history. It is time for this senseless violence, driven by disputes over the existence of God and His power, to come to an end."

"The truth will never reveal itself until humanity can coexist in peace and strive to stamp out hatred and prejudice," he concluded. "This is our sacred duty—to build a world where love prevails over hate, where understanding triumphs over ignorance, and where the myriad voices of our species can join in a chorus of unity and harmony."

Juliette's eyes shone with determination. "We must each play our part, no matter how small, in this grand symphony of humanity. It begins with us, in our homes, in our communities, and ripples outward to encompass the globe."

Derrick, feeling a surge of resolve, echoed his family's sentiments. "The journey ahead may be fraught with challenges, but armed with the enduring values of love, compassion, and integrity, we can forge a future where truth and unity reign supreme."

As the sun began to set, casting a warm glow over the horizon, the family stood united, their hearts aligned with a single purpose. They knew that their commitment to these ideals would not only light up their way but also serve as a beacon of hope for others. Together, they would navigate the complexities of the world, guided by the timeless principles that bound them to each other and to the greater tapestry of humanity.

Sebastian, his gaze unwavering, emphasized the urgency of abandoning the old ways. "The old ways of fighting, forcing one ethnic group to despise another, must end if humanity is to survive and thrive in the future.

As the family stood together, the horizon before them seemed to transform into a canvas of potential, painted with the vibrant colors of unity and love. They knew their journey was just beginning, but with unwavering faith and a shared vision, they were ready to face whatever lay ahead. Together, they would strive to turn their dreams of a united world into a reality, one step at a time. Killing every bad actor was not the answer; over hundreds of lives snuffed out under the guise of religious beliefs and territorial boundaries must be changed and reformed in unity and without malice. True progress demands that we transcend our differences and embrace our shared humanity. It is a call to action, urging us to dismantle the walls of division and to rebuild our world on the foundations of mutual respect and understanding.

The President's Killer Captured

*D*urbish's carefully devised plan seemed to be saving Sebastian's life for the time being, as he watched men burst into the small interrogation room. Sebastian held onto fragments of his past like a child unwilling to release his favorite toys. He imagined the beatings were only for the compassionate act for saving so many other lives. That was why they're angry, he kept thinking.

The guards were screaming for his attention. All Sebastian knew was that his guts were searing as if hot coals were ingested. The butts of rifles were being used to beat his sides and the back of his head. The taste of something bile rose within him, and something splashed across the room. He heard his ribs crack with each blow to his side. A sudden smashing blow into his groin sent Sebastian into uncontrollable spasms. The beating stopped. They picked him off the floor and seated him in the chair.

Even though they wanted to kill the prisoner, he had to remain alive. The lieutenant knew they needed to extract all the information possible from him first.

Barely conscious, Sebastian wished his heart would fail and prayed he would die before they resumed the beating. Any information he would give his captors he knew would not save him. All he had done was pull the trigger.

The lieutenant wanted to extract all the dirty details of the American' the vital information of this conspiracy to kill their President. His superiors were demanding that he obtain the plan from the prisoner before he was brought to face charges for the murders.

Sebastian knew if he were to die it would be by accident, not by their hand alone, not yet. The guards dragged Sebastian into the cell. His lifeless body was slammed into the hard concrete floor. He heard the cell door clang shut and the guards laughing and cursing him. They knew his true curse was the fact he would survive.

Sebastian knew they would return to beat him again. Each breath sent pain throughout his ribs and musculature structure. His steadfast attempt to not breathe was in vain. This hideous treatment of demented torture could not continue, he thought. With his eyes swollen shut, any impulse to move was of no use. The pain was unbearable. The stench of his own feces was a fetid attack on his senses.

Sebastian was so brutally beaten he didn't know he was near death. His ribcage had lost its supporting function. His ribs were severely broken. Sebastian thought if he had any ribs unbroken, he was lucky. The pain he felt caused him to plummet into unconsciousness. The wave of his misery was broken.

The lieutenant just glared at his capture, as he looked at his prisoner lying face up on the floor. He thought if he had not known what this man looked like beforehand, he would have never recognized him now. Sebastian's head was the size of an overinflated soccer ball.

Sebastián woke to harsh voices outside his cell. Something was familiar about the voice he heard outside speaking loudly.

Unable to control his temper any longer, the lieutenant said get this man medical attention immediately. If not, the Americans would hold the Warden responsible.

Sebastian was unsure if this was really taking place.

The guards' hushed voices mingled with the cell's damp chill. Sebastian felt a flicker of defiance surge within him, an ember buried beneath the rubble of his pain. He let his mind drift to the weight of secrets he carried—details that could unravel plans, names that could lead to unfathomable consequences. He would not part with them easily.

Slowly, he tested the limits of his broken body. His fingers twitched at first, and then he clenched his fists, a small but significant act of rebellion. He glanced at the puddle of water beside him, remnants of the guard's sweating, its cold reflection reminded him of the world outside this misery. Yet the effort cost him. The act of shifting even a fraction sent agonizing pain that clawed into his chest and ignited fire in his ribs.

The private was ordered to open the cell door by the lieutenant who gave his word he would be allowed to see the doctor. As he was leaving he exclaimed to the guards "If this man is killed, sanctions against our government will be enforced."

Sebastian heard the soldier enter the cell. The soldier checked the prisoner to make sure he was not dead. Barely able to see the young man kneeling over him. As the soldier shook his foot, Sebastian kicked him in the face. In an instant the soldier scrambled out of range of any more surprises. He quickly left the cell and relocked the door.

After kicking the guard, Sebastian began to cough up blood. He was hurting badly and the only thing that made him feel better was the thought of leaving his footprint on the guard's face.

Sebastian had a blurred image of someone near his cell. There were slight shuffling sounds near him. His eyes were too swollen to see who it was. Sebastian instinctively gasped for air as the guard splashed a cold bucket of water on him. Then they laughed loudly from this lousy trick that had bewildered him.

Sebastian was exhausted from the torrents of pain racking his body. Through bleary eyes he could tell some men had gathered around him. He heard one of them say, "He looks harmless." The guard said, "I wouldn't be so sure of that."

The doctor gently prodded his head and limbs. He placed a pillow beneath his swollen head. Sebastian thought the gentle care was a brilliant trick. This time was only a buffer devised to confuse him. Even though the men in the cell did not hurt him, the excruciating pain caused him to pass out once again.

Outside the cell, sounds woke Sebastian. He felt as though he had swan dived into an empty pool. The swelling in his eyes had lessened and enabled him to see a little better. He reached to grasp whatever was holding his chest. Finding no hold, he realized he was bound tightly around his ribcage. This gave him some idea of why the pain was different. With renewed confidence, Sebastian took a small breath. Someone had taken particular care of his injuries. He felt a bandage, as well, wrapped around his head. Any place he touched on his battered body was sore, swollen or broken. He noticed two teeth were missing and others loosened. Sebastian lay on the floor thinking of how the guards had half killed him. *"To a point, they have partially paralyzed me,"* he thought.

The sounds of keys made Sebastian tense involuntarily. The keys had someone holding them that could easily cause his pains to impale him. The sound triggered fear. The cell door was opened again. Out of focus, two people entered his cell. He noticed one man was wearing a white smock. Sebastian felt the sting of a sharp needle point. A few moments later the only urge he felt was to disgorge matter from his stomach. Having had no food in quite some time, the drug's effect altered his reaction. He tasted an unpalatable sour liquid rise in his throat.

In the ten or fifteen seconds of sadistic pains felt caused by his injuries, the morphine injection caused Sebastian to dream. The dreams sent him far from where he lay. He dreamed he was on his own bed with her. Incredibly, his breathing wasn't painful, nor anything else, but the arousal was an unimagined surprise. He was on the beach with her again, the same beach where they had gone years ago.

He visualized her lying right beside him. Her body was wet from the sweat caused by the heated rays of the sunshine. Her bathing suit shimmered; the material mixed with shades of different colors. She was naturally tanned, but the sun added luster to her stunning beauty.

He could hear her girlish voice as he placed an ice cube onto her stomach. The heat from her skin melted it quickly. A pool of water gathered in her lower belly right above her waist. Sebastian could feel the cool water on her hot flesh. He remembered how every part of him wanted to ravish her, to take this woman that instant and prove that he was learned in his skills of lovemaking.

She denied his natural right for the whole time they knew each other. He remembered on this occasion that day on the beach had been no different. Again, she had torn another piece of his heart from him. Sebastian wanted to stop the dream. His ability to do so did not transpire. What started out as a pleasant dream now was like the hell he had lived in because of her disapproval of his love.

Repeatedly in the dream he heard her saying she was afraid of losing their friendship. It had steadily been her reply and Sebastian understood the reasons why she would not completely accept him. He hated her chastisement of him. As he struggled to get himself out of his past, someone spoke to him. It helped him focus on the voice and brought him out of his dream.

A man stood right beside the bed. Sebastian heard him asking familiar questions. He, being drugged, made them depersonalized. The man asked, "Where do you live?"

He managed to say in a confident manner, "Houston."

"Really! Where in Houston?"

"No, I said Washington." Sebastian's heart was in his throat as he realized he had said the wrong thing.

"Where do you work?" Loudly, the man asked again, "Where do you work?"

Finally, Sebastian said, "The Washington Post."

"What brought you here to Abuja?"

"My job."

"What job?"

"To photograph."

"Where are you?"

Sebastian knew he had better do something.

"Where are you?" the man asked.

Sebastian waited, then said, as if he thoroughly understood the question, "I'm in Massachusetts."

"What are your parents' names?"

"I don't remember."

"Your parents' names? You must know their names. Tell me, what are their names?"

"My father is Bartholomew."

The man said, "Yes, you're correct."

"What is your mother's name?"

"Marie."

"Where do they live?" he said, impatiently.

"They live in Houston," I told you."

"No, that's not true, you live in Houston."

"No, I live in Washington."

The man burst out angrily and screamed, "That is a lie!"

"No, my job is in Washington, and I live in Washington. Why won't you believe me?"

"Shut up!" the man screamed.

Sebastian knew he messed up but only hoped to fix things by acting confused by the drug. He was frightened by the effectiveness of the drug's ability in making his thoughts uncoordinated. He pretended to doze off. He felt the emotional terror from knowing he was messed up. He did not mean to say he lived in Houston. Sebastian couldn't tell if he had tricked the man into believing his lie. He was held in suspense as the man quietly stared at him. He kept the truth hidden with shadowy false confidence.

Sebastian incoherently mumbled, "Water. Do you have water?" He hoped to deflect any more questions as he tried to fight both the drug and his inability to give straight answers. These two things were particularly trying on his uncooperating mind.

The man stood there and withdrew a cigarette package from his pants pocket. He slipped a cigarette from the pack and lit the dangling object held in between his lips.

Sebastian noticed as he did the man's teeth were large and unevenly spaced. The cigarette was held by his lips in an odd, crooked half smile. He was a large man with long eyebrows and graying bushy hair. His features were set off by the color of his deep-set black eyes. Their color almost looked like polished stone. The cigarette smoke swirled upwards and filtered up into his bushy hair as it rose slowly above his head.

He spoke as if trying to convince him of his words, "We will not hurt you if you tell us who sent you to kill the President. You may even be lucky enough to remain alive." He spoke perfect English as he continued the interrogation. His steps barely made a sound as he paced back and forth in the little cell. "I'm only doing this to help you," he said, adding, "Don't cause yourself any more harm. As you know, we can be very thorough." The man wore a long chain around his neck that swayed back and forth as he stepped in controlled, defiant rhythm. It was an old, elegant crescent shaped pendant that held Sebastian mesmerized.

Sebastian asked him, "What is it you don't understand?" Abruptly, he stopped and slowly turned to face Sebastian. His expression was guarded, obviously not feeling self-confident any longer. Not quite sure how to react, he hesitated and turned to leave the cell. He told Sebastian as he closed the door, "This was only a preliminary action. I will return. If I were you, I would take into consideration the ramifications of another interview. For your sake, take this time and try to find a reason to save your miserable hide!"

After the man left, Sebastian became aware of how tense this made him. His body shook feverishly. He was in an uncontrollable state and his teeth chattered as if he were freezing. He tried to gain control over his mind and body as he lay down, he just stared at the ceiling. Looking at nothing, he switched his focus from one spot to another. Now, he knew that the drugs were for two defined purposes. He struggled to recall vital facts he had memorized.

Soon, he gained composure. His wounded body began to ache and seemed to throb with each labored breath he took. His wish to die had not been granted. His suffering was clearly the outcome of his unanswered prayers. His mind was dulled by the distraction of the man's demeanor. At first, he had sounded friendly and even showed concern by his offer of advice, but slowly he had turned into an obvious dislike for Sebastian. He restrained from any further questioning and left him with his rigid advice to save himself. Sebastian thought something was not quite right with this person.

He was certain he needed to be careful and better prepared the next time this man returned.

A man approached the cell door with a tray in his hand. The smells from the food reached Sebastian before he ever saw the worker standing there. As he looked towards the door, he could see the man pausing, waiting for the guard to unlock the door. The worker entered cautiously, and he noticed he wasn't very old and seemed very scared. Sebastian smiled at him as he leaned over to place the tray onto the floor. The boy backed away from what he saw as a threat to him, then turned away from him as he neared the cell door. Once he was safely outside, the guard turned his keys to secure the captured killer. They stared at him as if he were something alien. The cell held the killer of the most powerful leader in Nigeria's history.

His hunger quickly became extremely evident. The meal, whatever it was, wasn't plentiful, barely enough to satisfy his hunger. The young worker who had brought Sebastians meal suddenly reappeared. As he did so, Sebastian heard keys jingle down the narrow hallway outside his cell. These unfamiliar sounds were becoming more routine. The guard made his appearance just long enough for the young man to gather his tray. He listened to the sounds of their tasks as they completed their chores. He could hear the guard making his way up the hallway again. He needed to speak to him. As he approached the front of his cell, Sebastian interrupted his passing. "Hey, mister."

The guard stopped, alarmed by the sound of Sebastian's voice. A tautness overtook him as he looked quickly in Sebastian's direction. Sebastian clearly could not trust this man, nor anyone, any harm would easily befall him, but their display of fear was evident. His ribs were bound so tight even though the effort to speak hurt him.

The guard asked, "What do you want?"

"Can you bring me a blanket? I'm cold."

"No," the guard said and as he turned to leave Sebastian, noticed above his left eye a gash about an inch long, a fresh wound. He did not press the issue of the blanket. He realized the guard must be the same man he kicked. He thought it was well worth his chills having had the satisfaction of kicking him yesterday. He knew it would be an error to be rude to this man or to do anything to cause him to retaliate for what he had done.

His treatment remained unchanged for over a week, two meals per day, no bath, and no blanket. His skin and lips cracked from severe loss of moisture this dryness was an apparent discomfort. During this time, he painfully began to walk upright. He only did this at night as he did not wish the guards to see him. Before long he had the feeling something was about to take place. He hoped to gain some insight as to what was being planned for him. He listened to everything said, but any real information that seemed to be said about him was quickly spoken in their native language. He became frustrated by this recurring treatment during his detention. Sebastian gave up hope for any information. He did not know how long he had been there or what day it was.

He formulated time by the constant changing from the different guards. Of course, he could tell day and night, but no specific time. He did not have the pleasure of being certain of anything. He guessed the time of day by the meal he was being served and could assume it was around noon. Only guesses. This was a frustrating time. Sebastian's usually organized lifestyle, this nullity in his life, gave him a sense of defeat. He felt this was a normal reaction to the succession of abuse of his rights. This abuse sent him scanning hideous corners of his mind.

The penal system of Nigeria had beaten Sebastian. A haunted look took possession of him. His eyes had sunk deeply into their sockets. He was giving in and growing weak. The steady efforts to rehabilitate what the beatings had temporarily caused him to endure began to resurface. The pain he endured, even his walking, was laborious. The conspired attempts to keep Sebastian completely isolated prevailed. The killer was a broken man because of their relentless mistreatment of him. Their prize was this development in Sebastian's mental condition.

His will to live was gone. All reasoning had escaped him. His weak mind made him feel less than a man. It showed by his inaction and loss of perception of his own predicament. Sebastian was moved several times.

By his best calculation, a month had passed, and they were moving him to still another place within the prison. The area he found himself in now was dark, almost like a dungeon. In fact, he was in a dungeon. He was completely unable to comprehend this.

His only key to freedom would be to regain his methodical type of reasoning. If not, he would be reduced to a lunatic if he remained in this current state of mind. The functions of his brain were very vulnerable and unstable. The slow destructive effects of isolation were reaching critical heights. He was in a phase now that if he did not stop his temptations of death, he soon would reach insanity. With his loss of hope, he lost the power that had been his throughout his lifetime. He must somehow find this power within him to bolster his will to live, or he would surely be thinking about a constat desire to die. He knew he must find a true desire to survive.

If he did so, he would find what life's essence could bring forth in him. Never had he questioned his own sanity like this, neither had he prepared himself for self-doubt to seep into his mind. His defenses were broken. These occurrences sent dreadful fears which continually shook his confidence.

Late in the day he realized his surroundings. A cold metal frame made up his place to sit or lie down on. There was a hole in the floor for his body's excretions. He used this as well for the inedible food they gave him. He sent it down into the unseen abysmal tube's entrance. The sounds from adjoining cells were distorted by echoes. A cry from some unknown individual who pleaded for help was unanswered. Only an identical echo replied in answer to his plea.

Sebastian thought, *"Why, how fitting. Every bit of this torture is deserved."* He was most effectively losing his mind in the bowels of the prison. The pleas for help and requests for food and medical attention were constant. The screams were at a peak level of disorder. For hours, these were the only sounds he heard, sounds from desperate men with no hope of any help. After invoking no assistance, the sudden quietness from the men was equally unnerving. This was a dangerous intrusion into Sebastian's thoughts, surely an omen of what was to come. The silence was broken by the sound of keys that snapped Sebastian out of his listlessness. The keys meant either the prisoners were going to be fed or worse, someone would be tortured.

Sebastian hoped it would not be him the attention was focused on. He knew by the sounds this was not food coming in. There was no clanging of trays or pleas for more food. He was tense and suddenly afraid as the keys were inserted into his cell door. Two guards entered his small cell. Sebastian stood wide-eyed against the back wall. Both men held his arms tightly and led him out. He knew his time had come.

The chamber door was opened, and the guards led Sebastian into a chair. He glanced apprehensively around the room and saw metal devices hanging from the ceiling. He didn't know what their purpose would be, he just sensed he was about to be beaten again.

He dared not challenge the guards with an attempt to escape. The guards stood in the alcove outside the room but steadily watched him. Sebastian's profound fear of what was about to happen never took place. The large man with the crooked smile and big teeth appeared. As before, his medallion swung in unison with his gait. He knew this arrogant man was a true antagonist. The man's voice thundered in the small room. Sebastian had a preexisting sample of this man's power and precision.

"Who are you?" His directness left Sebastian with no room for evasion of the question. "My name is Sebastian Gavenworth." The man turned and spoke to the guard. "Corporal, bring the evidence. And the girl put her in the other room."

Sebastian was jolted into reality by the man's words. Thinking quickly, he did not know what the evidence could be, but he knew his answers would remain the same. He was prepared to answer questions for this man, but he was suddenly concerned of what girl he was speaking of. He only knew one girl and he thought, *It must be Aneda (Juliette)! It must be her!*" Stark fear of her being there transcended his own mental limits.

A woman's cry was heard by all the men present. A moment later the corporal reentered the chamber. The big man told him to close the door as he handed him a folder. He extracted a passport and held it before him. He waved it in front of Sebastian's face, seemingly disgusted by having it in his possession. He screamed, "This is a false passport, Sebastian Gavenworth, as well as all the other items here! They are all fake! And like you, we have your friend, Durbish, upstairs now and the girl you met is in the next room. She will die and so will your accomplice."

Sebastian was beyond words and unsure of his sanity. This sudden realization stirred his emotions back to life. He thought if what this man said was true, he must try to save them both. He said, "There are no others. I have no accomplices I swear to you."

The man spoke in his own language to the corporal. Sebastian's mind was working feverishly to understand what was, in fact, true about what this man had said.

The man turned to Sebastian, "Mr. Gavenworth, these false documents were brought here by your accomplice and Durbish is his name. Isn't this true, Mr. Gavenworth?"

Incredibly, Sebastian heard his word, "No," denying the man's pronouncement of the truth. Sebastian asked the man to describe Durbish. After he did so, he said I have no accomplice.

The man's leverage was weak. Sebastian saw it in his black eyes. The man changed his direction of attack against Sebastian's defense. He said, "The girl is quite beautiful and very young. I will keep her alive if she can endure the wave of men. My corporal will be first. He will weaken her for the others. Let's just say he is very healthy, Mr. Gavenworth."

A woman's scream was heard throughout the dungeon. Sebastian imagined the corporal's forced entry had caused this chilling sound. He was getting pumped into a rage and feared he would reduce his stance that there were no others involved. Unfortunately, he endured this, not wanting to give in until the girl's screams ceased.

Unknown to Sebastian, Durbish was standing by his own free will on the third floor of the prison in the Warden's office. The visit to the Warden and his aides by Durbish was unexpected. They requested his credentials had been a formal transaction. A set of direct orders were received by a staff member of the Warden and presented to Durbish.

The issued credentials were validated and were official documents stating Durbish McFane was the Active Special Commissioner for N.A.T.O. In this capacity as Special Commissioner, his authority covered any country in Africa. Durbish was asking for answers about their prisoner. He was held in suspense by his act which was in check. He received some information and asked to see this man who had caused so much trouble in Abuja.

The supreme request was left up to the Warden to decide. His N.A.T.O. office officially had no interest in this man's fate. Durbish watched the Warden's reaction. He had taken in all favors owed him in Washington to obtain such a valid cover. His credentials were no real legitimate threat to this delicate matter. The Warden handed Durbish his IDs and passport and, as well, gave him a pass to permit his visit.

Durbish thanked the Warden as he was led from the office. He was asked to wait. They told him the prisoner would be sent for as he was led into a small tidy room. He graciously thanked his assigned attendant. Durbish remained in the room and acted as if he were truly annoyed by his mission.

Having now gained the advantage of speaking with the prisoner, he could secretly speak with Sebastian. He hoped the Warden and his immediate staff did not further check his credentials. If they did so quickly, they would be riddled, but if there was any deep investigation into his story, it would indicate his articles were a hoax.

He knew he must speak with Sebastian quickly or take the chance of joining him in his incarceration. The Nigerian government would have grounds against the Americans befitting the crime. This act of Durbish's was ground for a legal complaint if he were caught. Durbish was aware of his shaky disadvantage. He nervously waited for his chance to talk with Sebastian. Inwardly, he was gushing with confidence.

His plan had worked. He knew once he spoke with Sebastian, he could give him hope and tell him of his plan for his escape. Just to let him know there was a chance of it would make Sebastian confident he had people working with the court for his safety and return to America.

Meanwhile, in the small chamber, Sebastian stared into the big man's black eyes. His deep-set eyes were covered with a sheen; their polished luster was untinged and threatening. The man was about to speak when the Warden's assistant entered. This disturbance was followed by the man saying, "I have a direct order from the Warden. Take heed."

The corporal interrupted the big man further by asking for his attention. The big man turned from Sebastian and ordered them both, "Tell me what it is that is so urgent!"

Heatedly, the assistant said direct orders to the corporal, "The prisoner is to be brought upstairs immediately. There is a high-ranking official waiting to speak to this killer." The messenger was satisfied that his request would be conducted effectively. The door remained open.

The man was upset by the orders. His plans for Sebastian were postponed temporarily.

Sebastian was confused by it all and unaware of Durbish McFane's success in securing a meeting with him. He watched one of the guards leave the room. Moments later he could hear the cell door next to them being unlocked. He heard a woman's voice and noticed her heavy accent was not his lover's voice.

As the man walked by leading the woman, he knew Sebastian had not been deceived. As he passed, he gave him a piercing glare and Sebastian knew this man was someone he would be unable to avoid seeing again. Reluctantly the man left shouting an order for the corporal, "Prepare the prisoner." He outwardly showed his disgust for Sebastian as he spat out his command to be conducted and slammed the heavy steel door behind him.

All Sebastian could feel was relief. The man's awesomeness struck fear in him. He knew to spar mentally with this man was dangerous, yet he felt he had little to lose. From the moment he had been caught, he had been changed forever, but he felt at any rate defeating one more foe was a joy he'd try to accomplish.

The corporal ordered Sebastian to follow him into an empty cell. He ordered him "Wait for my return." Several minutes later the corporal returned with a jumpsuit and a razor. "Clean up quickly. You have a visitor." As the corporal left, he said, "How lucky you are," and went to do whatever corporals do.

Sebastian quickly shaved his heavy beard and washed up a bit. After he had put on the jumpsuit he called for the corporal. No one heard him. A few minutes passed, Sebastian yelled, "Get me out." Still nothing. Sebastian paced the floor for at least fifteen minutes. Not realizing how nervous he really was, he began to perspire. To calm himself, he sat down. He thought about what had just happened. He had almost caved in by the tricks played on him. At first, he thought they really had gotten Juliette, but it was only the cries of another woman. He managed to discount their helter-skelter treatment. He knew if he had seen Juliette there, he would have done anything possible to save her. He knew how much he loved her, and their brief adventure had been the most piercing form of love he had felt in twenty years. Before the guard approached, the sound of his key reached Sebastian. His wait was over. Sebastian stood near the door of his cell. There was no herald needed by the guard; it was unnecessary.

The guard told Sebastian to place his hands through the slot in the door and handcuffed him. He was then led to the exit. There, chains were placed around his waist and ankles. The guard inspected him as if he were a threat, even chained as he was. This cunningly devised psychological game was often played to make the prisoners feel distorted and insignificant. Sebastian said, "Who has come to visit me?"

The guard gave no indication of who he was to meet. He and the guard walked slowly up steps that seemed to have no end. Sebastian held back his desire to rush past the guard as he slowly plodded up the steps. This was another subtle form of torture.

Sebastian thought it was tolerable since he was out of his cell and meeting a visitor. He felt he had won the winning hand in a high stake's poker game. Just knowing he had a visitor was like receiving a gift of extreme pleasure. The steps led to an unfamiliar floor. Once inside another room, the guard unshackled his wrist. Looking up, Sebastian spotted his visitor behind a wall of glass. His first reaction was his complete loss of self-control. Tears even attempted a release. With this surprise of such a mix of emotions, he tried to hide his panic-stricken reaction. He was stunned and his strength wilted after seeing his closest friend.

Durbish sat still, shocked by his own feelings of powerlessness. The only help he could give his friend was some buoyancy to hang on, but Durbish had no intention of leaving Sebastian without his firm promise of his plans for his escape.

After seeing his friend, Sebastian panicked from the effects of seeing his only chance of being released about to enter.

Durbish had been thoroughly searched and now was led into the same room as Sebastian. The guard took the seat closest to the glass in the other room. This chain of events left both men alone. Durbish looked at Sebastian in his condition and said nothing to cause him further disgrace.

Instead, Durbish clutched Sebastian's paper light hand. He realized Sebastian had been treated with paganized bitterness. His first words were sudden and hushed as he drew Sebastian near him. He said, "Don't act like you know me. He let go of this subtle embrace and motioned for him to sit. Durbish took the seat next to him. He sounded off with a tactful approach as if in an official manner. He said, "So, your name, sir, is Sebastian Gavenworth?"

Sebastian nodded and Durbish asked, "Do you need a doctor?" He feared an approach that would give him vital clues to his plans that may be overheard. Nervously, to check Sebastian's response, he said, "I know a man named Sebastian, but he lives in L.A. I believe his girlfriend's name, if I remember, was Jennifer. Of course, you would not know him. His last name was Scott. Their mother lived in Houston, but the father of Sebastian lived in Galveston. He moved to Houston once he earned his medical degree and he is a fine surgeon.

All Sebastian could feel was an overwhelming sense of relief. The formidable nature of the man instilled a deep trepidation within him. Though Sebastian knew that engaging intellectually with such a man could be perilous, he felt as though he had little left to lose. Ever since the moment of his capture, his life had undergone a profound transformation, yet the prospect of defeating another adversary filled him with a determined joy.

The corporal instructed Sebastian to follow him into a vacant cell, issuing the command, "Wait for my return." After several minutes, the corporal reappeared, carrying a jumpsuit and a razor. "Clean up quickly. You have a visitor," he directed, befara departing with a cryptic remark: "How fortunate you are." Left to his solitude, Sebastian swiftly shaved off his unruly beard and freshened up. Donning the jumpsuit, he attempted to summon the corporal, yet his calls went unanswered. Minutes stretched on as Sebastian grew increasingly agitated. His voice echoed, "Get me out," but was met with silence. For fifteen lengthy minutes, he paced the cell, nerves frazzled to the point of perspiration. Seeking solace, he finally lowered himself onto the cold floor, reflecting on what had just transpired.

The psychological games played by his captors had nearly broken him, especially when they led him to believe Juliette had been captured. As it turned out, the cries of anguish belonged to another woman. Sebastian managed to push aside their chaotic tactics, yet he remained certain that if Juliette had been there, he would have risked everything to save her. Their fleeting time together had awakened in him a love so piercing that it eclipsed anything he had felt in two decades. When the guard finally approached, the metallic sound of the key reached Sebastian before the guard was visible, signaling the end of his wait.

Standing by the cell door, Sebastian felt the weight of the moment. The guard instructed him to extend his hands through the slot in the door and secured handcuffs tightly onto him. Chains encircled his waist and ankles as he was led toward the exit. The guard scrutinized him as though he were an imminent threat despite the restrictive chains adding another layer to their psychological ploys designed to strip prisoners of their dignity. Sebastian asked, "Who has come to visit me?" but his query was met with an indifferent silence. Together, they climbed a seemingly never-ending staircase.

As much as Sebastian wanted to rush forward, the guard's slow and deliberate pace forced him to endure the climb. Yet, even this subtler form of torment was bearable, as the promise of meeting his visitor felt like an unexpected gift. The staircase led to an unfamiliar floor. Inside a new room, Sebastian's handcuffs were removed, and through a glass partition, he saw his visitor. Overwhelmed by the sight, Sebastian lost his composure, feeling emotions he hadn't dared to confront for years. As tears threatened to surface, he fought to mask his panic.

Behind the glass sat Durbish, his closest confidant. Struck by his own helplessness, Durbish resolved to provide Sebastian with some semblance of support. His determination to ensure Sebastian's escape was unwavering. As Durbish was ushered into the same room, the guard stationed himself near the glass partition, leaving the two men alone. Durbish refrained from addressing Sebastian with pity; instead, he offered a subtle gesture of comfort, gripping Sebastian's frail hand. The bitterness of Sebastian's treatment was evident in his condition. Quietly, Durbish drew him closer and whispered, "Don't act like you know me."

Sebastian hesitated, his fear clouding his ability to respond to Durbish's words. Yet the conversation had an unintended calming effect, allowing Sebastian to replay their interaction later in his mind for clarity. Durbish spoke of civil matters in Africa and the Americans' perception of Sebastian as a madman. Despite their disdain for him, which Durbish claimed to share, he expressed a willingness to return the following Monday while en official business in Abuja. The visit ended with Durbish extending an offer of help and Sebastian responding with defiant pride and valed gratitude.

Off duty, of course, the man is hard pressed to lean on the bottle. I do not know these fine people. I barely know them myself. Excuse me, I did not just come to dally. I am here to say, Mr. Gavenworth, you're in quite a sticky predicament. I'm Durbish McFane with N.A.T.O. I'm here to advise you that the Americans refused to lend you support for your actions here. That's why I've come, to assist you in any shape form or fashion I can, but my help is meager, to say the least."

Sebastian listened to this, too frightened to speak to Durbish. What he could make sense of had a clear, soothing effect on him. Later, he could recount this discussion to make it clear in his mind.

"The Americans claim you are a madman, of course. You are an outcast in their eyes, and they'll be unable to get you extradited. Personally, I'm involved in the civil matters throughout Africa, Mr. Gavenworth, and I'm a busy man, but my commander wished for me to come by and offer our indifference towards this matter. We hold a common dislike for you, but of course it's just a matter of opinion. I think my visit is over with, but if I can, may I return here, say next Monday. I've got to come back into Abuja on official business, but now that I've found you and see you're not the same American I know named Sebastian, I'm thinking I'll give him a ring up and see how their families are doing. We will meet once more, sir." Durbish rose and hoped Sebastian knew what he planned. He said, "It's been a memorable event to have had the pleasure of speaking with you. Are you okay here in prison? If I can help in any way, please let me know now." Sebastian smiled, bewildered. He had to clear his throat to speak and in his best tone of voice, "Mr. McFane, your opinion of me is quite unbothersome and if you visit again, do so only if you're sure you would not mind doing me the favor."

He took a deep breath and tried to swallow back his response to his stomach lurching upwards. He was swollen with pride for Durbish, yet said, "You call yourself a humanitarian by showing your concern with your presence. But to come here and 'dally,' as you put it, is to say I'm the least of your worries. You were brought here by your own curiosity to see if I were some American you knew. Well, sir, your friends, I am sure as hell don't know but call them and send them my best.

And now, if this is suitable behavior to you, all I have to say is yours was ghastly and, goodbye, Mr. McFane." Durbish was confused by Sebastian's query, but as he reached to help Sebastian from his seat, Sebastian breached his own act of dislike for him as a broad smile spread across his face. Under all the stress he'd been through, it showed now stretched across his face. As fast as he smiled, it vanished quickly this personal gesture of appreciation as Durbish released his grip from under the side of his arm.

As the guard came in, Durbish reached out and shook Sebastian's hand. As the two men finished with their goodbyes, Durbish was led back through a fluted doorway out of the visiting area, out of the waiting room. The guard returned for Sebastian and reestablished his authority by placing the handcuffs on him in full view of Mr. McFane who stood behind the glass.

Behind the guard's back, Durbish waved to Sebastian. Retracting into a world apart, Sebastian gave no response to his friend's gesture. Back inside the cell Sebastian felt his loneliness creep in, brought on by the departure of his friend.

With thoughts about his visit, he recalled the painted hall, the only painted walls he had seen. He closed his eyes and saw the pale green color of his cell. He thought of the differences in contrasting spaces. This review entered his perception slowly as he saw tiles on the floors and brass doorknobs. The halls were brightly lit down the full length of the upper floor. His hopes swelled. The walk back had been with less dread. He lay in the darkest corner of the cell while inside the darkest memories. Once more the door had been locked and there was no escaping this reality. He was secure and only through his thoughts did he find some form of relief.

Sebastian struggled to unravel the meaning of Durbish's message. He didn't have a clue about his part in the plan. He had no choice but to leave it up to his friends. He worried about them becoming involved. They had been dependable friends for fifteen years. He knew if Durbish called them, they would come to his aid.

Durbish laughs aloud as he sped across Abuja, returning to his hotel. The idea of how to release Sebastian was being formulated. After parking the vehicle, he rushed into his suite, anxious to work out a series of plans.

The simple solution was to get everybody into Abuja, but to get the four of them out then eliminated afterwards once and for all was his dilemma.

Ideas rushed over him as he made his first call to his wife in the states. Secretly, the two had been married ten months ago. He became exasperated as the phone rang at their home in Washington. He dialed her apartment across the city where she preferred to work. After the third ring, Melonie picked up the phone. "Hello, Melonie, this is Durbish I've just seen Sebastian, I, well he needs our help."

"Durbish, my God I've been wondering how things are in Nigeria. Have you gotten any ideas how to get Sebastian out?" "Hold on a minute, one thing at a time, okay?" He continued by saying, "Melonie, we have some problems, I need you to call Scott. Have him contact Dr. Weston."

"She replied coolly, "Yeah I can do that." "How soon do you need me to do this?" "Now." Durbish said I am a little confused yet hopeful over his situation, he's like an unwelcome guest.

Sebastian pondered Durbish's cryptic message, its implications yet unclear. He trusted his friends, dependable allies for over fifteen years, but worried about the dangers they might face on his behalf. He knew if Durbish called them, they would come, no matter the cost.

Meanwhile, Durbish formularte a plan through Abuja, laughter bubbling up as his mind raced with plans to free Sebastian. Parking the borrowed car and rushing into his suite, he began piecing together a strategy. The simplest solution was to gather everyone in Abuja, but his ultimate goal was to eliminate all enemies and people envolved once and for all. Ideas surged as he picked up the phone to call his wife, Melonie, back in Washington. The two had been secretly married for ten months, a detail he had not shared with snyonr.

Exasperated by the ringing, he tried her apartment instead. Finally, Melonie answered, her voice calm and steady despite the early hour. "Durbish? My God, how are things in Nigeria? Have you seen Sebastian?"

"Hold on, Melonie. One thing at a time," he replied, his tone urgent yet controlled. "We have problems. I need you to call Scott and have him contact David."

"I need all three of you to help me free Sebastian," Durbish continued.

Melonie hesitated. "I'll help Sebastian—but Scott? You're asking a lot."

"Just call him and make sure he contacts David. I need them both here—and I need you too."

"Me?" she asked, incredulous. "What the heck is going on?"

"You'll love it here, Melonie. Trust me, I have a good reason for you to come. I'll explain everything when you arrive."

"You're asking me to fly halfway around the world with two people, one I don't even like, for reasons you won't explain?"

"Yes. Be sure to catch the first flight to Zaire. Today is Friday—try to be here by Tuesday. I'll meet you at the airport. I love you. Bye."

She hesitated, her reluctance clear. "Fine. I'll call them," she said with a sigh. "But call me back—it's very early here."

"Yes, I'll call back in six hours. Goodbye."

Wait, don't hang up!

She asked in a vicious tone, "What do you need me to tell Scott? You know I despise him."

"Please, dear, this is a serious matter, I must have the three of you to help me free Sebastian."

"Just call him and tell him to contact David. I need both of them here."

"There?"

"Yes. My other request is that you join us. I can't fully explain my reasons now."

"Durbish, you're asking me to come halfway around the world with two people, one I don't like, for reasons you can't explain?"

Before he could hang up, she asked, "How is Sebastian?"

He immediately felt jealous by her question.

She knew he was jealous. The two had been very close, but now it was very different.

As Melonie listened, Durbish's reply was cool. "I visited him a short while ago. He has been in constant isolation since he was captured. He looks emaciated and he is losing his will to live. I know he's strong and I just hope he can withstand the constant pressure. It's vital you call Scott. I know you don't like him, but if not for me, do it for Sebastian. It's his only chance of survival. I must go now. I'll talk to you later."

She said, "I love you," and hung up the phone. As she placed her phone back in the cradle, she made a mental note of the time. She got out of bed and drew the blinds. Outside her window, the clouds were dreary and gray. "Appropriate," she whispered to herself.

She felt a lump in her throat as she sat in her finely upholstered chair at her desk and dialed Scott's home number. The line rang for what seemed like a long time. She cleared her throat as the phone was picked up by a woman. "May I speak to Scott?"

Cheerfully, she said, "He's still asleep. May I leave him a message?" "This is Melonie. It's very important that I speak with him at once. Would you mind waking him and telling him I'm on the line?"

"He's a real bear when he wakes up. If you let me rouse him first, I'm sure your business with him will be more effectively handled once I've fed him his breakfast." "Fine," Melonie said, "Have him call me at my apartment. I'll be glad to wait. He has my number."

"Thank you," Wanda said and hung up. She went to the kitchen first to prepare his breakfast, virtually a feast. From the kitchen she watched Scott sleep. She could still see his naked form clearly outlined under the sheet. They had been together for two weeks. They had met in a bar where he was a bouncer. He said his profession causing bodily harm to others was an incredible thrill. Other than this expression of his, she knew very little about him. She thought about their night together and what an incredible lover he was. She hated to wake him, so she let him sleep another five minutes after breakfast was ready. In the time she had spent with him she learned quickly what pleased him. Massive amounts of any foods known to man was his purpose in life. He ate everything to stay in shape. She admitted to herself he was in perfect shape and wondered how any woman would not find him attractive. She thought about a serious problem he had, his ego. He knew his body was perfect and he was proud of it. Other than that, Wanda had no bad vibes from him. His being so conceited was something he had worked hard to gain, like his muscular physique. She watched him work out in the gym he had made himself. The room was filled with all the latest state-of-the-art equipment, and he had spent a small fortune equipping it. Wanda, born in southern California, thought very little about his extreme fetish. She was concerned about his use of injectable types of steroids. She had been around long enough to see how the use of steroids had affected some other people she knew. She had said nothing to Scott yet, but she was gearing up for it because she was so concerned about his steady use of the substances. She wasn't sure if she had anything to worry about or not. So far, his planned cycles have been carefully organized. Before she mentioned her fears, she was going to check his behavior patterns more closely.

She bent over to place the mountain of food beside his bed and quietly stood a safe distance away and said, "Scott, wake up." Scott didn't respond to her call. She placed her hands on Scott's forehead and gently pulled the strands of his long blond hair back from his eyes. Her gentle coaxing hadn't stirred him from his sound sleep. She tried shaking the big guy to wake him. This new attempt of hers aroused the athletic man rolled his eyelids upward.

Wanda had gained Scott's undivided attention, she knew she was in a very unsafe spot. He came out of the sheets and let out a beastly drawl of threats to her. She had been through this, and her next course of action had never failed. Forcefully, she pulled the sheets off him. She knew the only safe place at this time would be the open seas, but she was on shore.

Scott pounced from his bed and had her pinned to the floor. Through her pleas for mercy, he let her off the floor as he sat on the edge of his bed. Never once had he hurt her and before she could fully rise from the floor he was already eating and jolly. Naked and content now, the man was so easy to tame.

He had smelled the food and forgotten about the fact he didn't want to wake up. Wanda circled the bed, facing his tan body. Slowly, she neared Scott as he glared at her as if she were after his food. Her only desire was to look at him as he enjoyed himself eating breakfast. Once Scott realized she was no threat, he grinned at her and paused, leaning over his tray in offering her a kiss.

After this show of kindness, he quickly returned to eat. Wanda loved watching this man and sat on the bed beside him and rubbed his back. She gently rubbed his well-developed muscles. As she played with his pumped-up figure, her breathing grew rapidly louder. Scott's muscles did turn this woman on. Before she forgot, she mentioned the call from Melonie. The mention of her name made his entire body contract like a penknife had pierced a nerve. "Melonie? Melonie called here?"

"Yes, Scott, do you know her?" "Well, yeah, we're old friends. Not friendly friends, but, yeah, I know her. What about her?" Wanda was disturbed by his unclear explanation of friends and told him to call her. Between mouthfuls he said, "What about? Did she say?" "Something about urgent business, that's all she said. Call her at her apartment. You have the number."

She had never seen Scott move quite so quickly. He always functioned so slowly. He seemed confused by what to do. He grabbed the phone by the cord and pulled the whole apparatus close enough for him to pick up the receiver. He glanced at Wanda who was watching every move with an inquisitive stare. Scott didn't know her number by memory and had to open a drawer in his nightstand that she had never known was there. He pulled out a sheet of numbers and found Melonie's name on it.

Wanda stood there bewildered by all the evidence of something peculiar going on and if that wasn't bad enough, Scott heard her gently sobbing behind him. By the time he realized she was crying the phone was ringing. He turned to face Wanda and poked her gently in the ribs and asked her to be quiet. This was his way of displaying his concern for her. She knew he meant it, so she quietened and listened.

Melonie had laid on her bed waiting for Scott's call. Finally, when the phone began to ring, she lit a cigarette and blew out a puff of smoke. Slowly, she picked up the phone and said, "Hello."

Scott said, "Well, I thought you'd never call me. What do you want?" "Scott, listen, this is urgent. Durbish called me from Nigeria, he needs you to contact David."

Scott listened to her as she told him what Durbish wanted. "It is urgent that you and David be in Nigeria by Tuesday. Even I'm going." After informing Scott of this, he teased her by saying, "Maybe somehow, we'll be able to work on our differences."

"Damn you, Scott, this has nothing to do with our clashing personalities. Do you have a valid passport? "I do," he said, as he grasped the urgency of the matter. "Well, do you think your friend Sebastian is worth dragging yourself away from your girlfriend long enough so we can all help him?"

"Well, sure I do, Melonie, but answer this for me, do you really hate me or is it just an act?"

"Scott, you are coming, aren't you?"

"Not until you answer my question first."

"No, Scott, I don't hate you."

"Okay, then, I'll call David. How soon do you need to know if he can make it?"

"Today."

"All right," he said.

Before they hung up, she told him the whole idea scared her, but he just laughed. Scott's macho mentality disgusted Melonie.

He said, "I know David will be hard to convince, but I can do it." "Besides," he added, "If anyone could succeed in what Durbish wants, we can."

"That's true," Melonie said, "I just hope Durbish knows what he's doing."

"Don't worry," Scott said. "I'll find David and convince him to drop everything to rush off to the other side of the world and get himself shot!"

"What doctor wouldn't jump at the chance?" she said. "Well, I have a list of items and papers to clear up before any of us can go. By this time tomorrow I should know when we can depart." "Fine." Scott replied, while chewing his food. "Durbish didn't give me much to go on but tell Dr. Weston he is worried about Sebastian's health. Tell him he is in very bad shape."

Scott understood the reason for her plea. Years ago, she had dated Sebastian and the two of them had lived together for almost three years. "Well, I better get busy finding David. This might be fun for all of us being together again." "Well, I don't know about fun, dangerous is more like it!" "Yeah, that's what I mean by fun." Managing a slight chuckle, Melonie hung up the phone.

Ten minutes later Melonie's phone rang. This time it was Dr. David Weston who called her. He began by asking, "How are you?" "I'm fine, David, but it's not me who needs help." "Yes, I know. It is Sebastian. Scott told me. How he ever got so mixed up in this is what I'd rather not know." "Well, David, you know very well already, but you're right.

This was a little far out, even for him." "David," she said, and paused to reconsider the purpose that she had to gain his support. She said, "Dr. Weston, Sebastian needs our help and I'm going to help him. Scott's more than willing to go with me. Can you join us? Durbish says Sebastian isn't doing well. He has suffered both mentally and physically and your help is very important."

David already knew the whole time he was going to go with them. "Before I commit myself and place my life's work on the line, I want to know all the facts. My involvement in this will only be in a physician's capacity. You make sure as hell when you speak with Durbish he understands my position completely on this. If you need me any further, I'll be at my home office. You have the number, don't you?"

"Yes, David, I do." "If Durbish wants to call me before we leave it would help him to do so. I have questions for him concerning what my personal needs will be. I only want to carry what he thinks necessary. If I don't hear from you or him, I must assume I'm to guess what medical supplies I will need and that's a risk I'm not willing to take in this situation."

"Okay," she said, "I understand. Did Scott tell you we're going to travel together?"

"Yes, when are you going to leave for Washington to meet us?" Expect me Sunday, all right."

"Yes, I'll be expecting you. When is Scott coming to Houston, David?"

"He'll be here by Saturday evening. What is your position on going, Melonie?"

"Well, I'm not really sure, David, but if it were up to me, I would not go, but my friendship with Sebastian has been a great learning experience. Durbish said I would be needed along with you and Scott, so that is enough reason, don't you think?"

David was disturbed by her answering her question with a question. He examined his surroundings and told her another thought. "Melonie, are you going to pick up the cost for the tickets or do we pay our own way?"

"David, I'll buy the tickets for all of us and reimburse both of you for your fares to Washington, if that's what you concerned about."

"No, Melonie, I'm just concerned about the tickets to reach Zaire."

"Yes, David, I'll phone now for the three tickets. If I have any money trouble, I'll call you. I'm sure you can wire me any extra if I fall short. Can't you?" she asked.

"Hell, Melonie, you drive a hard bargain. Where did you learn to be so shrewd?"

"Well, just hanging out with the likes of you and the rest of your gender, David!" She imagined this stung his pride and said, "I really must go now to see if I can get the flights out for Tuesday."

David knew she held the upper hand and graciously slid out from under this uncomfortable situation before it became a battle of wits on a cross-country phone call. "We'll see you Sunday. Have Durbish contact me, would you?"

"Yeah, David, sure, as soon as I hear from him later today, I'll tell him."

****

Sebastian lay on his uncomfortable cot barren and cold he slept unrest fully as sweat fell onto the metal bed. Certain dreams were recurring. Even as a young child he dreamed of horrible things. He woke up terrorized, filled with suspicion from shadowy figures from inside his bedroom. His best guess for his dreams at that young age was that he had done something wrong. A consistent pattern had developed at the age of ten that whatever he did would return in the form of nightmares. His dream today was shockingly vivid. In his sleep he was trying to shut out reliving today's horrors. The man with the bushy hair had Juliette.

Sebastian was strapped to a chair, and she had her hands and feet bound together. She was completely naked, and the big man was laughing at her as she cried for help. He was unable to wake himself and was forced to watch as two men held her upright for the big man to enter her. In horror, Sebastian could do nothing but watch as she fought to get away. She could go nowhere because the other men were holding her and laughing. Bravely she struggled but had no chance. The big man was painfully reentering her with force. He could only hope for the straps to break as he shouted, *"I will kill you for what you are doing to her."* The big man was laughing as he raped Juliette. Sebastian's threats seemed to make matters worse. The man began to slap her, vicious blows to her face which caused her to be covered in blood. Each time he hit her; blood flew all over the men. The blood seemed to give them a thrill as she lost her will to struggle against them. The next man repeated the same foul treatment. All three men were raping her, and she looked as if at any moment she would die. Her face was beaten and gaunt.

Sebastian felt his hands free and jerked back his arms, awakened by his sudden movements. He fell off his cot. He hit the floor before he realized it was only a dream. With both hands clenched into a fist he pounded them against the hard floor in anger. Where he had been lying, the metal bed was completely drenched with his sweat.

The fury he felt was unleashed as he threw his water bucket several times against the bars in his cell. This caused a lot of noise and everyone in the other cells began doing the same thing. They were banging and screaming, filling the bottom floor with a flurry of angry shouts and direct threats to their captors. Sebastian's madness had caused a small riot to ensue. By the time he saw what was taking place outside his cell the screams were out of control. There were only about fourteen men, but in the small confining cells their screams caused an extreme amount of noise. Before he could do anything, he heard an alarm go off upstairs which alerted the guards of trouble. In fact, this was a welcome sound, a reason for them to gather.

Briskly, the guards descended to the bottom floor forming a single file, one objective diffuse the crisis. In full gear, a wall of prison guards stood beyond harm's way of the flying objects. They held their shields and clubs ready as their commander led them closer. Being guards was hard work, for most of them looked upon the prisoners as scum. In their eyes, they were the lowest forms of men, but to the inmates they looked at the guards like they were lowest of any human. A guard's job was to keep humans imprisoned and on constant edge. The more the prisoners would try to please the guards by obeying his orders, the worse their treatment towards the prisoners would become.

In a prison, a favor never led to a favor, only the twist of a knife that was in constant use, a knife's edge that was kept sharp. A guard's whole world revolved around adding to the misery the others had already endured. Two of the guards held a long water hose as the commander of the guards ordered the area to be shut down. The commander motioned for the water to be turned on. The blast of water played haphazardly around the small, confined hallway. The sounds from the pressurized water as it escaped the hose made the inmates grow quiet. The guards sprayed each cell as they dragged the hose down the hall. Being hit by such a forceful spray was a frightful thing. The spray would literally lift a 250-pound man off the floor. It could toss him like a pencil in the ocean or slam him into the wall and drop him to the floor instantly. When punishment such as this occurred, ligaments joints, even bones could be broken, and muscles torn just from the steady blast of the water. It left no proof of any act of torture evident, but the recipient of this type of discipline wore the scars of the beating. The prisoner left with fear and painful wounds. About ten minutes passed and finally the water was shut off. The cells inside the prison walls were deteriorated.

Compared to its original constructions lacking qualities it was not a safe place.

The commander walked the length of the room inspecting each cell. He ordered each man to clean up his cell or else. Of course, no one knew what this *'or else'* would be. At the time inside a cell with no defense was a good motivator to do what they were instructed. It meant a hell of a lot of things. A person could imagine a long list of restrictions and horrid punishments for bad behavior.

With his inspection completed, the commander saw there were no men in apparent danger. He asked each man who caused the disturbance. Out of all the men, none of them gave the same answer. The commander could place no guilt on any one man but said, in fact, they were all guilty. Before he left the commander said, "I will let this matter rest, but I promise if there is one more episode of this type, what you have just been through will only be the beginning. My promise will be kept." The guards left the basement floor.

Completely unaware of the activities unfolding across the city, Sebastian strained to complete one more repetition in his daily routine of 300 pushups. After 100 reps he would pause for ten minutes, then do another set until he reached his maximum, then he would rest until his lunch arrived. Since his ribs had healed the routine had gained in intensity. He devised simple techniques to perform in his cell on a regular basis. His last 100 pushups were done on a decline. He placed his feet on the edge of his cot, a simple maneuver to alter the effects of the muscles used. Unbeknownst to him, while he did the last reps, the group of his most trusted friends began a course heading straight to him. Fundamental exercise had provided his constant maintenance, keeping his strength up and his mind occupied. The most obvious benefit from the exercises was that it kept him fit and helped him from going stir crazy while in isolation.

Sebastian laid on his cot aware that since his arrest his weight had fallen drastically. The food yesterday was quickly eaten. As he anticipated his noon meal, this dependence on someone else seemed to burn more of his calories, draining his energy. Sebastian unfolded a piece of paper the young orderly had given him this morning. He wanted to read it once more. Hardly able to read the writing, it said plainly, "We all thank you for di kellin of di hi chief." 64 men had signed their name onto the paper or placed Xs to show their appreciation in what he had done.

The note gave Sebastian a sense of hope, their support for his accomplished killing gave him a lighter outlook on his death sentence. It was a brave act for those involved to risk being caught passing the note through the prison. The names meant nothing, yet they did signify the men stood behind him. Their support would give him the strength he needed during his trial. The proof was in his hand. Men in prison their absence from the outside world to a degree became more sensitive. An enormous show of support was enough to justify his actions, dying for his act would be worth it all.

The letter reminded Sebastian of how he missed Juliette. The absence of freedom and being loved in his life made him want to see her once more. He knew it was out of the question to dare try to communicate with her. This day was turning into an assault on his emotions, the last days ahead was unbearably the hardest days he would forego.

As Sebastian replayed visions of Juliette in his mind's eye, downstairs, passes were issued to the group granting them free movement within the prison. Durbish and Dr. Weston spoke with the lieutenant. As they entered the prison Durbish excused himself. Dr. Weston politely asked them to stand at ease until they were needed. Scott and Melonie casually walked the grounds of the prison front. Melonie commented on how spooky the prison appeared as Scott strummed his ID card, anxiously standing beside the ambulance. Melonie stopped the noise by clipping the ID back onto his shirt.

Melonie said, "Okay, this is not a test. I am heading closer" Scott asked, "What are you going to do?" Melonie answered him matter of fact "I'm going to find myself a man!"

Melonie turned the radio on and clipped it to her belt. She motioned for Scott to do likewise. Swiftly, she walked to the opposite side of the prison's entrance way. She looked over the grounds and saw how well maintained the islands across the prison looked. The display of marigolds and neatly trimmed bushes ran the full length of the prison lawn. In the center of each island there were hearty nicely arranged trees all the same variety and cut the same shape. The guards had an unobscured view from the towers. They could see across the whole finely manicured lawn from tower to tower.

Dr. Weston stepped from the elevator onto the second floor. The Warden had left him unaccompanied to inspect the prisoners. The doctor acted pleased with the offer and strolled down the hallway. He gazed into each cell he passed. This graphic display of malnourished humans sent chills all over his whole body. Suddenly, he became very cold inside the prison's corridor. As he looked at the men behind bars and saw their look of desperation and depravation, it was an unnatural contribution to his senses. Undoubtedly, this would compromise his sleep for many nights to come. He thought he knew what it would be like inside the prison, but this view had been unimagined and drew his attention away from the purpose of his being there.

He continued down the corridor passing each cell and was unwilling to look inside them any longer. He found a guard sitting at the end of the long hallway. He asked him, "Could you please lead me to the cell I'm looking for?"

Quizzically, the guard looked over this doctor and asked, "Wha' number?"

"H-A-208." Dr. Weston said.

The guard eyed him suspiciously and lumbered ahead of him to the cell. Dr. Weston felt like he was in another world altogether. The smells and sounds were all foreign to him, causing his breathing to be uneven. He felt that he could not control himself in this environment properly much longer.

The guard repeated the question, "What cell number?" in broken English and seemed to grow impatient with the doctor.

David repeated the number, "208," and looked anxiously at each cell they passed. As they reached Sebastian's cell, he showed the guard a pass and said, "Open the cell." The pass allowed him freedom of movement and unlimited time to visit cell H-A-208.

The keys came off the guard's waist to enter the slot in the door. The sound of the keys and the clink of the latch caused Sebastian to raise his head. Scott was shaking all over and prayed Sebastian was in control of his senses enough to remain calm. Sebastian started to say something. His expression on his face took on the look of being rudely awakened by a total stranger. Dr. Weston knew the crisis was over.

Dr. Weston turned to the guard and asked, "Do you have a set of portable scales so I can weigh the prisoner?"

In broken English, Dr. Weston understood him to say, "It will take a few minutes."

"Go get them."

The guard said, "No," adding it was lunch time.

Dr. Weston said, "Please, sir, I must weigh the man because the records need to be documented before tomorrow.

"But it is lunch time. I'm going to have to eat first!"

Dr. Weston said, "Never mind. I have a set. My assistant will bring them. Please wait here for him, then you can go eat."

Dr. Weston unclipped his radio from his belt and flipped the switch. The radio on Scott's belt was breaking up as he heard Dr. Weston say, "Scott, come in please this is Dr. Weston".

"Doc, this is Scott". "What can I do for you?"

"Bring my bag and the scales. Scott, did you get that? Over."

"Doc, I'll be there in a few minutes."

Melonie saw Scott digging in the back of the ambulance and rushed over to give him a hand. Inside, she found the bag as he lifted the scales. She placed the strap over his other shoulder and secured the heavy bag which contained very few medical supplies and the 10 gauge over and under shotgun.

"Here goes nothing," Scott said. "Take your position and be ready for anything."

She said, "Getting in is simple, but believe me, getting out is another. Have you noticed?"

"Yep."

"Take the towers for example. How are we going to get past those guns?"

He replied, "Grenades. Just get the inside guard's attention, all right. I sure hope shooting won't bother you. I'm getting out one way or another." He rushed up the steps holding the scales under his arm. The bag hung heavily across his shoulder.

Melonie shouted to him, "Wait." She rushed over to him and whispered, "Please don't get us all killed."

He just grinned as he headed toward the entrance. As the guard told him to halt, Melonie caught up with Scott. Seductively, she said to the guard, "I'm not going up."

Ever since Scott had known Melonie, he had never heard her sound so seductive. The guard looked at her and read the expression on her face. The guard was not very smart. The buzz from the electric lock released the sliding door. A wall of bars opened; Melonie could be heard laughing at the entrance as Scott slipped out of view. The guard took the bait. She would tease him to death.

Scott spoke on his radio, "Dr. Weston, what floor are you on. How do I find you? Over."

"Dr. Weston said, "Did you find the scales?"

"Yes. Where do I bring them? "Over."

"Second floor, Scott, Unit H-A, Cell 208. Over."

"Be right up, Doc."

Durbish was eating lunch with the Warden. He knew that at any moment the lunch could turn disastrous. If he didn't move and find out what was taking place, he'd be trapped, in seconds Durbish pushed his plate aside without eating a bite. "Sir, my appetite is off besides I had a large breakfast this morning. Would you be so kind as to excuse me?" I'm going to see what the doctor is doing. I must make a formal report. The truth is, it is all very unnecessary, but it's my job and I must. If I don't--"

The Warden interrupted him saying, "Fine, please go ahead. I'll catch up with you in five or ten minutes. I know where to find you. Where can you go anyway? You are in prison," he said as he laughed at his own joke.

Durbish left him as he continued to display his bad taste in jokes and manners. Disgustingly, he laughed with his mouth full of food. Durbish stood waiting for the elevator and mumbled, "You gross pig!"

The guard in the bulletproof booth downstairs was drooling to come out. Melonie said, "I find you very appealing and you turn me on." She pressed her body against the glass, putting her breasts in full view. The guard was dying to get his hands on her. He rubbed the glass and played the perfect part of a fool. Melonie unbuttoned the two top buttons of her blouse revealing a nice portion of cleavage. She thought, "All this for this jerk-off!" but smiled her sweetest smile. The guard was half out of his mind from being enticed by this luscious woman. He motioned towards the slot in the wall of the booth. Melonie didn't like it, but knew she had to get inside with the guard. He was gaining his wits too fast. Her thoughts were screaming to her that she had to move now so she moved to the slot.

The guard's hand shot out like some cannon had exploded from inside the booth. His hands were on her face; she saw his eyes bulging out of their sockets as they surveyed her body.

"Hi," she said. In return, he said, "Hi," as he held a strand of hair, gently urging her closer to the slot.

"My name's Melonie what's your name?" He stammered, My names Roy". "You sure are a pretty woman."

She said, "Why, thank you, Roy." She pulled free from him, looking up and down the hall. His hands were flapping in the air through the slot. He curled his fingers in and out so she would draw near the slot's opening again, she supposed for him to feel her off. Melonie ran her hand across her breasts just out of his reach. His hand was opening and closing like a wind-up toy on a spring. She thought, "Damn, I've got to get this over with or we're all dead!"

Roy's hand slipped inside her blouse down to her bra. He said in a husky voice, "You've got to come closer I can't reach you." He was straining to get to her.

She felt disgusted but said seductively, "Let me in Roy. I could hide below the glass if you let me in, nobody will see me." As he hesitated, she said, "Roy, I want you closer to me." She neared the slot again, just close enough for him to touch her breasts again. As his hand moved toward her nipple, she glanced back up and out the door. She stepped back. Roy stood in the booth staring at her disheveled blouse. Her bra exposed her voluptuous breasts. She was near the guard, but just out of his reach.

Suddenly, the buzzer went off and the door was unlocked. In the small part of her back rested a small caliber pistol. She stepped into the booth and flaunted her body in front of Roy who was in full pursuit of her. He was worked up into a frenzy, she knew she had to move fast while he was vulnerable. As she entered, she unsheathed the pistol and pointed it right between his eyes, saying "Roy step backwards" as she gestured with a shrug of her shoulders, "Believe me, you slime ball, I'll kill you if you move." Hatred spewed from the tone of her voice. The guard's features looked washed out, showing the terribly injured look, he felt. She said, "Back up!" He backed against the wall and a flicker of hope showed in his eyes. Melonie said, "Don't twitch a muscle or I'll shoot you." The pistol was cocked as she stood ready, saying, "Open the gates."

He said contemptuously, "You won't shoot, and I won't open the gates, you bitch."

Melonie sent a solitary bullet along the side of his thigh. The bullet ricocheted off the metal wall of the small room in her direction. Luckily, the bullet missed and hit the heavy steel door. The bullet's velocity was spent; it fell to the concrete floor spinning.

Savagely, Roy glared at her as he grasped his hand to his wound, the blood dripped down his leg. The sound of her pistol was muffled by the silencer; it was still loud inside the small space. Having no choice but to do as she said, the guard opened the gates. He grunted in agony as he pressed the electronic panel.

She said, "You better not move. Roy, I believe you just lost your job." She reached for Roy and pulled him to the other side of the booth.

He was completely aware that he had just committed the greatest mistake of his career. He would lose his job.

Melonie was grinning from ear to ear as she plundered through the desk drawers until she found some cord. She said, "Put your chest on the desk, spread your legs and put your hands behind you." After she bound Roy's hands, she pushed him to the floor and with a swift move wrapped the cord tightly around his ankles. "Now, Roy, how can you ever take me out on that date?"

Upstairs, Dr. Weston withdrew a four-inch needle he had inserted into Sebastian's chest. Durbish stood outside the cell, keeping watch for the guard who was on lunch break. Dr. Weston said, "The medicine won't take long, Durbish. Go find a guard or anybody." He tossed the syringe into the hole in the floor. Dr. Weston looked at Scott and said, "Be ready. This stuff is liable to send him into trauma."

Durbish returned with the guard, whose lunch had been interrupted twice today. Dr. Weston said, "This will be the last time we will intrude on you. Can you lead my assistant to a restroom?" He felt his respectable position as a guard was being abused. Their excuse to disrupt his lunch was weak.

Durbish chuckled at the lame excuse as the guard unlocked the steel door to show Scott to the restroom. As he watched them go down the hall, Dr. Weston's attention returned to Sebastian and thought, "The injected drug entered his bloodstream easily." Momentarily, Sebastian rested his left hand over his mouth and Dr. Weston saw he remained conscious.

Sebastian was making every effort to remain calm and not panic as the drug took its effect. He turned to look up at David and lay very still. His breathing became ragged. Dr. Weston checked his pulse. It, as well, had sharply decreased. Hurriedly, David whispered, "Sebastian, listen."

A vacant look loomed over Sebastian's face. Dr. Weston deliberately drew close to him and rubbed his face. Sebastian was disoriented as he tried to focus on the face of the doctor. Dr. Weston said, "It's a normal reaction, Sebastian. Stay calm. He looked at Durbish as he said, "My concern is that he won't stay this way." Moments later Durbish stood beside the cot next to the doctor.

Suddenly, they heard what their friend heard several times a day. The guard's keys rattled as he and Scott reentered the corridor. Durbish quietly asked the doctor, "Did you give him enough of the drug to do the trick?" The doctor said, "I don't know, Durbish."

The guard turned the key to let Scott in and was summoned to enter. Dr. Weston said to the guard, "Something was going on with the prisoner." The guard glanced over in the direction of the prisoner, unconcerned.

Dr. Weston said, "Really, there's something wrong with him. This may be baseless, but I'm the doctor here and I tell you this man is very ill." The doctor was stern in his manner as he got the point across. The guard said, "Nonsense."

As if on cue, Sebastian jolted on the bed. Durbish said, "The man is having an attack." David and Scott looked at the guard as a smile spread across his face.

Dr. Weston said, "What is funny? This man is in cardiac arrest!" David leaned over Sebastian and placed both of his hands together to manually pump Sebastian's heart. "Get the prison's doctor and a gurney, we need to take this man to hospital fast."

The three men watched as the guard ran to unlatch the cell door. He ran down the hall. The doctor was applying steady pressure as he counted in two second intervals. The guard retraced his footsteps down the corridor with what sounded like a stampede of people approaching the cell they occupied.

Dr. Weston looked at Durbish and quietly said, "Now, the show will begin."

The corridor gleamed to perfection from its daily wax and buff. One man fell on its slick surface and caused a pile-up. The Warden was the last to fall headfirst into the pile. The bushy headed psychologist wasn't very lucky. He lay under the pile and voiced the unnatural acts he would deliver promptly if they didn't get off. "Get the fuck off me, now!" He was screaming so loud but under eight other good-sized men, only a few words were understandably clear.

Warden Jarod Masser permitted this until he found his footing. At the top of his lungs he barked direct orders, "Clear the hall immediately." The lieutenant's head was visible under the pile. Putting his arm out a mock salute was attempted.

As more orders were being shouted in the corridor, Sebastian's struggle continued. The color of his complexion was a deep shade of gray. In minutes the blue had washed into the gray tone to completely cover his body like ash colored paint.

Durbish punched at the guard who had been sent to find the prison's doctor. The doctor's assistant was still on the bottom of the pile beside the bushy-headed psychologist.

Durbish yelled, "Let me out."

The guard whirled around, physically shaking with anger as he opened the door.

Dr. Weston was frantically pumping downwards on Sebastian's chest. He knew he was not in serious trouble if he helped the heart flush the medication out of his arteries. He said to Scott, "Sebastian is aphasic."

Scott said, "Then it's fortunate for him you're here, Doc. He asked, "What is aphasic?"

Dr. Weston said breathlessly, "He is unable to communicate, and he does not show visible signs of response."

The Warden cleared the hall outside of all the unneeded staff members then stepped into the cell. The doctor's assistant, psychologist and lieutenant stepped inside the cell. Behind him all eyes were riveted on the dying killer!

Perplexed by the circumstances, the Warden consulted with the psychologist, because the chief medical doctor had not been available. They spoke privately as possible inside the crowded cell. The bushy hair on top of the big man was shaking wildly from side to side. It looked like a ship tossing on the rough waters in an ocean swell.

It was apparent to Dr. Weston that the two men agreed that the patient was dying.

Scott stood close to the doctor's side and quietly asked, "Are you ready for Plan B?"

"I've been ready!"

"You just say when and give me a two second lead so I can slam the clip in."

Dr. Weston could feel Sebastian's heartbeat regulated. Minutes were critical to make the plan work. They had to move him before he woke up. His breathing was undetectable.

Stepping closer to the cot, the warden asked Dr. Weston, "May we take a look?"

The physician's assistant stepped next to the cot and bent over the killer to listen to his heartbeat.

Dr. Weston said, "He has suffered a heart attack."

The PA was a substandard assistant at best and agreed with Dr. Weston's opinion. He asked the Warden, "What do we do?"

The Warden asked the psychologist. The bushy headed man was determined to steal the show. He asked the lieutenant, "Can we securely move him without any help from the others? Also, can we be certain the man suffered a heart attack?"

Dr. Weston interrupted the lieutenant's train of thought before he had another chance to speak, "This incident, as odd as it seems, is a blatant neglect of the prisoner's well-being. Do you understand what I am saying? I certainly have cause to claim malpractice in full view of three United Nations witnesses. The condition of this man, killer or not, is very serious and he is dying. As a medical representative of the United Nations, I insist we take him to a hospital as soon as possible or heads will roll. Since you three gentlemen can't decide what to do, Randall, bring in the gurney." At the instant he barked his command, his subtle threat had worn thin on the Warden.

The Warden said, "Hold on--"

Before he could complete his thought, Durbish briskly shoved his massive body through the congested cell. As he began to move forward, he noted the tension was increasing within the cell. Tempers were flaring and seconds mattered.

Sebastian was clearly in a restful state, not one that looked like a heart attack. Any second he thought the medication might stop working. If he woke up and did not have a clear understanding of what was taking place it could become a fouled-up mess that would ruin everything, they had to move fast.

Durbish asked the Warden, "Can I speak to you in private?"

"Surely," the Warden replied.

Durbish followed him out of the cell. The door remained open. Two guards stood wide-eyed in the corridor. Both gave Durbish a bitter look. "Warden, this man is in a deteriorating state. I must insist that we help. Why do you continue to hamper our efforts in this matter? Furthermore, the crisis has already gone beyond what is considered timely. If it's necessary, I'm quite able to take full responsibility for the prisoner. We move dangerous individuals all the time. I can't seem to make you understand. The man in there is dying."

The Warden just stared at Durbish and then told the two guards to prepare the prisoner for transport. The two guards rushed into the cell and handcuffed Sebastian to his cot. The Warden turned to Durbish as he said, "You'd better find a large hole to climb into if anything goes wrong. I will have your head on a platter. The two guards will ride in place of your two men. You drive the ambulance. Is that agreeable?"

Durbish said, "Well, what do my men do, walk to the hospital?"

"How in the hell do I know? You juggle the issue now, Mr. McFane. You figure it out. I think this matching of wits has gone far enough."

Durbish yelled Scott's name. "Nobody move," was the next sound heard within the cell. "Damn," Dr. Weston exclaimed, then rushed to lead the Warden back into the cell with Durbish following close beside him. Scott had the ten-gauge leveled and held waist height against his hip. "Do as I say! Get on the floor, all of you."

A blast was heard downstairs as Scott shot one of the guards that charged him. The blast sent blood and particles of body fragments across the cell and onto the wall as it tore through the side of the guard's now useless brain. The others lay face down, confident the maniac holding the shotgun was serious. If they had any doubts, the blood that oozed across the floor under their outstretched bodies was a good reminder.

The echoing sound alarmed the guards in the corridors. The booming blast ebbed; the eerie seconds were just studied by all the tense men within the prison walls. The guards were frantically calling each other from their stations, trying to find out what had caused the sudden noise. As they tried to organize themselves, they found out the Warden had been taken prisoner.

Dr. Weston took control of Sebastian. He shook him hoping that he would voluntarily awaken and talk to him.

Downstairs, Melonie was terrified. She was downstairs with Roy; he was still tied up mad as hell. Her small pistol was of no use against the men inside the towers, one which stood directly in view of where she and the guard were. A well-placed spray from a submachine gun could easily riddle the booth with bullets. She was vulnerable if yet remained in view of the tower. She closed the slot to the booth to make certain she would be out of the way of any stray bullets from her gung-ho friend, Scott.

Upstairs, Scott still held the advantage. He held his gun on the four men, swearing, "If any of you even breathe too hard, I'll blow your damn heads off." Scott was satisfied with the results of his threat. He observed the men on the floor and none of them dared take a full breath of air. Satisfied, he smiled as the psychologist nodded in submission to his orders.

David was still trying desperately to revive his perished friend. Several minutes had passed by. Dr. Weston delivered a hard slap to Sebastian's jaw. His eyes flickered open only to close once more. David had passed his limit. He was uncertain of what to do. He violently shook Sebastian who now began coughing and gasping for air. As he tried to breathe through his congested lungs, he asked, "What kind of fucking specialist are you, man?" Durbish and Scott roared with laughter at David.

The dead guard a corpse was the first thing that Sebastian's eyes focused on. As he stood on his own the surroundings and the situation seeped into his brain, Sebastian fought the unpleasant urge to vomit. He took a deep breath, asking, "What do we do now?"

Durbish announced as he clapped Sebastian on his back, "You make an escape, alarms started ringing all through the prison. Outside, the wailing sirens signaled the guards of an emergency.

Sinking out of view, Melonie crouched near the control panel searching for a button that would override the alarms. Inside the security booth, the phone began to ring. She saw the guard outside holding a phone in the air, plainly a sign it was him calling her. The loud singing of the sirens was deafening. She found the buttons to shut off the alarms. Now she was about to pick up the receiver, she noticed Scott and Durbish rounding the corner down the corridor.

She jammed her automatic pistol into the waistband of her nurse's uniform and turned on the outside speakers. She took the microphone and yelled, "Be careful, Scott." She noticed he had attached a long clip into his ten-gauge shotgun. Melonie put the microphone down and waited as Durbish and Scott quickly made their way to the booth. Melonie opened the door and as they rushed safely in, she found the switches that controlled the gates. As the wall of steel clanged shut behind them, the two men knew she was in full control of the situation.

Scott and Durbish shook their heads as they inspected the man on the floor. Durbish said quickly, "The gates are closed."

"Yes," she said.

"Open it."

"Why, we're safe, Durbish."

He chuckled and reminded her that they were waiting for David and Sebastian before they all left. She hit the control button once again and the gates opened. Instantly, she apologized for forgetting. They all laughed at her embarrassment. She gathered her wits and they all waited for David and Sebastian to appear.

Durbish asked for Melonie's radio and switched it on and said, "David, come in." He quickly responded Durbish asked, "How much longer will you be?"

David replied, "We're coming right now. We just got what we were looking for. Sebastian is still a little groggy from the antidote, but he is okay."

Durbish told him they were inside the booth and the guard from the tower has us pinned down with a steady line of fire. He said, "I'm going to send Scott out to take care of the tower. When you are round the corner, be careful." Static was all that was heard.

As they waited and watched in silence, Melonie heard distinct sounds of paper rustling. It was a distinct sound within the confining booth. She traced the sound and found its source. Without a care in the world, Scott was leaning against the wall, straddling the guard, eating the man's lunch. He caught the look of disbelief in Melonie's eyes. He smiled innocently as crumbs trickled down his shirt onto the floor. He said, "Well, I'm starved, Melonie, and there's no telling how long it will be before we can eat." She was speechless and could not respond.

She turned to Durbish for support. He briefly stared at Scott and turned his attention back to the corridor. As he turned away from Scott, he told him to hurry up. Scott shoved the other half of the man's sandwich into his mouth. He unslung the shotgun from around his shoulder as he gulped the last bite of food.

It was moments like this that Melonie found it was easy to admit to herself that Scott was so cool. He clearly showed no signs of being nervous as he said, "I'm ready."

She was thoroughly amazed. Durbish offhandedly said, "Go," as he opened the door Scott eased his sturdily built body out into the open hall. He plunged himself across the opposite side of the hallway, sliding behind a desk. The guard inside the tower thought he had seen something but had missed his sudden movement. It was a grave mistake.

Durbish saw David peek around the corner. He opened the door just as Scott raised the barrel of his gun. He shouted, "Scott, hold up. "Scott's head snapped, turning in Durbish's direction, who was pointing down the hall. Scott glanced in the same direction and saw David was leading Sebastian who was limping slightly up the long corridor. Pressing against David for support, they slowly made their way, closing the gap ever so slowly.

Scott leaned against the desk with his back to it as he watched the two men inching their way down the corridor. He had no choice but to patiently wait for them to reach the booth. They were all startled as the sirens began their shrill noise once more. Melonie hit the button to shut them off. This time it did not work. Durbish rushed out of the booth to help David with Sebastian. He shouted for Scott to get to the gates.

Scott was not sure what was going on, but as Durbish fled down the hall, Scott sent a grenade sailing into the tower window. The blast sent the spotlight perched on the rooftop twenty feet above the destroyed tower. Gray granite stones scattered randomly on the road and lawn across the front of the prison. A chair landed, ending its spiraling and somersaulting, as shards of granite and body parts showered the street and lawn. The piercing sounds of the sirens continued.

David held Sebastian's arms, dragging him the remainder of the way to the booth. As Scott surveyed the damage to the tower, he mumbled to himself, "Impressive." At the same time, rushed to the entranceway, setting his sights on his next target, another tower down the edge of the prison's entrance.

He suddenly heard someone rushing down the corridor. His hands were clasped tightly around the grips of his weapon. One hand instinctively slid to the trigger. Quickly, he realized the sound came from not one but a multitude of men coming his way. His muscles tensed as he realized the danger, he left himself wide open in the doorway. As they rushed around the corner of the corridor, Scott counted close to at least eighteen men dressed in full shields, wearing helmets, and lowering their weapons in front of their bodies. He coolly observed the men and did not move.

Melonie saw him grinning and nudged Durbish as she said, "Scott's about to obliterate those guys. Are you going to stand by and allow him to do it?"

Before he could respond, Scott delivered his first shot. It was meant for a warning. He stood there holding his gun as the smoke drifted from the barrel tip pointed in the air above his head. Shards of plaster showered him as dust filled the air around him.

Melonie's fingernails dug into Durbish's forearm as the sound of Scott's weapon discharged. David asked, "Durbish, what do you suggest we do now?" As the two men tried to determine what to do, Melonie suggested speaking to the onslaught of men through the speakers. She said, "They can hear you." She placed the microphone in Durbish's hand.

He quickly tested her theory, saying, "Scott, hold your fire." His voice echoed down the corridor.

Behind the group of guards stood the Warden and lieutenant. Their entry halted halfway down the corridor. The group looked anxious to disburse, shifting their bodies from side to side. The lieutenant was not pleased and wanted the Warden to give them orders. The psychologist appeared and he was obviously angry as he noted the standoff. He began screaming to the Warden, "Get those bastards!"

Scotts eyes met the psychologists as he grinned at the furious man, he began cursing everyone including the Warden. Scott pumped a grenade into the chamber. The sound of it lodging into the tubular device was equally impressive as its destructive results. The Warden knew his men had to advance and urged the lieutenant and the psychologist to go back up the hallway and let the guards rush the madman before he had a chance to launch the grenade. As the Warden and the two others moved back, the guards rushed towards Scott.

Scott lowered his body just as something hit the doorway above his shoulder. The sounds reached him seconds after the bullets smashed into the wall behind him. "Damn," he said, "It's getting hostile in here."

Just as he took aim in their direction, Melonie hit the button closing the steel gates blocking their entrance. In the seconds before the gates closed, the grenade cleared the gap. The blast sent most of the guards screaming in fear. Their faces bleeding with limbs dangling from injured bodies. Shields were strewn like cards across the floor as the few remaining guards retreated.

Scott quickly motioned for the others to follow him outside. He yelled, "Come on! Let's go! Hurry!" He stopped just outside the doorway, covering the front entrance. He saw nothing and stepped back inside as the others reached him. David was the first outside and he said, "Hold up." Each of his partners cleared the doorway and when they were all outside, he laid his barrel between the steel crossbars and fired another grenade.

As they all were running down the steps, they heard the blast. Scott fled down the steps passing everyone. Durbish was holding Sebastian who had not regained his full strength. Sebastian was trying to sort out all the jumbled events going on around him. Melonie was running full out for the ambulance when she fell, smashing her left shoulder into the sidewalk. The pain spread slowly at first, then she felt a bolt of pain run the length of her arm. She said, "I can't drive. My arm is either dislocated or broken. I'm not sure which." Scott said "I'll drive. Get in." He opened the door and she lunged into the front seat the pain in her arm was excruciating.

The others scrambled into the back of the vehicle and Scott yelled, "Hold on everyone." As the vehicle gathered speed, Scott slammed another grenade into the chamber.

The silhouette of the guard in the last tower was barely visible. He sent a grenade in its direction. As Scott fired, the guard's bullets were punching holes in the roof and windshield of the ambulance. The windshield was shattered. Scott's grenade bounced off the tower into the road in front of them and never went off. He saw it spinning on the pavement, David yelled "Get the hell out of here there's a hot grenade on the road."

They all looked at Scott and held their breaths as they maneuvered around the unspent grenade. They bounced over the last speed breaker as Scott sped out of site of the prison.

Scott asked Sabastian "If he was all right?" He slowly replied, "Yes sure I am fine considering I've been in a prison for weeks, beaten daily, close to malnutrition, and some quack doctor half kills me and another idiot trying to save me is firing a grenade launcher at anything that moves-- and you ask me if I'm all, right?"

Durbish just looks at everybody and shakes his head and turns back to Sebastian and says, "I see prison life didn't change you much."

After Durbish made sure everyone hurt was going to be ok, he said to David, "Turn on the sirens."

One by one he flipped the switches, and the lights began flashing and blinking wildly as the siren wailed.

David asked, "Where's the map?"

Scott said, "I have it."

"Well then, where to boss?"

Scott said, "Cut those damn sirens off and I'll tell you."

After David flipped the switch, the sirens wound down to a purr and stopped.

Durbish said, "Well, this whole surprise--or should I say, so far, this escape plan for Sebastian has been a great success." His little speech was accompanied by a smattering of applause by the whole gang. "Now, you don't really believe we're anywhere close to getting out of this so easily, do you?"

While everyone thought about that Melonie said, "Someone needs to have a look at my arm." She had a cold expression a hard look on her face.

Scott said, " You will have to drive as he eased the ambulance over to the shoulder of the road.

Scott opened the rear doors and David told him to help him get Melonie in the back. David and Scott gently lifted her out and carried her to the rear of the vehicle. David opened his medical bag and gave her a shot for the pain as Scott closed the door. David gently laid Melonie's head on a cushion.

In the distance, David heard sirens wailing through the city streets. He ran to the driver's seat as he said, "Big time trouble, guys. I assume they have mounted their efforts to find us."

As they were speeding off, Durbish said, "That can be expected. Turn left here. Two streets down we have a land rover parked inside a building. You remember when I left?" Scott said "That's what you were doing this morning?" "Turn left here?"

The ambulance wasn't very fast, but Scott pushed it to its limit at 63 miles per hour.

As the ambulance roared down the street, David probed along Melonie's shoulder and arm. She said, "It feels strained I am glad it's not broken?"

David said, "I don't think so, Melonie, in fact, it's more likely as you suspect a strained muscle. I'm going to have to wrap your shoulder, I have to take your blouse off."

David tried to help as she pulled her arm out, she screamed. She rolled shifting to her weight onto her other side as she slipped off her blouse. David inspected her further. He said, "Your cold now?"

"Well, I'm half naked, David. What do you expect?"

David rubbed his hands over her, making certain no bones were broken. He said, "You seem to be okay. You never looked better. In fact, you look really good, Melonie."

"Give me my blouse, you pig." Everyone laughed, even Durbish. The stress from the last few hours was finally tapering off.

Durbish said, "Here--Turn here. This is where I left the land rover. There's the open door. Slow down, don't miss it, Scott."

Durbish watched his wife put on her blouse. He was also watching David who was gazing at her beautiful body. Durbish thought, "My God, he's not even trying to hide it. He's even flaunting it."

Scott slowed the ambulance to a crawl as the vehicle dipped, they entered the building. The slight dip tossed Melonie over to bump into David. He gripped her like he had just saved her life. She looked at Durbish and shrugged her shoulder to show her dislike of the apparent come-on.

Durbish said, "Drive up two levels and to the left there is a ramp. We'll all be perfectly safe here." He did not speak again. Melonie noticed his coolness. She was aware of his jealous streak which was more prominent now than ever. As the ambulance came to a halt, she forgot about the whole thing.

Scott backed the ambulance next to the land rover and pulled up hard on the brakes. He glanced around the empty building and then shut the motor off. It sputtered as he killed the switch. He opened his door and let his feet dangle freely as he sat sideways in the driver's seat. He was relaxing, enjoying the view over the edge of the abandoned building. He commented, "From here you can see for miles."

David reached into his medical bag and handed Jennifer a tube of ointment for her shoulder. He was animated as he suggested he could help her apply the ointment to her shoulder later.

"David, you're way out of line. Is your intention to rub this goo all over me and expect it to turn me on?" She grabbed the ointment from David's hand as he lowered his head like a scolded child.

He mumbled, "Oh, yeah, you'd be perfect." He looked up a second too late. Melonie's slap could be heard throughout the building. David was shocked. She was mauling him. None of them had ever seen her so angry.

Scott grabbed her by one ankle and pried her free of David. She yelled, "I want to smash your damn face in." Scott held her firmly, as she started scratching him. David backed off shutting his door abruptly, inside the ambulance David hoped Scott could calm her down. Finally, Scott made her promise not to hurt David.

After he let go David wasn't sure if she'd keep her promise. He licked his lips and tasted blood. He hated that coppery taste. He spat on the concrete, not that it was bleeding badly but bad enough, he decided to stay clear of the girl, hoping she'd calm down.

Melonie sat in the back of the vehicle glaring at the men. None of them dared say anything to her. It was obvious none of them wanted to find themselves in a scrap with this girl and the pistol stuck in her waistband made it that much easier to ignore her. With one hand, she tapped the butt of her pistol steadily, to some unknown musical beat in her head taunting them.

Scott joined in, patting the back of his seat. After a few moments she cooled down and apologized to everyone but David. She said, "You're such a jerk." Durbish said, "Look, he's uptight just like the rest of us so why don't we just cool down and forget it."

Sebastian asked Durbish, "What's your idea on how we get back to the States? I've about had it with these people and the way they've been kicking my ass lately. Frankly, I'm fed up with it and glad I won't be here to find out what else they had planned for me."

Durbish was tickled by Sebastian's outburst. He knew Sebastian was coming around. It was obvious he was choked up and said, "Hold on." He looked him in the eyes and said, "I'm glad you survived, and it seems you are your old self again, but you'll find I've taken care of everything as usual. So, please, let's all get some much-needed rest. I have another truck coming." He glanced at his watch and continued,

"We will leave in two hours. Wake me up in an hour and a half. All the others know the plan and they can fill you in, just wake me up the others will go over it with Scott, what you need to do is take the ambulance out of here, let's take out what we need and get it packed into the land rover."

Scott said, "It's a done deal." Scott had swiftly completed the transfer and was jogging back toward the abandoned building. Darkness had covered the city. As he kept a steady pace, his shoes made a loud crunching noise on the loose gravel street. The moonlight gave him a clear view of obstacles as he ran. He veered right and left to dodge an obstruction in his path. A girl stood outside a bar when he passed. She whistled, trying to gain his attention. Like a performer he turned his body and jogged backwards past her. The girl then eased her long dress upwards to show off her slender legs. He turned and ran placing one hand above his head as he waved goodbye. She cried out for him to stop. At the pace he ran, she knew this wasn't likely and cursed him in her foreign tongue. He had run two miles from where he had ditched the ambulance. They had agreed that it would be best if it were found and leaving it a few miles away gave them an advantage to slip out of the area. He was tired and slowed his pace as he neared the abandoned building. The others were dozing, but Sebastian woke as he heard Scott approaching. Scott bumped into the side of the land rover and knelt beside it catching his breath.

Sebastian stepped out of the vehicle. The door ajar left the interior aglow. The light did not disturb anyone. Melonie was in a fetal position against the back left side. David was in the front passenger seat sleeping soundly as he leaned against the window. Durbish reclined in the driver's seat. Sebastian caught himself staring at them like he didn't recognize them any longer. As he eased the door closed the moonlight cast shadows of both men's figures across the floor. Sebastian said, "You look like Tarzan, all pumped up from working out."

"A man's got to stay fit."

"I suppose so. I try, but lately my strength has been all but gone." "Yeah, well, you'll be all right," Scott said. "Is there any food in here?"

Sebastian laughed at Scott and said, "That's how I'll always remember you, eating or working out. Look in the back. I'm not sure if there's any food in there but be quite the others are asleep. When you finish, come over here close to the wall and let's talk." Sebastian walked to the other side of the building.

Scott could be heard saying, "Is there anything to eat in here?" as he rummaged through the back of the vehicle."

Pleasant memories flooded Sebastian's thoughts as a grin spread across his face, he swept the skies and watched the stars blinking, it made him glad to be alive. The whole sky above him was fixed to his position. To regain his freedom to gaze into the heavens was something Sebastian had sorely missed while in prison. He spoke softly to the world he looked on, "I bet you thought I'd never be here. It surprised me as well, but I'm very glad to see your magnificence again." He gently stepped forward, getting close to the ledge. He had a view through the open wall and sat next to the corner and just let himself release his fears and the immense sorrow he felt. He said, "Thank you God. As I sit beneath your domain, I suddenly feel your power again and that pleases me. Only hours ago, I was caught, and my life was in your hands, but even so my fear, Father, is for my friends' lives who brought me here. They will need your guidance, as I will, in the coming days. Do we stand a chance?" He sat there believing he had received an answer as he soaked in the wonders of the surroundings.

His mood suddenly turned defensive as beams of light flooded the street below him. A convoy of trucks had rounded the right corner of the building. He noticed two, no three trucks full of soldiers, their lights sweeping from side to side and up the buildings as they slowly made their way down the street. Quizzically, he stared up and said, "Well, you didn't say it was going to be easy, did you?" The floodlight's beam reached his position. He flung himself backwards onto the floor and rolled clear of the searchlight. He thought he had moved quickly enough.

Scott dropped his sandwich and froze instinctively at the sight of Sebastian's sudden movements and the presence of the light. In the eerie darkness both men looked at each other, realizing their position was not secure.

Sebastian told Scott quietly, "Wake Durbish" "Don't open the door just tap on the window and keep everybody calm and quiet. Scott leaned against the vehicle and furiously tapped. The constant tap, tap, tap caused Durbish to open his eyes. The sight of Scott so near the window momentarily startled him. Durbish's attention was quickly drawn by the sweep of the crisscrossing beams of light. The flashing lights flared up an old fear inside Durbish, reminding him of times he spent in the trenches. The flashing lights then were as real now, and he knew they carried the same dreadful result if the lights found their mark. The loud rumbling of the trucks faded. The seconds seemed like hours. Inside the vehicle everyone was silent, a little concerned, but none of them professed it. The fear was real those large diesel engines shook the building as they noisily rolled past. A sense of relief and triumph apparent as the thunderous roars faded. All the gang cheered. The pitch-black building was a welcome relief.

After all of them surrounded the front of the vehicle, Durbish said, "That was quite a tumultuous event."

Scott said, "I don't know about to-mul-to-us, but it scared the hell out of me." Everyone laughed at his remark.

Durbish enunciating the word tumultuous, then said, "Scott, the word means chaotic, turbulent, frenzied and any of those can be scary."

"Well, then, why didn't you say scared. It makes better sense to me if you'd--ah, forget it, Durbish. My education is fine with me. You can keep your big words for all I care and mulch 'em. I was scared, not tu-mul-tu-fied!" All of them burst into laughter loud enough to wake the dead.

"All right, you guys, knock it off," Scott said. He politely asked Durbish, "Would cha mind speaking in plain English for my benefit?"

Durbish said, "Since earlier today, and even now, you've been so benevolent, I'll be certain to use small words for your benefit, Sir Scott."

"Ah, shit, Durbish, you're such an ass, but I'm most aware of your bombastic style and I'm not stigmatized by your behavior towards me." A roar of laughter from Durbish was heard down the streets. He loved what Scott said and so did all of them.

Melonie said, "Hey, Scott, that was really funny. Where did you learn to be so prudent?"

"Mel-on-knee--"

"Just--Jus'--Jus kidding, Scott."

"Well, 'Jus' leave me alone, please."

"Hey," she said, "that was meant to be a compliment, if you didn't notice."

Scott turned to face her and looked down as if his feelings had been hurt.

Melonie approached him and said, "You're my friend. We don't always see things the same and I'm a bitch, at least that's how you've always treated me, but Scott, I'm not. You're not like I've envisioned you. You're more human than I thought and, well, I just want to thank you for saving my life today and I'm sure everyone else feels the same way."

Scott felt awkward and said, "Oh."

"Scott, what started the trouble upstairs?"

Scott said, "That Warden, whatever his name is, was acting really pissy, and he put us in a bad spot. That kicked it off. The next thing I know, I'd blown off half the man's head off."

"Did that bother you, Scott?"

"Well, not really, but yeah--yea, it does. It was sudden like."

"Well, what about the others?"

"I had no choice," he said. "What about the guy in the booth, what'd he do?"

Everyone seated in the land rover waited for Melonie's answer. Melonie joked about Roy. "The buffoon!" I couldn't hurt ole Roy. She misdirected attempts by any of them to find out the reason she hadn't done poor Roy in.

Durbish whispered, "It's apparent you're not going to give us any clear-cut reason."

She acted innocent at first and said, "Apparently, you've forgotten. You taught me that a long time ago."

"Taught you what?"

"How to avoid answering questions?"

Melonie got angry by their probing and tried to avoid the whole business which had now been blown out of proportion.

Durbish said, "Just let it go, everyone. Whatever happened, we all know she must have had good cause." He apologized for trying to dig so far and said, "It's all right if you don't tell us."

Melonie laughed and rolled down her shirtsleeves, crossed her arms, stretched out against the back seat and instantly appeared to fall into a deep sleep.

Durbish said, "Scott, let's get out of this building. Those troops may double back and search the building. We'll just have to forget about making the connection with the other truck."

The Warden was informed by the troops when they called saying they found the abandoned ambulance. Homes and offices were searched high and low in the surrounding area. The lieutenant scoured the city and was outraged that the group had vanished. All the evidence pointed to him that the group had outside help. The abandoned vehicle was full of bullet holes; punctured tires and the windshield had been smashed. He said to the Warden, "I'm certain there were other people involved." An all-out effort had begun to find the source of those unknown people. The lieutenant was angry at the Warden for being duped. The Warden's office was bombarded by phone calls.

The search was top priority throughout the country. A curfew was effective immediately in Nigeria, beginning in the city of Abuja. The troops' task grew in constant scope in Abuja and the city was litterly being torn apart.

Juliette saw light beams rapidly trace the sky out her bedroom window. She could think of only one reason for the lights. She felt the name, "Sebastian," escape her lips, like someone else had spoken it. "Sebastian," she said aloud and wept in joy, realizing he was free.

Sebastian said, "Durbish, I know this road goes to the village. I'm telling you, it's about 30 miles from here."

"All right," Durbish said, "Scott, follow this road but be careful. It does not look like much of a road to me. David, what do you think?"

David responded, "Do we have any other choices? We are out of the city and Sebastian said he knows where we are. What else do you want?"

Sebastian reminded all of them how he had entered the city by saying, "I followed the two roads back there. One river road met another. I crossed both waterways. Look on the map, David, one river goes south to Port Harcourt. It breaks out into several branches and dumps into the Gulf of Guinea."

"All right," David said, "I see it."

"Okay, then we're just above the Niger River."

"Okay, got it."

"But those were the main river roads. What we want is to follow the small area out there. He tapped on the map and sat back in his seat. Beside him, Melonie and Durbish were leaning in between the two front seats like kids. Scott drove slowly, following the river's course as it wound deeply into the jungle that Sebastian had walked through.

David asked, "Sebastian, how did you walk 100 miles in this terrain with no food except what you could shoot?"

"It only took three and a half days and a well-drawn map."

David said, "I've gotta tell you, Sebastian, I'm very impressed that you could carry out such a mission."

"Do you mean you don't believe I did it, David?"

"Yes." he said. He did not believe him, but he would not say it. He thought it."

"Tomorrow, we'll all be on foot. Our easy traveling will be over. As untimely as it may be, it will be impossible to continue in the land rover."

Scott said, "Listen, as long as it's all right with all of you, I'm going to make a road somehow. Somebody is going to help me cut, push or drag this truck out of these woods because I'm not planning on walking period."

Sebastian said, "You're wrong, but if we can, that's what we'll do. Let me be the first one to tell all of you, these aren't woods. This is a jungle and to quote my old buddy, the pilot, who dropped me in this hell hole, 'Mister, this is the meanest jungle in the world.' I've spent much time cursing the man and the day he dropped me here."

"Forgive me now for warning you, but I have no doubts now he was correct. Somehow, I made it and I know the way out. We all know the roads in the city and airports are surely being watched. There is no way we can attempt to leave, but we can hide in here for a long time. We could also die in this jungle, but my guess is, we won't. You see, I made friends with not only the people in the village of Kaduna, but with the jungle's creatures as well."

David said, "What the hell do you mean Sebastian? Made friends with what creatures?"

"Oh, you'll meet them soon enough, David."

David said, "What happened to you while you were incarcerated?"

Scott said, "What'd you do in there? Did you go a little crazy?"

"Hold it, one question at a time. If you really want to know, I'll tell you when we rest cause it is a long, long story. By the way, we're about to run out of road."

David said, "Real fine, messy place. Scott, pull over there."

"Wait a minute, Scott, let's check to make sure it's safe."

"Why?" David said, "It looks like a clear spot."

Sebastian was calm and replied, "If you check, you'll find out it could be quicksand."

"Fine. This is not funny, Durbish," David said. How did we end up in this God forsaken place. I thought we were going to Morocco. Suddenly, we're all in some damned jungle and the next thing you know we'll all be burned at the stake like we're in some old Tarzan movie."

Durbish said, "You're not kidding, are you Sebastian?"

"No, I'm not kidding. I'll check before you move. It's getting too dark to guess if it's just a sandy spot."

Brusquely, Durbish cut off Sebastian and said to David, "Check it out."

David said, "Why me."

Scott said, "Ah, hell, I'll do it. Let me go look at the spot."

David said, "Stop, Scott," then opened his door. Suddenly, the sounds from the jungle flooded their senses. Chattering lemurs, odd tones from exotic birds and far off roars and loud knocks filled the air.

Sebastian opened his door hung his feet outside in the darkness of the jungle and said, "David, come on."

David stepped out and placed one foot on the ground carefully. Sebastian remembered the familiar ground, its softness and leaped out into the muck. David swung his body from the vehicle and sunk ankle deep instantly and began screaming bloody murder. By the time Sebastian placed his hand on David's shoulder, he was shaking terribly. Sebastian was trying to calm him as he begged, "Please save me from sinking."

"Calm down, David, you're in mud. The bottom is firm. Don't you feel it."

"Damn, I thought I was a goner."

As Sebastian helped him tug his feet loose from the mud, they heard a hyena laugh nearby. Durbish was suddenly aware of this noise, one of his least liked species in the wild. His fingers dug into the cushion of the seat. No one noticed how frightened he was of the carnivorous creatures.

Within the hour, the conspirators all voiced their opinion about how lucky they had been, making Sebastian's escape a reality. The unfortunate deaths caused by their improvising Plan B had been instrumental in freeing all of them along with Sebastian. The curfew throughout the city was in full effect with 100's of troops was widening. The search for the confederates had turned up nothing so far. It had been a wise decision by Durbish to forget about the second truck.

As the five compadres sat around a roaring fire, the sparks trickled through the lower branches of the dense jungle. In the darkness they all felt secure by the fire.

Sebastian knew when dawn came, the group's safety net would vanish. Slowly one by one they began to realize Sebastian was the only one who fully understood the danger of their surroundings.

They all listened intently, waiting for Sebastian's plan of escape. They were fascinated with Sebastian's stories of his leap into the Kudana jungle and the recount of his prison experiences.

Sebastian thought it would be best to let his friends continue to believe they were perfectly safe. As he looked at their faces, one by one, he knew their awareness of the dangers were creeping in. He quickly thought of a distraction. He said, "David, Scott, help me get the tent out of the vehicle." As they busied themselves, the laborious chores burned nervous energy.

Sebastian sadly thought, "The morning's light would bring a host of problems." He did his best not to voice his fears.

When they finished putting the tent up Scott said, "Let's get some sleep. I'm bushed."

"Okay, " Sebastian said, "I'll keep first watch. I've had all the rest I need for a while."

As Melonie joined the other three in the tent she said, "Durbish, do you know you've severely broken your rental contract on the truck?" Everyone laughed.

"They'll just have to bear with me. I will call them in the morning. Sebastian can lead us to the nearest phone on the river."

Sebastian heard another blast of laughter as he settled down in a tree near the rushing waters of the river. He clearly understood the danger he could be in near the water, but the sounds from any animals or intruders could be observed best where he had situated himself. After his careful inspection of the area, he kept a sharp eye out for any signs of danger as the rest of the gang snuggled into their sleeping bags.

After a long, careful observation, Sebastian lowered himself quietly to the ground. He shivered as the moisture from the river misted him. He made his way to the fire and sat down. He stirred the fire and the sparks flickered like fireflies and the ashes died quickly.

The tentmates squeezed together and found it suitable and cozy. They were exhausted and settled down to sleep, Scott broke the silence, "Will someone call room service and order dinner?" Their laughter echoed throughout the tent.

Sebastian once again heard their laughter and knew it was better for them to laugh rather than realize the real danger, they were in.

Melonie's distinct laugh trailed off and caused Sebastian to think of Juliette. He thought he should have told them of his wish to return to her. As soon as they made it back and his mission was complete, he'd tell them he was retiring. He'd say, "I'm selling everything. I'm cashing in my stocks so I can start a new life with Juliette."

Alone by the fire, he tried to sort things out. The flames mesmerized him. He was lost in thought as the memories of Juliette flooded through him. He wanted to hold her again. He found it easy to imagine her profile. He could see her plainly, her lovely body next to his. He envisioned her sipping wine, the same wine they had shared so long ago. It never happened, yet it had. He knew she was thinking of him because she purchased clothes for him. While Melonie was at the hotel Juliette had given him the items he had left behind. The shirt he now wore was the same shirt she had worn after they made love. She felt her closeness. Her heart was filled with joy. The guarantee that he would always love her and come back for her was now stronger than ever. It was something to strive for, him returning to take her away. As long ago as this seemed, she knew this dream would remain prominent in her mind until it became a reality. As he gazed up into the stars, he found the brightest star and silently swore to himself he would return. He knew that she would be safe with her uncle until his return.

Thoughts of the night he drove to the palace to shoot Andras kept resurfacing, and he forced them out again and again. He only wanted to think of Juliette now and his reinforced love for her. Her blinding beauty and intelligence was wasted in her subservient life with her uncle. He relaxed and bathed in the absorbing pleasure that soon they would be together again. Entertaining himself with his new goals in life, he knew the 20 years of rejection and obsessive lust for his old love had fallen into the category of past stupidity. He began pushing his old memories out, filling the void with Juliette's love for him. Her love was complete. This knowledge overpowered the possession he once nurtured and with this came the renewed custody of his soul.

****

Unable to see beyond the firelight, Sebastian heard footsteps just loud enough to cause the slightest sound. He wasn't alarmed by the sound as he saw Melonie walking through the darkness towards the fire. The blazing fire cast an odd, but provocative alure on her. The reflective firelight enhanced her figure and beauty. He noticed the stirring in his loins and casted it off as normal. Any man would find her attractive and desirable. He put down this arousal, knowing he had found his true love. Little above a whisper, he said, "Why aren't you sleeping Melonie?"

She sat down next to him. "I'm too keyed up. It is too exciting out here. The sounds of the water's passing and sudden noises from the wild animals are something I want to enjoy. I don't feel tired any longer."

He chuckled and said, "You'll be tired tomorrow, and I understand what you mean by the sounds of the jungle. I suppose it is exciting if you look at it that way." He paid special attention to her, making sure she was not cold by throwing more sticks into the fire.

"Sebastian, I've got something to tell you."

"Oh!"

"Well, Durbish and I--Well, we--"

"What?"

She blurted it out. "Durbish and I are married!"

"What? Why did--When did--Well, that's great."

"We've been married almost a year."

"Why haven't you told me? Who else knows?"

"Nobody," she said.

"Why not? Why the secrecy?" He suddenly felt angry for not being told. He listened to the fire crackle as the flame spewed and the moist wood made hissing sounds.

"Durbish didn't want anyone to know Sebastian. I'm sorry."

"Well, Melonie, isn't that a decision both of you would make. I just don't understand the reason for the secrecy, but congratulations."

"Wait, that's not all of it. It is not working out for us, and as soon as I get back to Washington, I'm filing for a divorce."

"My gosh, well, hell, I don't know what to say. I'm sorry it hasn't worked out. Does he have any idea?"

"No."

With a heavy sigh he stared at the tongues of fire, then turned to face Melonie. "In all fairness of your trust in me, I'll be frank here. I want to retire, which all of you know by now, and I have already done it. I have been wanting to retire, but this job was of a nature that it could not remain undone. This mission was my last. I plan to come back to Nigeria."

"Why? Are you crazy? What on God's green earth would you do that for?"

"I've met a woman, and you know her. The young lady that gave you, my clothes."

"Anita, you mean?"

"Well, her name is Juliette and it's a long-complicated story, but Melonie, we love each other."

"My God, Sebastian, she's awfully young, but very lucky. It's understandable that you love her. She is very beautiful and seems intelligent, but is that enough for you? I know how you are."

"Well, what do you mean, know how I am?"

"I know you. You haven't committed to anyone in years."

"Well, I guess you don't get it. I've finally found a woman that loves me and if you're trying to say I could never get over my obsession with Darla, the answer is yes, I have."

"I'm very happy for you, both of you." She leaned over into Sebastian's arms. He drew her near and held her in a warm, friendly embrace. When Sebastian's released his hold, she held onto him more tightly. Sebastian sharply caught the look in her eyes. The firelight cast a sensual glow over her and was an unbearable sensation to him. Both had once been very attracted to each other. Melonie was full of life. Her breathing increased. "Sebastian, you know I've never stopped loving you."

Sebastian fought back his urges as she said, "You must have realized this. I've been so lonely and have worried so much about you all month. I thought I would die if anything had happened to you." She dropped her head and gazed down into the fire. He could clearly see tears forming in the corners of her eyes as she shook her head and released her hold on him. She looked away and said, "All I wanted you to do is just kiss me one more time."

"Listen," he said as he knelt and poked at the fire. "The next time we're in a jungle--if we're in a jungle, remind me not to reveal any of my secrets to you." The burning wood created a loud pop that startled them both. Instinctively, she found a safe lading into Sebastian's arms. They found themselves falling onto the jungle's soft ground. This, planned or not, was more than both adults could cast aside.

Their desires for each other, planted long ago, resurfaced. They restrained the urge to go beyond heavy petting, but both felt that old need for each other's love. Their friendship had been more important. Now, all their emotions were mixed up. Melonie was kissing Sebastian and in seconds the two of them were touching each other in frantic actions filled with desperation. He, because his love was far away and, hers, a desperation from her need for someone to hold her. Both stopped, but they knew this was something that should have happened again. Their love affair ended a long time ago. Now it was too late. Taking no chances, Melonie smiled as she pulled him near and slid her hand across his chest. With her slender fingers she delicately unbuttoned his shirt. Not wanting to stop herself, she opened his shirt and ran her soft hands across his body.

Sebastian knew this had to stop, but his weakness or his genuine wanting her kept him from breaking away. Her touch felt nice her touch felt hot like the fire that raged inside both of them. His body was willing to let this continue. Suddenly, he said, "I can't. Melonie, you can't. I can't help myself. No, Melonie--" His tone hardened. "This isn't right. As much as I wish it were, it just shouldn't happen again."

Exasperated, she broke away from him and said, "You're right," as she rolled over and sat up with her legs crossed under her body. "Damn it, we've always had awful timing, huh, Sebastian?" She slung a stick into the fire.

"The worst timing. Let's give this a lot of time and space. You know I'm crazy about you Melonie. It just wouldn't be fair to Juliette."

"You're right, still I'm not giving up that easily. I've known you a lot longer and Juliette is a long way from America."

"Yeah, but so are we."

She gave him an impish grin over her shoulder as she quietly retreated into the tent.

He rebuttoned his shirt and thought of his desires for Juliette and Melonie. All of this reminded him of his responsibilities, that he promised to keep his word to Juliette, to hold their love above all else. Relief spread over him as he realized his will had not been broken by Melonie. His stay in prison had made him miss the sensations of a lover's touch. This was obvious to him as he realized he had almost betrayed the greatest love of his life. He wondered then if Juliette would be as strong. He was sure she would try to be, but he knew what she had just begun to enjoy had ended quickly. He had been careful not to push too far too fast. Her sexual awareness had quickly developed into a strong desire for lovemaking. He hoped he had been successful in his show of tenderness for her and that her promise to wait for him would be as strong as his.

As he thought of her alone, he thought about what she was doing at that very moment. He looked at his watch and knew it was time for her to wake up to another busy day. He wished he could see her enter this new day as the skies were gaining light. A blue-green haze was prominently cast through the jungle's canopy.

What was taking place in the hotel across the city was that Juliette's uncle was being interrogated by the lieutenant as six of his soldiers stood guard. She cracked her bedroom door and nervously watched them. The lieutenant and her uncle were arguing. The front door of the hotel was hanging by one hinge.

She heard the lieutenant say, "Mr. Nannon, we have official papers, a warrant to search your premises." Calmly, Juliette's uncle acted as if the whole occurrence was a mere aggravation. Juliette knew she and her uncle had cleaned the hotel thoroughly in case this situation occurred.

"Before you begin, let me wake my guests. It is barely dawn and you will frighten them if your men just appear." He and the lieutenant argued.

The lieutenant said loudly, "Very well, but one of my men will go with you."

"Sure, that's fine, but what is all this about anyway? Why is it necessary to break my doors in?"

"Mr. Nannon, it is because your place of business is believed to have harbored a band of killers. This is not a routine search."

"What does that mean, not routine? I have done nothing."

"We also believe you housed the man that killed President Andras and gave his supporters help."

"That's absurd!"

"Sir, only this morning they were seen here, and you were seen with them. This is very serious and if you are found guilty, you face severe punishment. If charges are brought against you, you will be prosecuted to the full extent of the law. Do not hold me up any longer! I have most kind to you. My interests at this moment are only to capture these dangerous murderers. You will be questioned later."

"I have nothing to hide. Please, look for yourself. I have nothing to hide here." Mr. Nannon and the soldier stopped at Juliette's door first. Her uncle quietly opened her door so as not to frighten her. He calmly said, "Get out of bed, get dressed and meet me in the hall."

Juliette opened her eyes and saw the soldier standing next to her uncle. She was so afraid she could barely move from her bed.

They closed the door and made their way down the hall, waking their guests. The seven guests knew what was taking place and followed the uncle's commands. One by one they went down the stairs. The soldiers now situated at the foot of the stairs guided them into the dining room.

The lieutenant looked at Juliette and said, "We have been up all night and we could use some coffee." As Juliette made her way to the kitchen, one of the soldiers followed her. The guests seated themselves at tables in the dining room, quietly observing.

Juliette tried to remain calm as the guard made crude remarks and sexual advances. She continued making the coffee and ignored his advances. He sarcastically said, "You live in a whorehouse and what do you expect." He reached out and caught her by the arm. The moment he touched her, she began to speak in his language. Her uncle could not hear clearly what was being said behind the closed doors, but caught a word or so of the conversation, just enough to know she was being accosted. He realized she was using her usual defense; the same line she had learned from him. She was frightened and it was a signal they had worked out years ago.

Mr. Nannon hastily sought out the lieutenant. He collided into him as he rounded the corner of the long barroom. "You have a job to do, and your position is being carelessly undermined by the soldier in my kitchen. I will personally bring charges against you if you don't take steps to correct this. My niece, the young lady in the kitchen, is being propositioned this very second."

The lieutenant was angry and rushed alongside Mr. Nannon as he headed to the kitchen. The bat doors burst open. Both men rushed in, shoulder to shoulder. The lieutenant barked, "Attention!" The solitary word immobilized the soldier.

Juliette quickly passed both men and retreated to the dining room. The soldier stood erect as the lieutenant's anger grew rapidly. He walked over to the soldier and solidly hit him in the face. The first blow sent the man backwards across the kitchen. The lieutenant's wrath was evident as he continued striking the soldier.

Finally, Mr. Nannon stepped in front of the lieutenant trying to gain control of the situation and stop the beating that was in progress. The soldier stood up facing the two men. Blood oozed from his nose and lips. His left eyelid was cut so severely his eye was swollen shut.

The lieutenant said, "Mr. Nannon, I assume you are satisfied this worm has been punished sufficiently. If you don't think so, I'll have him shot!"

Mr. Nannon said, "He has been punished enough."

The lieutenant ordered the soldier, "Clean yourself up and this kitchen. thoroughly," he added, as he burst through the doors. "Now, we'll continue our search."

****

The sun was rising rapidly above the campsite. The struggle for life had begun anew. The lions, the water buffalo, the hippos, and the crocodiles ruled in their domains. In the never-ending cycle of the jungle, they ended heartbeats in a matter of seconds. The daily routine of searching for food and water was their only means of survival for the beasts.

At daybreak Scott and David left the campsite to search the area. Sebastian shook his head in disbelief as Durbish said, "Kudan is a large, thriving metropolis." Durbish tried to convince him the city was nearby.

"If there's a city out here, why did you have me walk a hundred miles in this jungle to reach Abuja?"

"Sebastian, we've gone over this three times. It was the safest way at the time for you to enter Abuja by way of the river."

"Then why didn't the pilot or I ever see this city?"

"Well, Darford knows this land and I'm sure he stayed just beyond sight of it somehow. Sebastian, no one is disputing you about how dangerous these riverbanks are, but I'm sorry, this is just not the Congo out here. It's a wide strip of thick cover I found suitable to hide your entrance. I, myself, told Darford to drop you here."

Sebastian yelled, "Melonie." She was busy pushing things into the rear compartment of the vehicle. "Melonie," he yelled, what did you do with my old map?"

"I never saw a--oh, yes, yes, a map. We looked at it in the hotel. I remember. David had it."

"Where is it now? It's my only proof that what I'm saying is true. Durbish says this isn't the wild jungle I forged, and I say it is. And, he also says there's a large city out here somewhere."

Compassionately, she said, "We all had the map at the hotel. We all looked at it and compared it with ours. I even retraced the markings you had on the old map. You of all people Durbish are the master of deception."

"Yes, he is, but I visited no large city on my way to Abuja."

"Sebastian, on your map there was a village. It existed before the turn of the century. Now, it is a largely populated city."

Sebastian stormed off. He tried to stay calm as he passed Durbish. He made his way into the heavy brush, seeking a clear view of the water. He was mumbling all the way, "This is a dangerous jungle." He viciously stomped the reeds along the bank to the river's edge. He remembered the snakes and crocodiles he had seen, realizing they were not there. The river was flowing slowly, not rushing past as he recalled. Sebastian's mind was spinning. He decided none of this was making sense. He knew there was a village out here but realized last night as they drove through the jungle, even that was different looking now. He looked at the ground closely and observed it was sandy, not muck. "What the hell!" he kept thinking. "These waters were full of crocodiles, not just a few here and there, but full." Precariously, he stood amazed as he looked down at the riverbank and swore softly.

His throat tightened as he thought, "What is going on?" He knew the boat was no dream and began to question that. He mumbled, "How confused I am." He chose to let this iron itself out, figuring there had to be an explanation, knowing he couldn't have dreamed of all his predator friends. "Friends?" he asked himself. "This whole thing just doesn't make sense. Who could make friends with wild beasts?" His attention was turned towards the sounds of someone making their way toward him. He continued to stare out over the water, refusing to admit this was not the infamous Kudana jungle he tamed himself, but only a heavily wooded area. He stood still as Durbish stepped beside him.

"Scott and David are back and we are ready to leave."

Still lost in thought, Sebastian said, "What?"

"We are ready to leave. They found the road and it's not far. Everyone is waiting for us." Durbish looked at Sebastian and could see the veins in his neck. He thought how pitifully thin he was.

"What do you think happened here? Did I have an episode, you know, like my mind does sometime?"

"Whatever happened out here, I'm sure you have cause to believe it occurred. If things were always the way people see them, it would be a boring journey indeed. Let's save that for now and run this gauntlet to get back home. When we reach Washington, I want you to stay for a few days before you go back home. There is a lot you and I haven't discussed, and I also have a lot to tell you. If you need a doctor, we'll go to my friend there and have him analyze what you've told us, but my opinion now is not fair to you. Considering all the stress you were under, I'm sure this played a large part in your perception of things.

A horn blared. The two men followed the sound, finding their way back through the woods. Before they reached the land rover, Sebastian said, "Thanks, Durbish, you're probably right. My nerves aren't as good as they once were and maybe this whole ordeal is something for me to remember in privacy, but it sure did seem real."

As they stepped out of the woods, the others stood waiting impatiently beside the land rover. They heard Sebastian say, "All I'm worried about is how to get us out safely."

"We'll find our way. The roads aren't safe, but we're going to make it on or off the road and, oh, yeah, I've got to find a damn phone to call the rental agency." They all burst into laughter and took their seats inside the vehicle.

After everyone settled in, Scott announced, "The road is washed out, but David and I decided it could be managed. It won't be smooth going, but it's a road.

"Let's do it," Sebastian said. This made everyone feel better. Sebastian was willing to forget about his experience and the gang had been pulled together once again as one. "Come on, Scott, go."

There was a road, but Sebastian had never seen it. The whole illusion or whatever it was he decided to keep to himself. He would sort it out later.

****

Juliette sat in the back room badly shaken from her experience. The lieutenant spoke with her and tried to reassure her nothing further would occur. One of the soldiers approached and Juliette stiffened. He reported to the lieutenant, "Our search has turned up nothing."

The lieutenant returned; his attention focused on addressing the frightened young lady. Beside her in the chair, something caught his eye. He thought it looked like a map stuffed on the edge of the seat. Beyond that he could not tell. He asked, "Would you mind getting up while I inspect your chair?"

She did not understand and was thrown off guard by the question. She rose as the lieutenant reached between the cushion and unfolded a piece of paper he found in the chair. He laid it on the table. This was the same map David had laid beside him as their crew was preparing to leave yesterday. Juliette was overtaken by a sick feeling as she saw the lieutenant's eyes brighten as he quickly refolded the map. He placed it in his pocket and as he left the room he yelled, "Load up. We're leaving now!"

It all happened so fast. The trucks raced off. Juliette was beside her uncle with her hand wrapped in his arm. She began to cry uncontrollably as she became fully aware of what had just occurred. She told the story of the map's discovery to her uncle, and he realized why the trucks had vanished so suddenly.

He said, "I can't be certain this will help them, Juliette. By now, Sebastian and the others have a huge lead. It will be difficult for that blundering idiot to find them. Sebastian will be safe, don't worry. I knew you loved him moments after you realized it." He stood there smiling before her. His head was held high.

She said, "I love you very much, uncle." She embraced him as tears streaked down her face.

"Often," he said, "we overlook things, but my dear Juliette, my responsibility lies in caring for you and this has been nothing but a pleasure from the day you came to live with me. When I realized you fell in love with him, this troubled me for a while, but soon I could tell Sebastian was a good man and gave you his love in return. Why else do you think he left here alive. I watched him intently but found it easy to see the hardship he placed upon himself. Yes, I know you know what I'm speaking of. His decision to kill Andras was a struggle. He did it for all of us and I respect him for his decision. Sebastian has fine qualities and has gained respect. Be proud, you have found a valiant man."

Her tears were dried by the old man's wrinkled hands as he spoke to her. They continued to talk a long time as they cleaned up and repaired the hotel door.

****

About two hours later the lieutenant and his troops splashed down the muddy trail. Their objective was clear. They were driving as fast as possible. The triangle Sebastian had drawn on the map led them dangerously close to the fleeing five.

The winch cable strained to its limit. The land rover, with Scott's steady hand at the wheel, was snaking the vehicle out of the mud. The road proved to be hazardous, full of ruts and mudholes. The group had walked ahead and waited. A brief shower had now passed and left the air heavily humid. Their urge to rest was not to be. Scott pulled up beside them in the truck. He stepped out and leaned against the door. David, Melonie and Sebastian were covered in mud as they approached the vehicle. The map was spread on the hood as Durbish, and Scott disagreed with their location. Durbish was certain they were between Bida and a place called Minna. Scott came up with a different location. He was sure they had passed Minna and said, "The city of Kaduna is not far." He cursed as he told Durbish this over and over.

Sebastian urged the others, "Come on before this gets completely out of control." All of them agreed and took their seats.

The soldiers had made swift progress. The men were hungry for blood and were on the trail. The war was over, yet their urge to kill was still very strong. The lieutenant kicked the ashes that had been left a short time ago and ordered the troops to restart the search.

Having no choice in the matter, the group had left a steady trail, easy enough for anyone to follow. Luckily, the showers hampered the troops, so both parties traveled slowly.

Sebastian reached over and nudged David. Melonie and the two men in the back seat quickly noticed what prompted the gesture. Off to the northwest the tall buildings inside the large city of Kudana stood majestically etching the skyline.

Durbish hadn't noticed. He was involved watching Scott's driving. He turned in his seat to look and noticed a change in their expression. The once gloomy and sad looks were now suddenly cheerful. Melonie said, "I'd bet money we're almost out of here."

Durbish informed her, "We are miles away from any city."

Melonie happily broke the news to him, loving every minute of it because he was never wrong. "The city is just over the next hill."

He looked upwards and caught sight of the city, right before the vehicle dipped down into another downward grade. "Well, I'll be damned," he said. "Melonie, you were right. Kudana is just over the ridge. You'll see it in just a few more moments."

"Hot dog."

He floored the land rover, quickly gaining speed as he topped the hill. This sent mud flying, sending a rooster tail 15 feet in the air behind them.

The city was there but did little to change the group's circumstance. They were still sought after and knew if they were caught it would be suicidal. They had needs to fulfill in the city. There, on the outskirts of the city, they agreed to enter at dusk. Sebastian stared at the city and said, "Well, this is the city of Kudana." He was puzzled. He didn't see the village that he was familiar with. He had looked all day for familiar signs and found nothing.

In the failing light, the troops' pursuit remained constant. The group had a four-hour lead that was dwindling as they watched the dramatic sun setting in the west.

As the sun set each of them talked about what each of them would be doing if they were home. Durbish broke up the senseless chatter and, like a father scolding his children, raved on about the imminent danger they faced. He had a good point, and each person promised to hold back the excitement they felt inside until they reached Morocco.

Durbish informed them, "When we reach Morocco, I will be happier than all of you, but until then I don't want to hear another word about home. Is that clear?"

He sat inside the land rover by himself, unsure of what caused him to snap at all of them. His sudden outburst had come about so harshly. Melonie made her way to the vehicle and stood outside next to the door. She spoke sweetly to him, saying, "None of us meant to upset you." Durbish confided in her, then asked, "Send David over. I want to talk with him."

Once she found David, she went to get Scott. Scott's eyes lit up instantly as he saw Melonie preparing food. He rushed to give her a hand, and they finished preparing some quick sandwiches. Scott said, "I've been so busy all day, I completely forgot about eating. Frankly, now I'm starving."

As they finished eating, Durbish told them to hurry up and get ready to leave. He closed the three-ring binder he had been looking at while he ate his sandwich. He placed it under the dash.

David noted it was the first time he had seen the binder taken out and made a mental note of its whereabouts. At least, he thought, Durbish had hidden the binder. He was aware of what a lethally dangerous book they held in their possession. Its mere existence was bad enough, he thought, yet to have it in their possession was unthinkably dangerous.

Durbish said, "Are you all ready to go?"

"Just jumpin' for joy," David said.

Melonie added her bit, saying, "Well, my oh my, Durbish, I can't tell you how thrilled I am, sir, and I just don't believe that as a lady I can find the appropriate words for this feeling I'm having."

Scott said, "I'm ready." He was chewing, walking, talking, and swallowing all at the same time.

Sebastian said, "Just look at that, would you? I've seen it all now. I thought I'd go through life and find newly discovered feats."

Scott glared over his shoulder and tossed his plate into the trash bag. Sebastian grinned at Scott and said, "Why does everybody get mad when I goof around." Sebastian was talking to Scott, but everyone took the hint.

"Let's just go," Scott said as he cranked the land rover. David asked Scott if he would let him drive tomorrow. Scott told him to buckle his seatbelt and then said, "No."

Twenty minutes later they were in the city limits of Kudana. A commercial airliner, coming in for a landing, crossed their path. As the jet plane's engine rumbled overhead, Sebastian said, "Durbish, your offer of my staying in Washington sounds good about right now."

"Sure, Sabastain I'd be happy to have you stay with uh-us-uh-me."

Melonie showed no sign of being upset. She just sat still with her head positioned in her hands on her lap.

Durbish said, "Scott, find a street called Jaharan. It should be close." As they wound their way through the city, Sebastian watched Durbish sit calmly. He acted as if it were on a Sunday drive.

Sebastian hadn't forgotten that this was Friday, the day he was supposed to go to trial and more than likely be shot all in the same day. He reminded everyone of that fact and not a one of them remembered. As he spoke, Melonie lifted her head and said, "Doesn't Abuja seem very far away now, Sebastian? I'm already finding it an easy place to forget. I hope you can."

Melonie slowly rested her head on her knees and Sebastian thought about last night, realizing she was serious and would not give up. He knew her mind well; once Melonie had decided, nothing was sacred, nothing at all. He knew he was in for a fight, and she would not give up on being with him. He thought she was a nicely built woman. There was nothing unattractive about her at all and it disturbed him to the point where he had to stop looking at her.

As they turned onto Jaharan, Durbish said, "Turn right on Callaway Boulevard." And that's how it went, right, left, left, right, for thirty minutes through the streets. The city lights were effective. They could see very clearly all around them. As they pulled up alongside the curb, ghostly figures from beneath the street made a steady climb, as hot steam was dispensed and scattered by the subtle breeze. They were parked in front of a small house, one in a row of many that all looked the same. This would have the number 93. There were two small nets on each end of the yard. Obviously, the nets were there to stop the soccer ball that lay beside the steps.

Durbish informed them, "I will return in a few minutes." He approached the door and released the door latch.

Melonie commented on the freshly cut lawn, "It's smell always stirs excitement in me." No one replied. "It's just like a new beginning. Do you know what I mean, Sebastian? The old is cut down to make room for the new. It's a fresh start."

The underlying meaning gained his attention. He looked towards her, smiling calmly, watching her. He shifted nervously in his seat. She could tell her suggestive remarks were taken for just what they were and this pleased her. She knew he was agitated and rolled down her window to take deep breaths of air.

Sebastian was becoming impatient with her conniving little tricks. He knew he could say nothing to her. He was thinking how she would handle things if the tables suddenly turned.

A middle-aged man emerged from the house and stepped onto the front porch with Durbish. The man was of color, a good-sized person. Unhurriedly, they talked for quite some time before the man returned inside.

In a few seconds, a yawning young man came outside. He shook Durbish's hand and tossed a light jacket over his shoulder and led him towards the road. Suddenly, the young man raced down the narrow sidewalk and tipped the soccer ball to roll towards him. His feet were dancing this way and that. He positioned the ball and sent it rapidly across the freshly cut lawn. The ball hit and gave a solid impression of the boy's youth. He leaped into the air, filled with joy as the ball was stopped inside the net.

Durbish took his seat in the truck and once again the smell from the lawn entered the rover. The instant he was seated, the boy headed down the long walkway and began to race along the street. Durbish said, "Scott, quick, follow the boy."

Melonie laughed at the sight of the lanky youngster, saying, "It's not fair, Durbish, the boy has a sizeable head start." She was suddenly surprised by Durbish. He was instantly on the defensive.

"I guess you're the only girl who could outrun him, huh." She didn't reply, only stared at him. "Well, aren't you, Melonie?"

The group was dead silent. The close quarters had suddenly turned very uncomfortable, thanks to Durbish and Melonie's apparent quarrel. The underlying meaning of the remarks they passed back and forth was unknown. Not another word was spoken.

The boy kept up a furious pace. Scott wanted to pass him so he could get him in the vehicle.

Melonie asked, "David, what do you know about the city? Anything we need to be aware of?"

David stirred uneasily in his seat. "Well, Melonie, I read a brief and limited amount about the city. I had no prior knowledge that we were even going to be here, but I do remember it's heavy into chemical development and natural fertilizers. The chemicals developed here, and fertilizer produced specifically for their needs in the area because the soil has such a low acidic quality.

There is a severe lack of nutrients. That's all I remember. This is a large agricultural area. The people's number increases far too rapidly for this region and that has caused a lot of debate about the lack of conservative agricultural measures not being used. The land is threatened by such an explosive population and methods are constantly being revised to update trade and protection is a must for their depleted soil and environment. As for the type of food and size of the population, I really didn't read a lot about the place. Their political structure is like most found in this part of the world. The larger families have more respect. I believe that was a fact of some form or it varied, I think. Oh, I'm not sure, but plans are important for some reason or another."

The boy stopped running. A few seconds later, Scott stopped the rover and turned off the ignition. The young man held both of his hands on top of his thick quadriceps. His head hung low as he was heaving in large amounts of air, trying to regain his spent energy. His shoulders rose and lowered with each deep breath. He lifted his head and smiled. He appeared taller than he had earlier. In his heavily accented language, he said, "My normal language is Hausa, but now in the city we speak your native tongue, English. My name is Satma or in your language Tom. For now, I am at your service, until we reach our goal in Zaire. My brother there will take over as your guide. I regret we have no time to spare in Kudana. We have heard reports all day of your passage through the river road. We were all surprised to see you here.

"Why?" Durbish asked.

Tom spoke rapidly as he led them into a small building. "First, bring your vehicle in here, please."

Scott turned on his heel to oblige him. He thought, "Joyous young fellow."

Barely visible inside, the group stood beside a large truck. Across the room, Tom turned on a loud switch which lit the room. Before them there was a big diesel truck, a Mercedes-Benz logo in the center of the front grill. The building was so small, the trucks barely cleared the doorway. With five people in the building, it was very crowded. Scott backed the rover into what little space remained. Everyone was pushed closer together. Melonie was right behind Sebastian. In fact, she was pressed against the back wall of the building. They fit snugly in a single file between the vehicles. Sebastian stood in front of her and she took full advantage of this. She held him with his belt loop and pulled him tightly against her body. He had no way to escape this sudden advancement. Sebastian sought an escape in the dimly lit garage and found none. She held him in a death grip by his belt loop. With her free hand she casually slid her hand around his waist. He couldn't believe what she was doing. He could feel the blood spread over his face as he blushed with embarrassment. The lady was seducing him as she ground her body into him, sending him into a complete arousal, but angry at her for putting him into such a state, especially since there was no hope of continuation. This is just too much, he thought. Of all the ways she could be so seductive, this was way out of any such permissible time to carry on. He was getting very turned on but had to end it. By sheer luck, the bodies ahead of him started forward. Instantly, he followed David. Melonie had no choice but to release her tantalizing hand from his groin. Sebastian looked back to see her in the dim light. Her facial expression said it all too clearly. She ran her hand over her forehead into her hair. Her eyes were partially closed, and these were just the obvious things he noticed immediately.

It took thirty-five minutes to unpack the land rover as Melonie supervised the placement of her computer. The laptop and printer were still inside their factory boxes. Melonie handled them with extra precautionary measures. "Scott, tie the boxes securely. We will be dependent on this computer system later. Be very careful."

A beam of light penetrated the inside of the truck. It was Durbish checking on their progress. He said, "Hurry, we must leave in the next few minutes."

David and Sebastian jumped inside the rear of the truck. Quickly, the two of them arranged their bedrolls and tents, along with several duffle bags. Durbish laid his flashlight on the bed of the truck and hefted the ten-gauge over and under shotgun to Scott. They worked in a flurry to complete the transfer. Durbish called, "Melonie, help me." In his hands he held two very large sponges. "Melonie, we have to wipe down the rover. I'm in quite a pickle. Would you please help me--quickly." She leaned outward. Durbish let her fall into his arms. The pace in which they cleaned the rover was admirable. She noticed he was acting in desperation. She stopped just long enough to study him. He was very pudgy. It seemed odd that he'd lay on his back to clean the underside of the rover. He edged his way as far as possible under the vehicle. All she could see was his two feet. He was carrying this to a scary extreme. She knelt to see him as his hands worked vigorously wiping any exposed metal. There was dirt falling all over him. She crawled under the land rover, realizing full well that he was unaware of sending an urgent signal. She slid right next to him as dirt fell into her hair and eyes. She called out, "Stop!" She opened her eyes. The garage was balmy. What Melonie sensed was plainly seen in his face. She asked him not to move. "Please, Durbish, I want to talk to you. Hold on a second." She yelled, "Sebastian. Sebastian." His head appeared and Melonie asked him to finish wiping the inside of the rover. "Just go back over it." She pushed the sponge towards him.

He picked it up and wasted no time as he wiped the interior. With the bottom of the land rover inches above their faces, Melonie said quietly, "Durbish, what did you mean when you said you were desperate?"

"Did I say that, Melonie?"

"You said it, Durbish. Don't deny it. Now, tell me why."

He looked at the bottom of the truck and slowly detailed what was bothering him. "Melonie, I've made some awfully big mistakes in the last few weeks. My name is known by the authorities and, hell, so is Dr. Weston's. This mission has been doomed for the two of us. We will only reach home to be arrested. That's why I've been so edgy and I'm sorry I've taken it out on you. I will have to leave and go far away."

"Where?"

"I don't know yet. I didn't plan on this, but in order for me to protect you I must ask that you end our marriage." Melonie was convinced he was truthfully sincere, and she kissed him. Both sensed the total reckoning between them, and they understood the situation.

"The truck's all clean," Sebastian said. He stood a few feet from the rover, unseen by the two under the vehicle. He had heard most of their conversation. He was truly disturbed that Durbish had made such vital mistakes. He planned on asking Durbish why he ever let such things happen. It was a question that deserved an answer. He thought that in his whole life there had never been a sadder occurrence. Durbish had sacrificed in the process of saving him. He knew David hadn't realized his pending capture. "Why?" he thought. He couldn't understand why David hadn't made this connection. It must be from the constant movement of the group that kept him so occupied. "That must be it," Sebastian thought.

Melonie crawled out and Durbish followed. Sebastian moved, aiding both from the dirty garage floor. Sebastian was extremely choked up but managed to convey a lot by his stance and the few words he spoke. "I'm ready to take us home and, Durbish, you will be beside me every step of the way until this is over. David will have the same, but you will both have me always to protect you, whatever it takes."

"Okay, are you ready to lead us home, Sebastian?"

"Yes, let's go."

The evening after President Roxmir Andras was shot, Durbish purchased a newspaper. He regularly gathered all the information about the deaths of Sabastian's expert marksmanship.

President Roxmir and his cabinet members deaths had caused quite a stir, Durbish opened the newspaper and read a law was instilled that allowed Sebastian to be publicly beaten or shot by a firing squad. Sebastian was looked on as a martyr in the people's eyes, but the conservatives who had supported Andras believed his style of killing had been unprecedented and they would accept nothing but his public execution. So far this had been the only choice for close friends of Andra's.

The only story he found about Sebastian today was on page four. The caption read, "KILLER'S TRIAL STIRS MORE VOWS OF VIOLENCE." This was the first story to mention a trial.

Durbish read it feeling disgusted. The mention of Sebastian being the cause of more battles was all nonsense. He could be blamed for his killing of the President, not the aftereffects. It was an ongoing battle, one that escalated after the rebels felt a surge of victory had been gained.

Of course, he had been blamed, but it was a clever political cover-up for what was really in progress throughout this country and in the streets of Abuja. The whole complexity of the story was a build-up to his upcoming trial. There had been a date disclosed, but no mention of where the trial would take place. The trial was set for one week from today, next Friday.

He was getting cabin fever, feeling caged in, caused by the tension of the trail being so nearby. He sat in a chair and felt confined, even in his massive suite. He felt with all their combined efforts they could possibly save Sebastian before the people brought him to trial. He knew Sebastian was guilty, but he felt the least they could do was try to save him. Durbish had only motivation and his love for money. He had made millions from Sebastian's dirty work. Durbish had become corrupted after the years of cleverly planned methods devised to fight inadequacies in powerful men. The independence of his procedures left him in point blank range to monopolize Sebastian's killings.

While Durbish thought about Sebastian, he was getting plenty of exercise and getting over his fear from the violent spray from the water hose. The aftermath of the water torture was excessive. He tipped his cot on end to release the water which had been funneled into his cell. The heat from the afternoon sun had caused the air to be heavy. The humid condition hindered his breathing. Gasping from the lack of enough oxygen, Sebastian stood on the edge of his bed frame to reach the fresh air entering his small window above the floor. It was impossible to see out the window, yet the fresh air drifting in was warm. It was a relief.

Durbish looked eagerly at his watch, wanting to go ahead and call his wife, Melonie, but she wouldn't be expecting his call for two more hours. He felt an urgency to call her sooner and picked up the phone. After his conversation, Durbish hung the phone back in its cradle. The only thing left now to be done was for him to pick all his friends up once their plane arrived in Zaire. Their time had also been cut short one day in advance.

Durbish would have to return to personally warn Sebastian. The trial was making things very complicated. His dilemma was how to get to see Sebastian again. Professing more NATO matters could cause problems, and the risk was far too great. Durbish reviewed his options and gained nothing but contempt for having such a role in this mayhem. He had resources in America which were unlimited. He was well known for being tough while handling business. Perplexed forms of political niggling were his specialty. Durbish needed to devise a plausible plan of action to show David and Scott they would be safe. All the way-out Sebastian would stay in a hornet's nest of the likelihood of recapture. The whole idea was a stupendous attempt.

Durbish was paving a subtle cause of destruction for all his associates. Sebastian was the reason he now put his goal into action. He and his friends were being led into a disaster.

Durbish was sitting on the bed in his hotel suite. It was unpleasantly hot and sweat dripped from his forehead onto the maps he prepared for his three confederates. Durbish left his work which was near completion. He had developed a well-designed plan to clearly define each route of each person's escape. He left the stuffy room to purchase his favorite newspaper. He carefully searched the headlines. What caught his attention was a story on page 6A about South Africa. The headline gave Durbish a great feeling and improved his outlook on the situation for the people. It read South Africa would adopt a new constitution. The planned occurrence would guarantee equal rights for all. This is what Durbish's group had strived to accomplish. The plan being proposed by the government would complete its official transformation from Apartheid to democracy.

As he stepped out into the street, he sensed a renewal in the people's expressions. He noticed the hard edged looks on their faces had softened. The death of Andras had restored human rights.

Sebastian's mission had been a success. Durbish knew all along death or, at least, his imprisonment was a given. He hoped his promise to release him was not the death of all of them.

His return to the hotel lobby was met by a surge of heat. Now his overall outlook gave him a new perspective. The vulgar conditions the people had been faced with had turned from rude violations to the surrendering of the government. The new constitution proposed would eradicate the obstacles in their way.

As he sat in his room, the plans seemed to glide onto the paper, making it less of a chore. His plans joined and fit together in reasonable working order. His plan seemed plausible. Not one of them would be left behind but would eventually succeed in reaching Morocco.

Durbish's nerves felt singed. South Africa would be affected by this new development.

He clipped the article about Africa's party leaders detailing the ratification in a promise by pledge statements of protection of the people's rights. The new leader, President Nelson Mandella said in the newspaper, "Victory is sweet." Chairperson Cyril Ramphosa had been quoted by the press to have said, "Today, this is the day when South Africa is truly born." His work on the details of the plan had been completed only hours before the ratification ceremony began. The Constitutional Assembly had worked two years to draft the 150-page document. It had been overwhelmingly approved. After the vote, delegates leapt to their feet. This Associated Press article further stated there were loud cheers from the delegates, accompanied by dancing and singing. This show of happiness took place in the same Parliament chamber where Apartheid laws were once passed. The pledge given by President Nelson Mandella was, "Never and never again shall the laws of our land rend out people apart or legalize their oppression and repression." Other reports from Johannesburg, South Africa, crowned the transition from Apartheid to democracy.

The real challenge facing the country is very complicated. Unless the government acts to boost the economy by the creation of jobs to spur growth, the constitution's promise of a miracle would make very little difference to the ordinary people. The constitution being no better than the paper it is written on, although a very important piece of paper, by itself it can't change things unless the economic challenges are dealt with.

The years Roxmir Andras reined in office and his misuse of power had created a huge budget deficit and caused unprecedented inflation. Job creation is by far the biggest problem facing the newly elected president today. Durbish read the print enthusiastically. The threats of more violence were never versed in today's paper.

Considering reactions to the upcoming trial, Sebastian's future was the cause of violence by some radical groups. This fact was a gift and the influence he needed to feel less negative about his and the others' chances of successfully freeing Sebastian.

The President's effort to overcome what the National Party had imposed by Apartheid and rule for the past 46 years would take a massive effort, in view of the less than full withdrawal by the old party members. This has had some negative effect to the new constitutional glory. Speculation on the outcome in any short-term rebound of the economy was poor. The members now installed knew the old Nationalists still had influence. Their form of reaction to the new constitution could spell trouble.

As Durbish continued reading, he was drawn into yet another story of a renewed clash in Monrovia, Liberia, in western Africa. It read the same of the war that was in regression throughout other southern African countries. Another battle involving millions of people was breaking out in the neighboring the Republic of Côte d'Ivoire, 300,000 Liberians had fled their country over the last six years of civil war. This upsurge in new fighting began on April 6th when the State Council tried to arrest a Krahn faction leader for murder.

Durbish finished the maps, and his plan was complete. He hoped these were his last days to be there. In the morning the three would arrive in the Congo (DRC) from the United States. Of the three people, his wife, Melonie, would lift his spirits the most. Of course, none of the others knew of their ten-month marriage. This was just another one of Durbish's carefully planned arrangements. Melonie had been against their secretive joining, but with his steady persistence she caved into his wishes.

Now that ten months had passed, she found herself under constant stress from the arrangement. She thought her reasons for marrying Durbish had been valid, but now as she reviewed them, they looked awfully shallow. Her reason for going to the Democratic Republic of the Congo was for Sebastian's benefit alone. Durbish would be surprised by the difference in the wife he left behind over one and a half months ago.

In his hotel suite, Durbish laid out routes and drew maps for the members of the party and Sebastian. Sebastian's escape route would be more complicated than the others in the group. He thought the route was almost foolproof. Sebastian would be on his own except for Scott who would shadow his friend in a last-ditch effort to provide extra cover for him and send information to Melonie. Scott was familiar on how this would be done. Scott had helped in various other ways before with others Sebastian had shot. This varied now differently because of the increased danger and involved three other members which put it on a larger scale.

Durbish placed Sebastian ahead of the rest of the group to form a checkerboard stratagem. As one man moved into an area the others would follow his lead. Sebastian's first and, worst, struggle was to escape Abuja. In the event this failed the game was over and he would be the loser. Melonie's expert hacking skills was paramount. She would have to access clearances if needed, making sure the men stayed out of areas unsafe that would cause them to surface. The plan called for none of them to leave together. If Sebastian were wounded, it would be up to him to reach his destination. If he were unable to meet this demand, Scott would be there following closely behind him. If there was a reason to surface it would be their fault. Durbish hoped that this would be avoided at all costs. The whole route Durbish had devised would be effectively carried out in a relay out of Africa. A three-way shuffle was the only safe way to ensure all of them escaped. He and Melonie would reach the last destination first. The other three men would have to reach this point safely before they could proceed with his plan. If they made it to Morocco Durbish knew all five of them would make it home.

Durbish had another plan developing in his mind, one that none of the four would survive. Durbish found that this was a great time to do what must eventually be done anyway. One day his life would be in danger if he did not eliminate Scott, David, and Sebastian. In the event the three men survived, Melonie would reach home only to die on American soil along with the others.

The hopscotch across Africa developed by Durbish was a hopeful entrapment or death by hands other than his own. He envisioned their attempt to escape would not succeed. He was sure death awaited Sebastian. His usefulness was over. Scott would die along with Sebastian in a vain attempt to save his life. David, he thought, would be lucky enough to reach his destination. He would end his life in America. Durbish had a simple plan for him in America.

He already knew two men willing to do his bidding and their desire to step up in the world made them eager to hear from Durbish. If the need arose, the two men would perform any form of killing for him. Of course, Durbish placed little hope for their future. He would send for them to kill, only to be later terminated by his own method, a lingering, agonizing death.

From his years of increasing wealth brought on by Sebastian killing for him, Durbish was thrilled with the thought of no ties remaining to his organization. He knew he would never have a better chance to eliminate Sebastian. It would never be the same, not now or ever. If Sebastian made it to Houston, he would die there. It was over.

The sweat rolled onto the sheets of paper before him. He made three different plans. It gave each of them a slim chance to accomplish their goal.

Melonie would fly with him to Morocco forming a vital component in his confederation. He hoped she would be successful in keeping all three men moving. If they were able to unite this would be serious. His hopes were to cause an illusion for the others and her, one he wished would not be obvious. He knew to give the men continual help would not be wise, but Melonie's wish would be to see them victorious. Durbish was in the virtual position of playing both ends. All the information would be fed to Melonie and under his control. He would misdirect her with false accounts of news and her chore would be to send the men where he wished. He would navigate the men into danger, and she would never know until their deaths had been pronounced. Unknowingly, she would send her friends to their deaths, her prudence would be for naught.

Durbish gathered his belongings. It was time for him to be on his journey to Zaire. He had planned on leaving for the airport tomorrow, but he had changed his mind. There were things in Abuja he must take care of for his future escape. Before all the others arrived, Durbish would set in motion the things that would hamper the others' escape. Those who helped Sebastian to escape would die.

He entered the streets of Abuja to fulfill his last transactions at the stock exchange. When he finished there were preparations to attend to for the arrival of his three associates.

Across the city, Sebastian found himself being transported to a new location in the prison. His new location was a cleaner cell upstairs. He wondered why they had brought him there. He spotted a guard and tried to gain his attention. Since he didn't speak their language, this was not so easily done. The guard ignored him as he walked past his cell. His attempt to find out information failed all day and into the evening.

He lay on his cot confused and angry, waiting for something to occur.

In another part of the prison the Warden's private line rang. It was a call from Durbish wishing to introduce a doctor from America. The warden granted his appointment and Durbish hung up the phone saying the doctor would be appreciative for an audience with the prisoner.

From here on out things would be hectic, a sheer scramble for their lives. Durbish hailed a cab as his plans were in motion throughout the city. His mind was fully loaded with problems. A sudden smile appeared as he rode through the streets. The streets were quiet, and he saw no battles anywhere. This and the fact that all his plans would soon fall into place, gave him a sense of relief. Sebastian was the key to the others' deaths.

Durbish asked the driver where he could rent a vehicle. Quizzically, the driver seemed confused. Durbish explained he wanted to take the vehicle across Africa's wilderness, and he needed a strong form of transportation like a big land rover. The cabbie sped by the old barricades as they set out on their journey to rent a vehicle.

Durbish looked forward to his trip away from Abuja. The return trip with the others sharing his problems would also be a nice diversion.

In his rented land rover, Durbish stopped to speak with the owner of the hotel. He was assured that by the time he returned the things he had requested would be ready. He chose to leave Abuja and drive all night into Zaire. He knew once he reached there Scott could drive on the return trip. This would give him time to prepare the others of the detailed plans.

Halfway to the airport, Wanda's suspicions had not been satisfactorily addressed by Scott and David. Their reasons for leaving had been vague. The two men continued babbling on about meaningless things, not giving her any better idea of where they were going or what they were doing. She thought the two men had planned all of this as an act so Scott could fly to Washington to meet Melonie. Scott tried to assure her there was nothing to be jealous of. It was strictly business. Dr. Weston agreed and completely ignored Wanda. By the time they reached the airport, Wanda was glad to leave the two men behind and just drive away.

Inside Houston airport, Scott and David had reformed the old bond between them. They thought the whole encroachment by Wanda was hilarious. Scott said he was not so sure she believed them, and he would pay dearly for his antics. He told David he really hated not being up front with her and causing her to be alarmed by his responses. He added, "She is a great woman."

David agreed she was as the two men ordered a drink at the bar. Scott ordered orange juice and in one hour he drank five glasses of it. David had two glasses of brandy. They were amazed at the different type people and how crowded the airport was on a Sunday night.

Little did they know that once they converged with Melonie in Washington, it would be the start of a spiraling ring of mishaps. The two men boarded the plane with no unordinary delays. In the air, on their way to Washington, both men fell fast asleep.

Twenty-two hundred miles away Melonie was amusing herself with her beloved feline. She was tossing a small ball filled with catnip to the cat for pleasure. It had taken only a short time for her to prepare for the arrival of her two associates.

She kept her studio apartment to get away from Durbish so she could handle her business affairs with no distractions. On foot, she was only thirty minutes away from their home or six to eight minutes by car. If she tried to work in their home, Durbish constantly summoned her for some trivial matter. She had grown tired of their marriage. Durbish had fallen short of her expectations. She was glad she had been wise enough to retain her apartment. Before they had gotten married, she had taken a stand before she agreed to marry him.

The decor of the apartment was simple; unlike the home she shared with Durbish. His tastes were an excessive show of apparent wealth. Her apartment was arranged simply to meet her needs in a computer-oriented profession. For her luxury was fine to a point, but his tastes consumed not only him but the house as well. Durbish had acquired an abundance of both riches and material gains in the last fifteen years. Melonie disliked all the material wealth he displayed. It made her feel she, as well, lived a repulsive life. She knew all Durbish had done was pillage these prize possessions from private sources or so-called respected dealers in arts and finery. She felt the ambience of his showcases of arcane dubiously purchased prizes compromised her. Off the record, Durbish had priceless, primitive collections of pristine eras. Every other article he owned was a quality piece. The home they shared was an aggravation for her. She spent much of her time away from it and Durbish. His tolerance for her actions was forbidden things he even encouraged friends to watch them in bed. She never did this unspeakable act and never would. The marriage was all but over. She had voiced this fact but found no relief. She played a role sought for his pleasure. Her submission to him finally was as repulsive to her as the house.

Once she returned from Africa with the others, she would resolve her role as wife. She knew a divorce would not cause any filth to harm his reputation. As for any of their friends, no one even knew the marriage had taken place. Everyone just thought the two lived together. As her cat became tired from rumbling across the floor, Melonie prepared herself for her guests.

She thought if Durbish cared for her there would be no sense in hiding their marriage. If this were the case, things might be different. The men arriving would be more comfortable in the home she shared with

Durbish, but the pied-a-terre would have to remain a secret to her guest. Her small apartment would serve its duty to house the three of them. In less than twenty-four hours all three of them would leave for Zaire.

She was uncertain of what lay ahead of them. She could only guess how Sebastian's release would come about. Her love for Sebastian was deep. It was caused by his self-induced devotion to humanistic values. The two of them shared many of the same opinions. Of course, she did not support the fact he was a killer, but his concise methodical style led her to trust in his concerted belief. This seduction in recantation was known by Durbish, his jealously was pitifully distasteful of their friendship.

Rojo pounced onto the counter and began to clean his fur as Melonie locked him in the utility room. She knew he would be content as she listened to him purr. Melonie padded through the apartment to the front door, ready to leave for the airport. Her bags were already packed and placed near the door for their departure tomorrow.

As she made her drive across Washington's back streets, Durbish, with no map to aid him, set out across the country maverick-style beginning his journey. His land rover was well suited for this type of travel. The tires hummed wickedly as he sped along on the desert roads. The high-pitched hum reminded him oddly of a hyena's cry. He thought this was another good reason to have such a good form of transportation in Africa. The hyena, a carnivorous creature, lurked in this area of the world. The animals' jaws are very powerful. Like most of the animals in Africa, an encounter would be a very dangerous situation.

With the distractions from the last hours spent in Abuja, his decision to leave a day earlier relaxed him. Driving alone, the environment was dormant. He watched the sun's rays ricocheting off the mountaintops ahead of him. As the sun set, his surroundings were surreal. He was absorbed by everything around him. This overabundance penetrated and stimulated his mind.

The outcome for the others was his own personal gratification which ensured he would be protected permanently. The brilliance of his plan possessed him as the sun fell out of view behind the mountaintops. Durbish knew all the dangers, the wild beasts that roamed the mountains and plains. Much the same in life, he thought, how only the strong survive. He visualized great plumes of smoke rising from behind the mountains and on the ground below smoldering piles of bones. His thoughts tracked deeply into this disgusting life's lesson. The bones shattered in flames, formed by sorrows of others' misfortunate luck. He drove silently as the darkened skies caught remnants of the retreating sun's resonance.

Melonie waited in the area provided for new arrivals. She is gritting her teeth to keep the steadfast smile on her face. Passengers swarmed through the entrance of the airport waiting area. Dr. Weston saw Melonie first and waved as he and Scott emerged from the dissecting portico. Her forced smile instantly changed from laborious into her glamorously genuine smile. She rushed to greet the two men.

It was forty-five minutes later before all of them left the airport. Stepping outside a light misty fog blanketed the area. David asked Melonie the time as he set his watch and advised Scott to reset his watch as well. Scott restrained himself from exhibiting his informal characteristics and reset his watch. She announced the ride to her apartment would take about thirty minutes. Scott's concern was for food. Melonie assured him she had plenty of food at her apartment for his consumption.

In the seclusion of the vehicle the group courteously limited their conversation. If any of them were experiencing impulses to mention the intensity of the upcoming events, they never expressed it. Melonie entered the freeway taking the closest route to their destination. The tension of the situation provided each of them with ample exposure to stress. It caused inner paranoia and extraordinary fatigue. She shook a cigarette free from her pack in hopes to ease her outbreak of fear. David detested smoking but politely allowed this practice. His defense against her unfavorable habit was simply to roll his window down. Twenty-three minutes later, she exited the freeway into her area of town. This lessened her nervousness. Smoothly, she maneuvered her car through the streets. The streetlights displayed beautifully manicured lawns. Most all the estates were owned by the prominent politicians. "A few of the craftier members of the community have fallen from grace through scandals recently. Their reputations have been damaged by false, malicious statements."

A few minutes later they reached their destination, Melonie manipulated the car into her parking space. The men took only their carry-ons into her apartment for their convenience.

Scott asked, "What time does our plane leave tomorrow?"

Melonie said, "We will take off at 9:00 A.M. but we must arrive one hour earlier. By 7:30 we have to be ready to leave here."

Scott and David just looked at one another and Scott said, "Gee, Melonie, couldn't you have made a later flight? I'm beat."

She excused herself without further comment. She called out, "The couch folds out into a bed."

Both men stared at the couch, knowing very well one of them would be sleeping on the floor. Rojo leapt onto the couch as David unfolded it. The cat startled David as he saw a flash of red land on the sheets. David disliked cats as much as cigarettes. He called Jennifer and in an exasperated tone said, "Please, would you mind removing this animal from where I must sleep?"

"Sure, David. You're not awfully fond of cats, I gather, by your rejection. This is Roji's favorite place in my apartment."

"I said, please, Melonie. I'm allergic to cats. I'm sorry if I was rude."

Melonie scooped Rojo into her arms and the cat eyed David with suspicion.

"Melonie," David asked, "How much does your cat weigh?"

"Oh, David, everybody makes fun of my cat, but he is big, isn't he."

"Well, how much, Melonie," David quizzed her in a challenging tone.

"He weighs twenty-eight pounds, David."

"My God," Scott said in amazement. "That's the biggest cat I've ever seen in my life."

Melonie proudly announced that Rojo would sleep in her room. She told Scott she would be right back. She would bring the extra blankets for someone to use on the floor. Scott commended her for her quick study of the situation. Moments later Rojo was secured in her room, and she picked up the blankets she had placed there for her guests.

As she handed the blankets to David, she said, "I'm sorry for the lack of beds."

"Who cares?" David said. "Just let me settle in a place and I'll find a new day."

"Okay, you guys, the bathroom is down the hall, first door on the right. As for myself, I'm turning in. Oh, Scott, there's food prepared in the refrigerator and in the cabinets, you'll find assorted snacks." She left the living room in their care, saying as she left, "I'll make breakfast before we leave."

"Goodnight," was all she heard as she closed her bedroom door. The illumination from her bedside clock read 12:17. Rojo curled beside the edge of her extra pillow, was already asleep. David's invective attack about the size of Rojo had irritated her. Looking at the cat, she supposed he was big. She compared him to the pillow he laid; beside her his outstretched body was as long as it was. At 12:21 Melonie turned off the lamp on her bedside table. She lay on her bed and worried about the upcoming days. She fought to block these uncertainties out of her mind.

The controversy over Sebastian killing the President of Nigeria, as well as his entire entourage, had had its effect on her. Some of the men he had killed had been exalted since young ages. They were raised for those specific positions in power, entrusted to no one's control but theirs. Seven men, all skilled and trained in exhibiting charm, their shrewd ingenuity had been cunningly crystalized to nullify the larger picture of debauchery.

By 12:30 Melonie was fast asleep, and her cat snored beside her.

Miles of desert, and many miles driving east remaining ahead, Durbish bared down on his accelerator, happy to put a full day behind him. The decreasing miles before him gave way for loopholes ahead. His senses were numb as his mind played down his acceptance of the prevailing gloom. Durbish felt like a villain coming out of seclusion. The challenges he faced couldn't be spoken of. They were worries only he could face alone. His dealings with Sebastian, an outcast, hung over him. It gave him a sick feeling that he understood Sebastian so well but was now ready to step out of his past. Durbish had to leave him behind and step forward, undefeated. As infrequently the two men's lives had crossed paths, the encroachment was now dangerously close to Durbish. This upsetting shred of witticism now became a setting for his advantageous conclusion of Sebastian's. Graciously, the plan to release Sebastian was just a show of courtesy. He would be keeping his word. It would mean very little because the outcome would remain the same. Tentacles must be severed. Durbish's time alone slowly overcame his sanity. His seeking salvation with no regard to his vulnerable friends' lives reared above his strategy to penetrate his mind. Stricken as made to order, the man and mastermind over this plan fell into his own moat. This protraction was heavily surrounding him. Hideously Durbish knew, but though purposely admitting this to occur, he regained his mental control.

What Sebastian faced now made him draw the last remaining strength within himself to muster up courage and hope to see him through. The upcoming trial was off-handedly mentioned to another prisoner by an orderly as he mopped the floor. Sebastian did his best to ignore them as they made bets on how he would die. Instead, he tried to recall any words that may have been mistaken in his conversation with Durbish. After a while he realized that if he had missed something it wouldn't make any difference to the trial's outcome.

Sebastian knew he was not the beast as he was perceived. He deliberately took a deep look into his past. He had been imprisoned for over a month and had thought very little of it. He sat on the edge of his cot and thought of his poor judgment in choices he had made in the past. The chain of events had only intensified his manic-depressive state of mind. From childhood he had always seemed to embroider situations out of kilter. His mind replayed his past life events in slow motion. Compared to his memories of childhood, his incarceration was a cake walk.

The good things he skipped. He was looking deep into his memory, seeking once again the bear. He knew so long ago something valid must have caused him to be as he found himself today. He whispered, "What?" A feeling arose within him, and he was taken back by an unfamiliar force as he shook in fear. "Why?" Sudden images flooded his mind's eye. Uniformly, he retraced his memory recall. A siege of sickness captured him. This exploration was critical. He realized what he saw in his mind was acceptable, but what he was experiencing was hard to believe. It was an age when he was still innocent.

Trembling with terror, Sebastian considered the concept as he tried to find meaningful implications to what all of this meant. He squeezed his eyelids tightly closed, unfamiliar in this sector of his mind, to consider his senses had survived from such a young age. He saw the inside of his baby crib. It was as if it were yesterday. He was in his grandmother's room against the wall. His stomach pitched and rolled uncontrollably. As this memory surfaced, he felt slightly concerned and very disheartened. He was lying in his crib crying or pleading. Less than ten months old, all this suddenly became very important to him.

He had never felt so stricken with fear. He thought of what he had caused others to endure because of his anger. The repulsiveness of his vision had caused a mixture of emotions accompanied by the outpouring of reasons. Other reverent quixotic snippets joined directly plethorically fitting, each procuring something unsettling. His revelation was so simple. His grandmother gave him no supervision. Instead, she had left him alone to cry in total fear, terror administered by and with no contemporary definitions. A ridiculous degree of fear and hate was in her possession coupled with the hate for his own mother. Sebastian knew this was true and that it all fit well in the maze of his personal feelings and the feelings of his grandmother. She had deliberately set out most purposely to harm him and his mother through means she had access to. Sebastian was left for her to protect her while his mother worked and now, he realized he had been emotionally abused. He saw an empty room in his mind and knew this was the abuse. There was clarity in his vision which was proof nobody ever appeared. She dares not give in by giving any aid to the baby in the crib.

Sadly, Sebastian knew it was true - what, who and why. Quizzically, he wondered if it was just the lack of affection that had caused so much pain in his life.

He gradually sensed real relief. It was continuous and pliable. The copulation would last until he hung for his crimes. His trembling stopped; a host of immediate dangers tore through his mind further. He knew a specialist, depending on their licensing and training, could accept his interrelationship. Combined with circumstance and opportunity his thoughts very well could have been programmed for his degeneracy.

By accident, Sebastian had been so absorbed in his past, he had not heard breakfast being slid under his bars. Blocking out any reason to feel sorry for himself, he ate his cold meal in an equally cold place. Like the cell, the meal gave nothing in value.

As Sabastian ate the lieutenant appeared. Sabastian continued eating ignoring him. The lieutenant stroked his hand through his small goatee as he stared at Sabastian. The lieutenant struggled to keep his composure. He suddenly stopped stroking his beard. This awareness of his hand in his beard must have annoyed him. Instead, the lieutenant pinched the tip of his goatee delicately between his fingertips as he began to speak.

He carefully chose his words asking Sabastian what gave him the right to kill the president and his loyal followers employed by his office? Sabastian's heart rate increased as the question was asked. The lieutenant deserved a conclusive answer, but the question threw him off guard. Unprepared for the question he tried to respond calmly but his breathing had rapidly increased. This caused him to temporarily lose his composure.

Sabastian's first instinct was to avoid the question. But he knew he had nothing to lose by giving an honest answer.

He said " Lieutenant if I tell you why I killed the president it will put me in a fiercely compromising position. If your desire to discuss this matter is strong, it's customary in my country to do so only in the presence of an attorney."

Why, sir, I see your point to wish for a representative of the law present here for you but, I suppose it is purely for my own curiosity I've asked you. I agree the ramifications could cause you difficulty. My curiosity to hear your reason or excuse to kill those men got the best of me. Their memories are all that remain now.

Sabastian thought about his response and said lieutenant, against my better judgement I'll tell you something off the record if you agree to it. Honestly? Yes honestly. Well fine, to satisfy my curiosity I'll agree to it. Sabastian gave the lieutenant a list of reasons why the so called six prominent figures were cast into the same category with the president. The association pertaining to the six men with the president was not easy for Sabastian to justify for the lieutenant. Sabastian hoped to clarify to him they were not in his initial plan.

His constant profusion of reasons was not proving enough for the lieutenant, he exploded into a rage as Sabastian spoke.

He shouted at Sabastian to shut up. Then calmly the lieutenant said. You materialize form know where and the nature of your acts have sent seven men to their graves. As macabre in nature as it was, I find it hard to believe you had no intention in doing just what you did as you did it.

I furthermore don't think you did this without outside help. Sabastian understood how the man fought to make sense of his actions. The reasons for the massacre of the whole assembly of men. Sabastian spoke without losing eye contact. I freehandedly choose to kill the six men lieutenant, much for the same reasons I killed the president, all of them were guilty of serious acts against the country as well the people living here.

Sabastian knew the man was convinced; his corroborating statements were commonly known facts throughout the nation.

The lieutenant did not respond, Sabastian thought he gained some amount of commiseration from his explanation. The lieutenant spoke in a civil manner, Sabastian listened relaxing his posture. He felt better after he told the lieutenant his side of the story. The lieutenant looked wearily towards Sabastian, he said you are not a very good photographer. The pictures you took were unclear, perhaps you were a better lawyer.

Of course, what we have said here will remain between us, if you say anything about this incident, I will deny it.

Sabastian wanted to be friends with this man for now, he asked the lieutenant how he learned to speak English so well. The lieutenant informed him of some facts by telling him he had spent time in America. The lieutenant said I understand the customs of your country and you, believes vary. The composition of your reasons to kill those men are acceptable to me, if what you say is not gibberish. Under the circumstances

I'm inclined to believe you in the matter. I commend your fortitude if this story is not all fabricated.

When he finished speaking, he left without another word, he disappeared down the corridor, his arrogance was not compromised by his show of understanding Sabastian's story. Sabastian felt that whatever the man had been seeking was found, the lieutenant had not ridiculed him for his comments, this raised hope for Sabastian even though it would not change the outcome of his upcoming trail.

Sabastian wondered if he could be as convincing to give the details during his trial. If he could dissuade one member of the jury the truth behind his killings would be heard one day. Long after his death someone might examen the case and enter the facts correctly in the history books. He hoped the books would show conclusively he had been right in doing what he had done.

History had been made but the heading would remain the same, THE PRESIDENT WAS SHOT.

Sabastian knew his memory and the history would remain as it was, he would be remembered as a murderer! Sabastian knew specialists at this moment would be involved in a huge cover up, the truth never would be known. Records that could prove the president was corrupted would all be destroyed, anyone who could gain access to those records could never form a conceive conclusion.

Sabastian wished there was a way to recover any records of the presidents, if there was any it would be doubtful, they would survive very long. He tried to think ahead of what Durbish was planning. His voluntary discussion with the lieutenant might cause him to make a mistake Durbish could catch. His guess was the lieutenant was involved in something but how to prove it was nonexistent without Durbish.

The smiling orderly stood still as the guard watched him slide the tray full of food into Sabastian's cell. The tray was piled high with food.

Sabastian was sure there had been a mistake; the tray of food needed side boards to hold it all. The orderly shifted his weight from foot to foot. In broken English he said, "the food was sent by order of the lieutenant." To Sabastian the message was clear the lieutenant undoubtedly had something to hide. He accepted the food from the orderly as he shuffled away Sabastian handed him some of the fruit. The young, orderly smiled revealing a set of bright white teeth. He slid the fruit into his pockets then whirled around to rush off down the corridor to catch up with the guard. Sabastian could hear them make their way down the steps. His situation in isolation had taken a turn for the better.

Unable to believe his luck Sabastian formed a large pile of assorted foods. He placed some of it in the corner of his cell, the temperature against the wall would serve well in keeping the food cool. For a start he chose a bunch of grapes and two bananas, his taste buds proved to be intact, the exquisite fruits pleased him and his deprived stomach. Silently he ate and wondered why he had been given such a feast, then the thought occurred this was his last good meal before the trial. Depending on the outcome of the trial it would also mean these were the last days he'd spend alive.

Accustomed to his privacy in the cell, he supposed the lieutenant gave him the food to help him relax. If it were known in the prison that he had done this for the killer of the president, the lieutenant might draw himself administrative difficulties. Sabastian would not say a thing to anyone in front of the lieutenant but decided to thank him if the chance arose.

Inwardly Sabastian braced himself for the coming events, if Durbish failed the trail would go on without incident, at least a firing squad was a quick die. He thought of the prevailing trial and his execution with no real idea of when these events were to take place, he began to feel uneasy. He knew the trail would be quick and things would soon come to a head. His life hung on a thread for now all he could do was hope Durbish was close to a way in freeing him.

While eating his third sandwich, Scott drives south towards Abuja. The group was one hundred and fifty miles away, Scotts' only concern was food and his weight. He weighed two hundred and twenty-seven pounds, because his height, which was just under six feet tall, the doctor said his weight was correct. Scott was sure his doctor was wrong. He thought he needed more weight, so he constantly ate and worked out to build muscles. Even though Scott ate so often, Melanie made the remark that Scott had no fat anywhere on his body.

Melanie was mad, every two hours the group helped Scott find a place to buy food. The trip would never end if this continued, Melanie told David that Scott was stalling. Durbish made the group happy, he advised Scott to buy a cooler and fill it with food, Scott found the largest container he could, and his food selection ranged from vegetables to the meat of a wart hog. He had enough food to feed a family of six adults!

Scott asked Melanie to fix his snacks. She had up until he requested the meat off the back strap of the wart hog. Melanie drew the line there and she refused to fix one more thing for Scott.

Durbish reviewed his plans for the group, convincing David to visit Sabastian confused him of his true purpose in being there.

David questioned Durbish three times on his mission's necessity, Durbish knew David understood his importance in being involved, David wanted the group to know how valuable he was to the outcome of the plan. The constant persuasion was his way of letting the group realize it. Durbish explained how important he was and pumped him up for the group, all this did was swell his ego, David rendered his reward for this he gave in and said he understood the plan.

Durbish clearly pointed out that Dr. Weston would do fine, he stated that he had told Melanie to call him specifically. No one else had been considered. Dr. Weston grinned as these facts were revealed for the group to realize his importance in being there. He said with all the respect directed towards the group his responsibility was not the most perplexing part to him, the fact remained that once the four of them were inside the prison how were the five of them going to just walk off with the most hated person in Abuja?

With all respect, Durbish was not stretching the importance of David's part. The success and deception the doctor must perform was vital. He had to administer a drug into Sebastian that would cause his heart to fail. This was a dangerous procedure, and it had to be done quickly with no margin for error. If the delivery of the drug was an inkling too much, Sebastian would have a massive stroke. This was David's concern that Sebastian's incarceration would double, even triple the complexities involved in estimating the dosage of drug used.

Melonie's participation was also significant. She had to be a decoy drawing any unwanted attention away from David and the situation. It was an intricate plan with many unforeseen possibilities for failure. All in all, the plan was not much better than an outright scam.

The group was now 80 miles outside of Abuja's city limits. All their concerns had been answered, and doubts had been covered. There were no problems remaining and each knew their role. Many questions were answered concerning flaws in the plan. The what ifs was everyone's main concern.

Durbish felt his nerves exposed. He finally closed the discussion, making it perfectly clear that in the event of any misunderstanding or disruption on a whole, each of us will do whatever is needed. "Scott is here for just that reason," Durbish said.

Scott said, "Don't worry if the plan collapses, I won't let any of you down. You bet cha, I'm the last person, besides Sebastian, these people wanna fool around with. If anything goes wrong, just hold your position and do not be in my line of fire. Durbish says the weapon that will be here for me can control any situation quickly."

Durbish had promised Scott an inline over and under 10-gauge shotgun with a grenade launcher. The lead fired from this weapon could tear a person's limbs off. The latitude of the grenades in such close quarters, if used, would have no limitations.

Melonie had seen Scott in action. She knew his willingness to use such a weapon. She also figured he hoped he would have that chance as Scott enjoyed these types of excursions. She admitted to herself if any one man she had to choose, Scott would be her first choice for a backup. To look at him you would mistake him for a jock, easy-going on the surface, but beneath his outward appearance lay a highly trained operative. He was highly skilled with a level of expertise that was unconventional. He was the only one cognizant of the methods he used.

The Nazis and Russians have their elite groups. The United States have the Marines, the Navy with its Seals, the Army, and Air Force, then there is the CIA accounting for the world's best classified or unclassified organizations -- as Melonie thought of all these groups, Scott was a one-man enigma devoted to one thing, his pursuit of pleasure in gruesomeness and mocking no one.

Twenty-five minutes away from the hotel, he told Scott to follow a deserted road. He turned to his left onto a barely visible trail if you were not looking for it. The road would easily be mistaken for a break in the landscape. The vehicle descended a steep hill, bouncing viciously as the suspension bottomed out in the ravine. Scott's remedy for the trouble was applauded as he engaged the vehicle into four-wheel drive. The truck was at an unnatural angle, but with all four wheels pulling them, he managed to pull them out of the ravine.

Durbish looked out the side of the narrow rut filled road and spotted the reason they were there. On the driver's side of the road an ambulance was parked. It was perfectly marked and secure. He told Scott to hold up beside it and the whole group got out of the land rover to inspect the hidden vehicle. Durbish said, "Everyone needs to hurry. The sun is almost down; we need to try on our uniforms.

"None of them are perfect fits, but suitable. "David inspected his medical bag. It was a large bag containing some surgical equipment and medicine for emergencies. The paramedics' clothing had been laid neatly on the front seat, along with identification papers for each of them.

Drubish said, "From here on out, until Sebastian is safe, we will remain in these roles. We will be considered officials for the U.N. Of course, Melanie, you are the nurse here to assist the doctor and Scott, your role is the driver. Now, let's prepare to enter the city." Durbish rushed to get them moving as darkness blanketed them.

Each of them looked at the part they had to play; it would serve the purpose of gaining the confidence of any curious observer. As they all piled into the ambulance, they could barely hear anything but the grinding starter, as the motor made its final protest started. As it cranked, thick black smoke bellowed from the exhaust pipe. He revved the motor, cleared the carburetor and the smoke stopped.

Durbish was ahead of them in the Land Rover, making the incline, about to reach the main road. Scott gave an efficient amount of acceleration for the ambulance to make the grade. The ambulance and its occupants had no choice but to sway and growl as the vehicle negotiated the hill. Slowly, they made the top.

Durbish waited for them and waved them on to follow him. He turned on his headlights and the lights flashed brilliantly in their pitch-black surroundings. Once Scott gained full control of the ambulance on the road, he did the same thing. Melonie studied each set of IDs, then handed them to her partners to familiarize themselves with their fake names.

Melonie's new identity now became Cheryl Estes, a registered nurse from Birmingham, England. She was a volunteer aide to the U.N.

Peace Corps. "Scott," David said, as he read the information to brief him of his new identity, "You are Randall Cope, a university graduate from the U.S. Marine Corps, a technical sergeant. You've been granted permission as a volunteer for a three-month tour for the U.N. peace effort." At last, David read his and exclaimed loudly, "Why, I'm Dr. David Weston!"

Scott asked, "Why would you be you and we are different?"

Melonie reminded both men, "Scott and I are different only for anyone who may be suspicious. If you recall, Dr. Weston is scheduled to be here in the prison and last, but no less important, we are in this scheme only as props. Until we get fully organized, we play out this scenario and David, being the physician, will remain under his identity. It makes perfect sense to me," she said. "Besides, who we are makes very little difference in the overall plan anyway."

"The whole idea and its purpose are just for an introduction into the hotel setting," David reminded them. He added solely to stroke Scott's ego, "Remember your flexibility in the matter. You, my friend, will just be there waiting for any signs of trouble outside while we're inside the prison with Sebastian. Once we're there, I'll have to make the decision on the dosage, then you'll be called in by a guard if everything goes well. Melonie will ask the guard to take her outside to get you, Scott. As Melonie distracts him you take his keys and come inside. Be sure you bring your gun. Melonie will stay outside in the ambulance, making sure the guard is well hidden. Once I know you're coming with the gurney, I'll have administered the shot to Sebastian and will act as though we're finished. How long the drug takes are underdetermined, but we won't make it out until it's had its effect. That will leave us there to be called back alongside of their staff, hopefully."

"David," Melonie asked, "do you think these plans will work or do you think we're all crazy to attempt this."

"Melonie," he said sternly, "This whole damn mess looks doubtful that we'll succeed, but I'm willing to do it for one reason. I owe it to Sebastian. Plus, the fact that the trial is just a formality and he's surely going to die, and I'll be damned if I can just not try to help him escape."

"Melonie, you'll need to secure the guard and return downstairs. Joke around with the guards and keep them busy. I'll have my hands full trying to persuade their doctors of the need to move Sebastian. If they don't buy my story, Scott--I mean Randall has the solution for that. If you hear any loud blasts, be sure to keep the prison operational by whatever means possible. Don't let security get organized enough to shut down the system. If they do, we'll all be trapped and, as well, separated. When you see us coming--if you see us, begin to make your exit as we planned. You drive and Scott will cover our backs. As we leave, Scott sends a few grenades in the corridors to delay their pursuit. That's a worst-case scenario and that's what we don't want to happen to cause the plan to collapse. "But" David sighed, "Melonie, if things go right, you'll be downstairs flirting with the guards as Scott, and I rush out with our patient having a massive stroke. All in all, it's a simple plan and it's understandable that we'll have an emergency release for the prisoner. Of course, you realize they may add a guard to send with us."

"What if that occurs David?" Melonie asked.

"Well, we'll have one guard in the ambulance already and two will just make it cozier."

Scott said, "This is the craziest idea Durbish has ever come up with and I smell trouble, but I like it."

The group tailed closely behind Durbish as he pulled into a side street parking next door to a rundown hotel. All that was said by any of them as they exited the vehicles was how glad they would be to get inside to sleep. Their conspiracy was in full progress, but now it took a back seat until the group rested.

Durbish said, "We all need a good night's rest." Then quietly, he said, "Once we enter the hotel keep quiet about any of this. Don't even speak of it in the privacy of your rooms. We are safe here, but we can't afford any foul-ups. Inside you'll find you can get anything you need. The man that owns this place is very efficient. Each of you will remain in your room until we are ready to depart in the morning. Now, let's go and be on your best behavior. It depends a lot on it."

They all followed Durbish into the hotel. As the four of them entered, all eyes were instantly drawn to the doctor, nurse, and paramedic. The rough interior of the hotel had not changed, and Melonie stared at the girls who willingly bared their voluptuous breasts. The large gathering of men was totally unrestrained as they shouted promises of satisfaction to the dancers on the tables.

Melonie looked at Durbish totally stricken by what was going on but held her attention to her secretly married husband's raised eyebrows as he noticed her dislike for the swirling figures before them. Durbish quickly pulled her alongside him. Holding her gently, he led her up the stairway. Several minutes later Durbish returned downstairs after being ridiculed by Melonie for his obvious enjoyment of what was going on downstairs. He joined Scott and Dr. Weston having a drink while a woman danced on their table. The girls who danced had been trained to negotiate their moves with sophistication as their heels were planted firmly on the tabletops. The slowness in which they revealed their bodies could hypnotize anyone. Both David and Scott were mesmerized by the dancer and unaware that Durbish had taken a seat beside them. They stared blankly as the dancer's routine grew more furious. She bared her breasts and brushed her nipples across each man's face.

Durbish saw Anita and her uncle out of the corner of his eye. He quietly left the table as her uncle led him into a back room. Anita was disturbed by her uncle's sudden disappearance. She had seen him walk through the swinging doors with Durbish. She was filled with dread and thoughts of more problems but filled with hope that Sebastian would return. She then quietly peeked through the doors to see what was taking place in the barroom. She searched the crowd, quickly discarding the familiar faces, she saw what she was looking for. She knew the two new faces she saw were there for one purpose, other than the obvious.

Her heartbeat rapidly increased as thoughts of Sebastian flooded her memories. She could see him in her mind so vividly. She staggered as she backed out of the doorway and had to lean against the wall as her breathing was erratic. She tried to catch her breath; she imagined the two of them together again. Not a day or a moment had gone by since Sebastian left that she hadn't believed he would return to her. He had promised that his love for her was undying and that he would return. She knew he had meant those words. Now, with Durbish's arrival and presence of the two men in the other room was her assurance that Sebastian would soon be free.

The timing was perfect. She had read the trial of the President's killer would begin in two days. For whatever reasons these men had come, she knew she must keep it secret. She knew these people, whoever they were, would save Sebastian and lead him back to her. She was unwilling to expose herself to them out of fear of getting killed. She had to purposely act as though nothing unusual was going on. She would do nothing to jeopardize her love for Sebastian and the safety of her uncle. Deep down she just knew Sebastian would be saved soon and he would return for her. Juliette's heart was soaring from the renewed hopes of Sebastian being saved. She had a burning desire for him, a flame of love that rekindled the inferno inside her. Now she was entertaining herself with fantasies of their being reunited. Juliette's uncle entered the kitchen and brought her back to reality. When their eyes met, he smiled at her, amazed by the expression on her face. He had not seen her smile in weeks.

With no need for words, her uncle crossed the room and reached out for her hand. The two of them were instantly in a loving embrace. Her uncle held her like a child and soothed her with words that she could now relax her worried mind. Quietly, he told her what he knew. "What we don't know for sure is if their plan will work. Everything possible is being done to save Sebastian, Juliette, and you must be brave for him. The chance of this occurring is uncertain. The rescue itself or any attempt such as this has never been made. To accomplish what these four people have come to do--"

"Four?" she asked. "I saw only Durbish and the two others."

Her uncle said, "There is a girl much like yourself in age, as well as beauty, upstairs. She is part of their group and quite a friend to all of them."

"What are you implying, Uncle. Is the girl more than just a friend?"

Her uncle quickly attempted to diffuse the fury Juliette hid and said, "No, Juliette, that wasn't what I meant. She is a friend, nothing more. You'll see. You know Sebastian much better than I do and surely you believe that he loves only you. Trust me."

Juliette left the kitchen. She did not return for quite some time.

Melonie sat staring at the expensive laptop computer Durbish had arranged for her to use. It had all the bells and whistles she wanted for her own personal use. This computer would become a gift to whomever stumbled across it after they fled Morocco. Her objective was to outsmart the heads of state, officials of each country which the group would pass through, and the government personnel involved in the recapture of Andras' killer.

The computer, if used to its capacity, would be their only means to implement their plans. As she stared at the computer in front of her, she felt more now than ever part of the plan. The computer would become her friend, and her task would be to use that friendship in a way friends would never use one another. Every one of these men will be depending on me. She now clearly understood it was up to her to gain control of her part in the mission.

The pressure was weighing heavily on Melonie's mind, suddenly someone knocked loudly, it shook the door.

She opened the door cautiously, Durbish entered the room perturbed over a trivial matter. It seemed to her to be nothing, but Durbish carried on. "My room has no facilities, those in my room were installed in 1900's and haven't worked in years."

She listened to Durbish become more infuriated over his predicament. When she could no longer contain herself, she fell back onto her bed roaring with laughter.

As mad as this man was, the sight of his wife rolling on the bed instantly had a positive effect. Durbish joined her on the bed as both broke out laughing hysterically. The two of them were in tears and had to finally force themselves to regain control.

Juliette walked down the corridor and stopped beside the doorway. Since their arrival, Juliette had been quietly observing their every move, something she disliked but felt a need to do. She did not want to sabotage their mission's success. Her jolt of fear of the other woman had caused her to snoop. All she could hear was giggles and soft whispers. The sounds she heard were Durbish adoringly making love to the woman inside the room. This was sufficient evidence to end her prying curiosity. She quietly continued down the hall to the stairs. This episode had set her mind at ease, her doubts quenched Juliette retreated into her room.

In her room she stood naked before her mirror inspecting her unborn child, yet barely noticeable, even to her. Sebastian would be a father, regardless she would bear his child. She knew her pregnancy could remain secret for just so long. She wasn't to the point of telling her uncle; he would soon be a grand uncle. If Sebastian died, she thought this way his legacy would continue. His child would be respected throughout the country.

Flatteringly beautiful as she was, the slight awareness of conception was viewed by her at all angles. Juliette was aching for Sebastian. She gently pressed against her stomach, making her feel a part of him. Somehow from this motion a true sense of togetherness was found. She then lay naked on her bed. Comfortable with her own body's sensations, she dreamed it was Sebastian touching her. A glimpse of Sebastian's image warmed her senses. The emanation of her pleasure eased her mind. With her needs left unattended and worries binding her, she was drained. All this vanished as Juliette did a natural act automatically. The pressure released within her satisfied her emotional and sexual desires.

As she lay nude the hotel's construction creeped with the occupancy of others upstairs. Few guests stayed over on a regular basis. A few kept companies with the girls downstairs and had for years. With four new people, it would be busier than usual in the morning. As Juliette began to fall asleep, she softly whispered encouraging words to her unborn child. As she stroked her belly, she whispered of how her father had saved thousands of lives and was the bravest man ever. She told the baby how its father let God be his guide in any important decisions.

Scott and David, after their drinks were emptied, walked upstairs to retire in opposite rooms, down the hallway from Melonie where Durbish was asleep cradling his wife.

David stopped at Scott's door as he opened it. Both men experienced a surge of adrenaline, they saw supplies neatly stacked against the wall. David said, "Scott close the door, gently," as he stood behind him aware of the smell of weapons drifting in the air. David's impression was that it was a visible display of authority. Significant, since they would be the possessors and responsible, no doubt safe with plenty of fire power.

"Impressive," Scott said.

David said, "Yeah. By the time we use this much ammo, I'll be very surprised if the ground around the country will be safe to walk on."

"I heard that."

David sighed wearily and walked to his room in the moonlight. The moon illuminating his side of the hotel. Stirring under the covers he escaped the light shining in almost shattering the silence. The hotel was quiet.

Scott could sleep anywhere, and his snores were heard throughout the second floor. David was tossing and turning in his bed unable to sleep. As the clock approached 11:15, Scott snored with less determination which gave David enough of a break to fall asleep. Scott slept in charge of the weapons snoring…

After a delectable breakfast, the group lounged in the back room as the last minutes before their rescue mission. Outside the hotel, two vehicles bared the weight of all their supplies, their suspensions strained under the load.

The morning had been full of activity. Each of them in the early hours labored as they loaded the supplies. Everything was now ready. All that remained to be done was the execution of the plan. The possibility of abandonment would not be considered beyond this point. They were now bound inflexible in full agreement, now became united a unit, not an easy joining considering their differences. They were psychologically prepared to save Sebastian from certain execution.

With all their accumulated skills an enormous effect set them at ease, quiet disciplined environment. As they sat spellbound, gathering their wits calming their nerves no words had been whispered for over ten minutes.

Durbish broke the silence as he placed a call to the prison. He gained access to the Warden's office in a matter of moments. He secured permission for the United Nations doctor to enter the prison with him. Abruptly, Dr. David Weston heard his name clearly spoken by Durbish, giving the Warden pertinent information and time of their arrival time. Durbish advised the warden, "A staff of two other volunteers will accompany the doctor, a nurse and an assistant." Durbish slid the phone tonelessly into the cradle as he completed the call. As he spoke the group consciously tuned for any sounds of trembling in his voice. "Be sure all of your paperwork is in order. Other than that, our entrance is granted with full cooperation as promised." Juliette's uncle appeared in the doorway. In his hands he held a three-ring binder. He displayed its contents to Durbish. As the other three observed, Durbish looked pleased returning to the group. Durbish told them the significance of the binder's contents. It listed friends of the uncle who would help them hide as they escaped the country.

Juliette approached the room cautiously, holding a tray of specialty drinks. Durbish ushered her into the room. Instantly, Melonie's and Juliette's eyes met. She sat the drinks on the table. Melonie and Juliette stood beside one another. Each woman introduced themselves to the other. Melonie said her name was Sheryl Estes. Juliette said her name was Anita. Both women were nearly the same height. Their features varied; both were beautiful to gaze at, lethal women combined beauty could conjure up pleasingly naughty thoughts. The men in the room were all trying to dismiss the effects of them standing before them. Melonie looked at Juliette's pert figure and envied her beauty. Even she could not deny Juliette was astounding with perfectly defined inherited traits.

Durbish announced, "He would return in one hour." I suggest you find your form of relaxation the best way you can. I'll be back shortly."

Juliette and Melonie joined in friendly conversation. Juliette claimed she was bored and had nothing to do. The two of them sat next to Scott and were introduced to Juliette. As Randall sat close to Juliette, he found her a pleasure to listen to. Her voice was delicate and precise. He stuck to every word and savored the sounds. He was not listening to the words she spoke, but the melody in her voice. His attraction towards this lovely young lady Melonie pointed out to Juliette, "Don't pay any attention to Randall's diminished loss of his senses and lack of respect."

Scott never flinched women easily sensing a fondness with nothing but good intentions. Both were patient with his lost senses and just giggled and enjoyed each other's conversation.

Dr. Weston chose not to become involved. His nervousness was difficult for him to cope with. He was reading the morning paper as he dealt with his personal situation. He agonizingly forced himself not to dwell on the danger he and the others were about to embark upon. He controlled his fear. He would not let anything break the pattern. If he did so, it would punch holes in his tactic. The information in the three-ring binder was bothering him as well. If the police arrested Durbish while in possession of the binder, all those listed would be in imminent danger. The police could easily track the five fugitives.

Also, the names of the people and safe houses of the intricate underground network would instantly be in the hands of the police. David knew that the information should not be in existence. To lose the list would ensure many arrests, including the people who have helped them now. He could not fathom the recording of such volatile information. He wondered why it was being entrusted to them. He was sure the property was too valued to be so flagrantly displayed. Even if that was the only course Durbish had left in securing their escape, the binder with its ramifications, if found, was just too risky to possess. Dr. Weston didn't like his life riding in one person's care. Durbish had complete control over their lives and David knew his eyes would be on him just to be sure nothing was amiss. For now, he chose not to mention any of his thoughts to the group, but certain he would in the event of any major screw-up.

Completely unaware of the unfolding activities across the city, Sebastian strained to complete one more repetition in his daily routine of 300 pushups. After 100 reps he would pause for ten minutes, then do another set until he reached his maximum, then he would rest until his lunch arrived. Since his ribs had healed the routine had gained in intensity. He devised simple techniques to perform in his cell on a regular basis. His last 100 pushups were done on a decline. He placed his feet on the edge of his cot, a simple maneuver to alter the effects of the muscles used. Unbeknownst to him, while he did the last reps, the group of his most trusted friends began a course heading straight to him. Basic exercises had provided his constant gain in strength. The most obvious benefit from the routine was that it kept him from going insane.

Sebastian lay on his cot. Since his arrest his weight has fallen drastically. The food yesterday was sparse, quickly eaten and forgotten. As he anticipated his noon meal, this dependance on someone else seemed to burn more of his energy. Sebastian unfolded a piece of paper the young orderly had given him this morning. He wanted to read it once more. Hardly able to read the writing, it said plainly, "We all thank you for di kellin of di hi chief." 64 men had signed their name onto the paper or placed XX's to show their appreciation in what he had done.

The note gave Sebastian a sense of hope, their support for his accomplishment killing gave him a lighter outlook on his death sentence. It was a brave act for those involved to risk being caught passing the note through the prison. The names meant nothing, yet they did signify the men stood behind him. Their support would give him the strength he needed for the trial. The proof was in his hand. Men in prison became affectionate in their absence from the outside world. It was all very touching to a degree and an enormous show of support, enough to die proudly for.

The letter reminded Sebastian of how he missed Juliette, her absence in his life made him want to see her constantly. He knew it was out of the question to dare try to communicate with her. This day was turning into an assault on his emotions; the last day was unbearably the hardest day he had foregone.

As Sebastian replayed visions of Juliette in his mind's eye, downstairs passes were issued to the group granting them free movement within the prison. Durbish and Dr. Weston spoke with the lieutenant. As they entered the prison Durbish excused Randall Cope and Sheryl Estes. Dr. Weston politely asked them to stand at ease until they were needed. Scott and Melonie casually walked the grounds of the prison front. Melonie commented on how spooky the prison appeared. Scott strummed his pass as he anxiously stood beside the ambulance. Melonie stopped the noise by clipping the visitor's pass back onto his shirt.

Melonie said, "Okay, Randall this is not a test. I'm heading in closer.

Scott asked, "What are you going to do?"

Melonie answered, "I'm going to find myself a man!"

Melonie turned the radio on and clipped it to her belt. She motioned for Scott to do likewise. Swiftly, she walked to the opposite side of the prison's entrance way. She looked over the grounds manicured islands maintained and groomed nicely by the prisoners. The display of marigolds and neatly trimmed bushes were across the full length of the prison lawn. In the center of each island were hearty and nicely arranged trees of the same variety and cut the same shape. The guards had an unobscured view from the towers. The guards could see across the whole finely manicured lawn from tower to tower.

Dr. Weston stepped from the elevator onto the second floor. The Warden had left him unaccompanied to inspect the prisoners. The doctor acted pleased with the offer and strolled down the hallway. He gazed into each cell he passed. This graphic display of malnourished humans sent chills over his whole body. Suddenly, he became very cold inside the prison's corridor. As he looked at the men behind bars and saw their look of desperation and depravation, it was unnatural the contribution to this mission heightened. Undoubtedly, this would compromise his sleep for many nights to come. He thought he knew what it would be like inside the prison, this drew his attention away from the purpose of his being there.

He continued down the corridor passing each cell unwilling to look inside them any longer. He found a guard sitting at the end of the long hallway. He asked him, "Could you please lead me to cell #208 I'm looking for it?"

Quizzically, the guard looked over this doctor and asked, "Wha' number?"

"H-A-208." Dr. Weston said.

The guard eyed him suspiciously and lumbered ahead of him to the cell. Dr. Weston felt like he was in another world altogether. It was apparent he was each second, as he moved through the corridor the smells and sounds were all foreign. Voices, shouting with all this noise, his heart rate began causing his breathing to be uneven. He felt more in control of himself in this environment but probably not much longer.

The guard repeated the question, "Wah cell number?" in broken English and seemed to grow impatient with the doctor.

David repeated the number, "208," and looked anxiously on each cell they passed. As they reached Sebastian's cell, he showed the guard a pass and said, "Open the door I have freedom of movement and ten minutes to visit this inmate."

The keys came off the guard's waist entering the slot in the door. The sound of the keys and the clunk of the latch caused Sebastian to raise his head abruptly. Scott was shaking all over and prayed Sebastian was in control of his senses enough to remain placid. Sebastian started to say something. The look of recognition disappeared from his face as he took on the look of being rudely awakened by a total stranger. Dr. Weston knew the crisis was over.

Dr. Weston turned to the guard and asked, "Do you have a set of portable scales so I can weigh the prisoner?"

In broken English, Dr. Weston understood him to say, "It will take a few minutes."

"Go get them."

The guard said, "No," adding it was lunch time.

Dr. Weston said, "Please, sir, I must weigh the man because the records need to be documented before tomorrow.

"But it is lunch time. I will eat my lunch first!"

Dr. Weston said, "Never mind. I have a set. My assistant will bring them. Please wait here for him, then you can go eat."

Dr. Weston unclipped his radio from his belt and flipped the switch. The radio on Scott's belt was breaking up as he heard Dr. Weston say, "Randall Cope, come in please. This is Dr. Weston.

"Doc, this is Cope. What can I do for you?"

"Bring my bag and the scales. Cope, did you get that? Over."

"Doc, I'll be there in a few minutes. Cope out."

Melonie saw Scott digging in the back of the ambulance and rushed over to give him a hand. Inside, she found the bag as he lifted the scales. She placed the strap over his other shoulder and secured the heavy bag which contained very few medical supplies and the 10 gauge over and under shotgun.

"Here goes nothing," Scott said. "Take your position and be ready for anything."

She said, "Getting in is simple, but believe me, getting out is another thing. Have you noticed?"

"Yep."

"Take the towers for example. How are we going to get past those guns?"

He replied, "Grenades. Just get the inside guard's attention, all right. I sure hope shooting won't bother you. I'm getting out one way or another." He rushed up the steps holding the scales under his arm. The bag hung heavily across his chest.

Melonie shouted to him, "Wait." She rushed over to him and whispered, "Please don't get us all killed."

He just grinned as he headed toward the entrance. As the guard told him to halt, Melonie caught up with Scott. Seductively, she said to the guard, "I'm not going up."

Ever since Scott had known Melonie, he had never heard her sound so seductive. The guard looked at her and read the expression on her face. It was a promise the guard should ignore if he was smart. The buzz from the electric lock released the sliding door. A wall of bars opened, and Melonie could be heard laughing at the entrance as Scott slipped out of view. The guard took the bait. She would literally tease him to death.

Scott spoke on his radio, "Dr. Weston, what floor are you on. How do I find you? Over."

"Dr. Weston said, "Did you find the scales?"

"Yes. Where do I bring them. Over."

"Second floor, Randall, Unit H-A, Cell 208. Over."

"Be right up, Doc."

Durbish was eating lunch with the Warden. Knowing at any moment the lunch could turn to disastrous. If he didn't move and find out what was taking place, he'd be trapped. Durbish pushed his plate aside without eating a bite of it. "Sir, my appetite is off. Besides, I just had a large breakfast. Would you be so kind as to excuse me?"

I'm going to see what the doctor is doing. I must make a formal report. The truth is, it is all very unnecessary, but it's my job and I must do it. If I don't--"

The Warden interrupted him saying, "Fine, please go ahead. I'll catch up with you in five or ten minutes. I know where to find you. Where can you go anyway? You're inside a prison," he said as he laughed at his own joke.

Durbish left him as he continued to display his bad taste in jokes and manners. Disgustingly, he laughed with his mouth full of food.

Durbish stood waiting for the elevator and mumbled, "You gross pig!" The guard in the bulletproof booth downstairs was drooling to come out. Melonie said, "I find you very appealing and you turn me on." She pressed her body against the glass, putting her breasts in full view. The guard was dying to get his hands on her. He rubbed the glass and played the perfect part of a fool. Melonie unbuttoned the two top buttons of her blouse revealing a nice portion of cleavage. She thought, "All this for this jerk-off!" but smiled her sweetest smile.

The guard was half out of his mind from being enticed by this luscious woman. He motioned towards the slot in the wall of the booth. Melonie didn't like it, but knew she had to get inside with the guard. He was gaining his wits too fast. Her thoughts were screaming at Well come closer to me right here! Now he said that. She had to move now she moved slightly towards the slot. The guard's hand shot out like some cannon had exploded from inside the booth. His hands were on her face, and she saw his eyes bulging out of their sockets as they moved down her body.

"Hey," she said trying to control the situation,

In return, he said, "Hi," as he held a strand of hair, gently urging her closer to the slot.

"My name's Sheryl, what is your name?"

He stammered, "Roy. You sure are a pretty woman."

She said, "Why, thank you, Roy." She pulled free from him, looking up and down the hall. His hands were flapping in the air through the slot, reminding her of a magic show. He curled his fingers in and out so she would draw near the slot's opening again, she supposed for him to feel her off. Melonie ran her hand across her breasts just out of his reach. His hand was jerking, opening and closing like a wind-up toy on a spring. She thought, "Damn, I've got to get this over or we're dead!"

Roy's hand slipped inside her blouse down to her bra. "Sheryl," he said in a husky voice, "You've got to come closer to the slot. I can't get to you." He was straining to get to her.

She felt disgusted but said seductively, "Let me in Roy. I could hide below the glass. If you let me in, nobody will see us." As he hesitated, she said, "Roy, I want you. I must have you closer to me." She neared the slot again, just close enough for him to touch her breasts again. As his hand moved toward her nipple, she glanced back up and out the door. She stepped back. Roy stood in the booth staring at her disheveled blouse. Her bra exposed just enough of her voluptuous breasts. She was near the guard, but slightly out of his reach.

Suddenly, the buzzer went off and the door was unlocked. In the small of her back rested a small caliber weapon. She stepped into the booth and flaunted her body in front of the guard who was in hot pursuit of her. He had worked himself up into a frenzy. She knew she had to move fast while his guard was down. As she closed the door, she unsheathed the pistol and pointed it between his eyes, saying, "A dead man if you twitch, Roy our you should be wiser." He stepped backwards as she gestured with a shrug of her shoulders, "Believe me, you slime ball, I'll kill you if you move." Hatred spewed from the tone of her voice. The guard's features looked washed out, displaying a terribly injured look, he felt so stupid. She said, "Back up!" He backed against the wall and a flicker of hope showed in his eyes. Melonie said, "Don't twitch a muscle or I'll shoot you." The pistol was cocked as she stood ready, saying, "Open the gates."

He said contemptuously, "You won't shoot, and I won't open the gates, you bitch."

Melonie sent a solitary bullet along the side of his thigh. The bullet ricocheted off the metal wall of the small room in her direction. Luckily, the bullet missed and hit the heavy steel door. As the bullet speed was spent, it fell to the concrete floor. Savagely cursing her, the guard clasped his hand to the wound as the blood dripped down his leg. The sound of the pistol was muffled by the silencer.

Having no choice but to do as she said, the guard opened the gates. He grunted in agony as he pressed the electronic panel controlling the doors.

She said, "You better not move. Roy, I believe you just lost your job." She reached for Roy and pulled him to the other side of the booth.

He was completely aware that he had just committed the greatest mistake of his career. He would lose more than his job.

Melonie was grinning from ear to ear as she plundered through the desk drawers until she found some cord. She said, "Put your chest down spread your legs and put your hands behind you." After she bound Roy's hands, she pushed him to the floor and with a swift move wrapped the cord tightly around his ankles. "Now, Roy, how can you ever take me out on that date?"

Upstairs, Dr. Weston withdrew a four-inch needle he had inserted into Sebastian's chest. Durbish stood outside the cell, keeping watch for the guard who was on lunch break. Dr. Weston said, "The medicine won't take long, Durbish. Go find a guard or anybody." He tossed the syringe into bag on the floor. Dr. Weston looked at Scott and said, "Be ready. This stuff has the potential to send him into cardiac arrest.

Durbish returned with the guard, whose lunch had been interrupted twice today. Dr. Weston said, "This will be the last time we will intrude on you. Can you lead my assistant to a restroom?" He felt his respectable position as a guard was being abused. Their excuse to disrupt his lunch was weak.

Durbish chuckled at the guard as he unlocked the steel door. As he watched them go down the hall, Dr. Weston's attention returned to Sebastian. "The injected drug entered your bloodstream easily." Momentarily, Sebastian rested his left hand over his mouth and Dr. Weston saw he remained simi conscious.

Sebastian was making every effort to remain calm and not panic as the drug took its effect. He turned to look at David and lay very still. His breathing became ragged. Dr. Weston checked his pulse. It, as well, had sharply decreased. Hurriedly, David whispered, "Sebastian, listen."

A vacant look loomed over Sebastian's face. Dr. Weston deliberately drew close to him and rubbed his face. Sebastian was disoriented as he tried to focus on the face of the doctor. Dr. Weston said, "It's a normal reaction, Sebastian. Stay calm. He looked at Durbish and said, "My concern is that he won't stay this way long enough." Moments later Durbish stood beside the cot next to the doctor. Get the Warden in here, we have to move fast!

Suddenly, they heard what their friend heard several times a day. The guard's keys rattled as he and Scott reentered the corridor. Durbish quietly asked the doctor, "Did you give him enough of the drug to do the trick?"

The doctor said, "I don't know, I think so Durbish.

The guard turned the key to let Scott inside the cell. Suddenly the cell was too small for everyone to enter. Dr. Weston said to the guard, "Something was going on with the prisoner." The guard glanced over in the direction of the prisoner, unconcerned.

Dr. Weston said, "Really, there's something wrong with him. This may be baseless, but I'm the doctor here and I tell you this man is very ill." The doctor was stern in his manner as he got the point across.

The guard said, "Nonsense."

As if on cue, Sebastian jolted on the bed. Durbish said, "The man is having an attack." David and Scott looked at the guard as a smile spread across his face.

Dr. Weston said, "What is funny? This man is in cardiac arrest!" David leaned over Sebastian and placed both of his hands together to manually pump Sebastian's heart. "Get the prison's doctor and a gurney, we need to take this man to a hospital fast."

The three men watched as the guard ran down the hall. The doctor was applying steady pressure as he counted in two second intervals. The guard retraced his footsteps down the corridor with what sounded like a stampede of people approaching the cell they occupied.

Dr. Weston looked at Durbish and quietly said, "Now, the show will begin."

The corridor gleamed to perfection from its daily wax and buff. One man fell on its slick surface and caused a pile-up. The Warden was the last to fall headfirst into the pile. The bushy headed psychologist wasn't very lucky. He lay under the pile and voiced the unnatural acts he would deliver promptly if they didn't get off. "Get the fuck off me, now!" He was screaming so loud under other good-sized men, only a few words were audible.

Warden Jarod Masser permitted this until he regained his footing. At the top of his lungs he barked direct orders, "Clear the hall immediately." The lieutenant's head was visible under the pile. With his outstretched arm a mock salute was attempted.

As more orders were being shouted in the corridor, Sebastian's struggle continued. The color of his complexion was a deep shade of gray. In minutes the blue had washed into the gray tone to completely cover his body like ash colored paint.

Durbish punched at the guard sent to find the prison's doctor. The doctor's assistant was still on the bottom of the pile beside the bushy-headed psychologist.

Durbish yelled, "Let me out."

The guard whirled around, physically shaking with anger as he opened the door.

Dr. Weston was frantically pumping on Sebastian's chest. He knew he was not in serious trouble if he helped the heart flush the medication throughout his arteries. He said to Scott, "Sebastian is aphasic."

Scott said, "Then it's fortunate for him you're here, Doc. He asked, "What is aphasic?"

Dr. Weston said breathlessly, "He is unable to communicate, and he does not show visible signs of response."

The Warden cleared the hall outside of any unneeded staff and he stepped into the cell. The doctor's assistant, psychologist and lieutenant stepped inside the cell behind him. All eyes were riveted on the dying killer!

Perplexed by the circumstances, the Warden consulted with the psychologist because the chief medical doctor had not been informed yet. They spoke as privately as possible inside the crowded cell. The bushy hair on top of the big man was shaking wildly from side to side. It looked like a ship tossing on the rough waters in an ocean swell.

It was apparent to Dr. Weston that the two men agreed the inmate now was a patient dying.

Scott stood close to the doctor's side and quietly asked, "Are you ready for Plan B?"

"I've been ready!"

"You just say when and give me a two second lead so I can slam the clip in."

Dr. Weston could feel Sebastian's heartbeat regulated. Minutes were critical to make the plan work. They had to move him before he woke up. His breathing was stable but barely apparent.

Stepping closer to the cot, the Warden asked Dr. Weston, "Let me take a look at him"

The physician's assistant stepped next to the cot and bent over the killer to listen to his heartbeat.

Dr. Weston said, "He has suffered a heart attack."

The PA was substandard the assistant at best agreed with Dr. Weston's opinion. He asked the Warden, "What do we do?"

The Warden asked the psychologist. The bushy headed man was determined to steal the show. He asked the lieutenant, "Can we securely move him without any help from the others? Also, can we be certain the man suffered a heart attack?"

Dr. Weston interrupted the lieutenant's train of thought before he had another chance to speak, "This incident, as odd as it seems, is a blatant neglect of the prisoner's wellbeing. Do you understand what I'm saying. I certainly have cause to claim malpractice in full view of three United Nations' witnesses. The condition of this man, killer or not, is very serious and he is dying. As a medical representative of the United Nations, I insist we take him to a hospital. And as soon as possible our heads will roll under any investigation. Since you three gentlemen can't decide what to do, Randall, bring in the gurney." Instantly he barked at his commanders. Durbish with his subtle threat had worn thin on the Warden's authority.

The Warden said, "Hold on--"

Before he could complete his thought, Durbish briskly shoved his massive body through the congested cell. As he began to move forward, he noted the tension was increasing within the cell. Tempers were flaring and seconds mattered.

Sebastian was clearly in a restful state, not one that looked like a heart attack. The medicine had dissipated throughout his system. Any second, he'd wake up and not have a clear understanding of what was taking place. This could foul things up and they had to move fast.

Durbish asked the Warden, "Can I speak to you in private?"

"Surely," the Warden replied.

Durbish followed him out of the cell. The door remained open. Two guards stood wide-eyed in the corridor. Both gave Durbish a bitter look. "Warden, this man is in a deteriorating state. I must insist that we help. Why do you continue to hamper our efforts in this matter? Furthermore, the crisis has already gone beyond what is considered timely. If it's necessary, I'm quite able to take full responsibility for the prisoner. We move dangerous terrorists all the time. I can't seem to make you understand. The man in there is dying."

The Warden just stared at Durbish and then told the two guards to prepare the prisoner for transport. The two guards rushed into the cell, handcuffed Sebastian, and stood next to his cot. The Warden turned to Durbish as he said, "You'd better find a large hole to climb into if anything goes wrong. I'll have your head on a platter. The two guards will ride in place of your two men. You drive the ambulance. Is that agreeable?"

Durbish said, "Well, what do my men do, walk to the hospital?"

"How in the hell do I know? You juggle the issue now, Mr. McFane. You figure it out. I think this matching of wits has gone far enough."

Durbish yelled out Scott's name. "Nobody move," was the next sound heard within the cell. "Damn," Dr. Weston exclaimed, then rushed to lead the Warden back into the cell with Durbish following close beside him. Scott had the ten-gauge leveled and held waist height against his hip. "Do as I say! Get on the floor, all of you."

The blast was heard downstairs as Scott shot one of the guards that was charging him. The blast sent blood and particles of body fragments across the cell and onto the walls. The blast tore through the side of the guard's now unusable brain. The others lay face down, confident the maniac holding the shotgun was serious. If they had any doubts, they were reminded by the blood that oozed across the floor under their outstretched bodies.

The echoing sound alarmed the guards in the corridors. The booming blast ebbed; the eerie seconds were just studied by all the tense men within the prison walls. The guards were frantically calling each other from their stations, trying to find out what had caused the sudden explosion. As they tried to organize themselves, they found out the Warden had been taken prisoner.

Dr. Weston took control of Sebastian. He shook him hoping that he would voluntarily awaken and talk to him.

Downstairs, Melonie was terrified. She was alone downstairs with the trussed-up guard. She knew her small pistol was of no use against the men inside the towers outside, one which stood directly in view of where she and the guard were. A well-placed spray from the submachine gun could riddle both. She knew if she remained in view of the tower she could die. She closed the slot to the booth to make certain she'd be out of the way of any stray bullets from her damn gung-ho friend, Scott.

Upstairs, Scott still held the advantage. He held his gun on the four men, swearing, "If any of you even breathe too hard, I'll blow your damn heads off." Scott was satisfied with the results of his threat. He observed the men on the floor and none of them dared take a full breath of air. Satisfied, he smiled as the psychologist nodded in submission to his orders.

David was still trying desperately to revive his perished friend. Several minutes had passed by. Dr. Weston delivered a hard slap to Sebastian's jaw. His eyes flickered open only to close once more. David had passed his limit. He was uncertain of what to do. He violently shook Sebastian who now began coughing and gasping for air. As he tried to breathe through his congested lungs, he asked, "What kind of fucking specialist are you, man?"

Cheers were heard from Durbish and Scott as their buddy roared at David.

The dead corpse of the guard was the first thing that Sebastian's eyes focused on as he stood on his own. Sebatian fought the urge to vomit. As the surroundings and the situation seeped into his brain. He took a deep breath, asking, "What do we do now?"

Durbish announced as he clapped Sebastian on his back, "You make a lousy corpse. Let's find out if we all can complete this transition without any more disastrous results. Dr. Weston, get the keys from the dead guard and unlock Sebastian's handcuffs."

Dr. Weston said, "That will be a pleasure." He slouched over the dead guard. He said, "Damn, Scott, you sure made a mess of this guy."

Scott said, "Yeah, a hell of a mess." The four of them were alerted by sounds coming from downstairs of intermediate chatter made by machine gun blasts.

Inside the bulletproof booth, as Melonie reloaded her automatic, she asked, "Why did you go and do that, Roy?"

Inside the cell the men listening heard no other shots being fired. Hastily, they handcuffed all the men on the floor to the cell bars.

Roy's escaping blood was filtering from three neatly placed shots from Melonie's pistol. She had shot him across his chest. Roy's body slid down the wall onto the floor. He rolled over sideways into a pool of his own blood. As he did, he groaned and tried to speak. He managed to say, "You'll never make it out alive."

Melonie said, "Roy, that's what you said about me not shooting you, remember?" She heard the last bit of air escape his lungs. She carefully observed the tower outside across the narrow street in front of the prison. As she nervously peered over the control panel in the booth, the guard in the tower outside riddled the bulletproof glass with his machinegun. At that moment, alarms started ringing all through the prison. Outside, the wailing sirens signaled the guards of an emergency.

Sinking out of view, Melonie crouched near the control panel searching for a button that would override the alarms. Inside the security booth, the phone began to ring. She saw the guard outside holding a phone in the air, plainly a sign it was him calling her. The loud singing of the sirens was deafening. She found the buttons to shut off the alarms.

Now she was about to pick up the receiver, she noticed Scott and Durbish rounding the corner down the corridor. She jammed her automatic pistol into the waistband of her nurse's uniform and turned on the outside speakers. She took the microphone and yelled, "Be careful, Scott." She noticed he had attached a long clip into his ten-gauge shotgun. Melonie put the microphone down and waited as Durbish and Scott quickly made their way to the booth. Melonie opened the door and as they got safely in, she found the switches that controlled the gates. As the wall of steel clanged shut behind them, the two men knew she was in full control of the situation.

Scott and Durbish shook their heads as they inspected the dead man on the floor. Durbish said quickly, "The gates are closed."

"Yes," she said.

"Open it."

"Why, we're safe, Durbish."

He chuckled and reminded her that they were waiting for David and Sebastian before they all left. She hit the control button once again and the gates opened. Instantly, she apologized for forgetting. They all laughed at her, embarrassed she gathered her wits and they all waited for David and Sebastian to appear.

Durbish asked for Melonie's radio and switched it on and said, "David, come in." He quickly identified himself and Durbish asked, "How much longer will you be?"

David replied, "We're coming right now. We just got what we were looking for. Sebastian is still a little groggy from the medication, with the antidote he will be okay."

Durbish told him they were inside the booth and the guard from the tower has us pinned down with a steady line of fire. He said, "I'm going to send Scott out to take care of the tower. When you round the corner, be careful." Static was all that was heard.

As they waited and watched in silence, Melonie heard distinct sounds of paper rustling. It was a distinct sound within the confining booth. She traced the sound and found its source. Without any care in the world, Scott was leaning against the wall, straddling the dead guard, eating the man's lunch. He caught the look of disbelief in Melonie's eyes. He smiled innocently as crumbs trickled down his shirt onto the dead body. He said, "Well, I'm starved, Melonie, and there's no telling how long it will be before we can eat." She was speechless and couldn't respond to this obvious display of a heartless narcissist.

She turned to Durbish for support. He briefly stared at Scott and turned his attention back to the corridor. As he turned away from Scott, he told him to hurry up and finish eating. Impatiently, Scott shoved the other half of the dead man's sandwich into his mouth. He unslung the shotgun from around his shoulder as he gulped the last bite of the sandwich.

It was moments like this that Melonie found it easy to admit to herself that Scott was so uncool being cool. He clearly showed no signs of being nervous as he said, "I'm ready."

She was thoroughly amazed. Durbish offhandedly said, "Go," as he opened the door.

Scott eased his sturdily built body out into the open hall. He plunged himself across the opposite side of the hallway, sliding behind a desk. The guard inside the tower thought he had seen something but had missed his sudden movement. Discarding the idea of it was a grave mistake.

Durbish saw David peek around the corner. He opened the door just as Scott raised the barrel of his gun. He shouted, "Scott, hold up."

Scott's head snapped, turning in Durbish's direction, who was pointing down the hall. Scott glanced in the same direction and saw David leading Sebastian limping slightly up the long corridor. Pressing his weight against David for support, they slowly made their way, closing the gap ever so slowly.

Scott leaned against the desk with his back to it as he watched the two men inching their way down the corridor. He had no choice but to patiently wait for them to reach the booth. They were all startled as the sirens began their shrill. The noise once more stopped by Melonie. She hit the button to shut them off only this time it didn't work. Durbish rushed out of the booth to help David with Sebastian. He shouted at Scott to get the gates.

Scott wasn't sure what was going on, but as Durbish fled down the hall, Scott sent a grenade sailing into the tower window. The blast sent the spotlight perched on the rooftop twenty feet above the destroyed tower. Gray granite stones scattered randomly on the road and lawn across the front of the prison. A chair landed, ending its spiraling and somersaulting, as shards of granite and body parts showered the street and lawn. The piercing sounds of the sirens continued.

Durbish and David held Sebastian's arms, literally dragging him the remainder of the way to the booth. His features were wilting. As Scott surveyed the damage to the tower, he mumbled to himself, "Impressive." At the same time, rushed to the entranceway, setting his sights on his next target, another tower down the edge of the prison's entrance.

He suddenly heard someone rushing down the corridor. His hands were clasped tightly around the grips of his weapon. One hand instinctively slid to the trigger. Quickly, he realized the sound came from not one but a multitude of men coming his way. His muscles tensed as he realized he was in danger. He had left himself wide open in the doorway. As they rushed around the corner of the corridor, Scott counted close to at least eighteen men dressed in full shields, wearing helmets and lowering their weapons in front of their bodies. He coolly observed the men and did not move.

Melonie saw him grinning and nudged Durbish as she said, "Scott's about to obliterate those guys. Are you going to stand by and allow him to do it?"

Before he could respond, Scott delivered his first shot. It was meant for a warning. He stood there holding his gun as the smoke drifted from the barrel tip pointed in the air above his head. Shards of plaster showered him as dust filled the air around him.

Melonie's fingernails dug into Durbish's forearm as the sound of Scott's weapon discharged.

David asked, "Durbish, what do you suggest we do now bossman?"

As the two men tried to determine what to do, Melonie suggested speaking to the onslaught of men through the speakers. She said, "They can hear you." She placed the microphone in Durbish's hand.

He quickly tested her theory, saying, "Scott, hold your fire." His voice echoed down the corridor.

Behind the group of guards stood the Warden and lieutenant. Their entry halted halfway down the corridor. The group looked anxious to disburse, shifting their bodies from side to side. The lieutenant was not pleased and wanted the Warden to give them orders. The psychologist appeared and he was obviously angry as he noted the standoff. He began screaming to the Warden, "Get those bastards!"

Scott's eyes met the psychologist's gaze. Scott grinned at the furious psychologist who had begun cursing everyone, including the Warden. Scott pumped a grenade into the chamber. The sound of it lodging into the tubular device was equally impressive as its destructive results. The Warden knew his men had to advance. He urged the lieutenant and the psychologist to go back up the hallway and let the guards rush the madman before he had a chance to launch the grenade. As the Warden and the two others moved back, the guards rushed towards Scott.

Scott lowered his body just as something hit the doorway above his shoulder. The sounds reached him seconds after the bullets smashed into the wall behind him. "Damn," he said, "It's getting hostile around here."

Just as he took aim in their general direction, Melonie hit the button to close the steel gates. The heavy metal gate slid blocking their entrance. In seconds before the gates closed, the grenade cleared the gap. The blast sent most of the guards screaming in fear. Their faces were bleeding, and their limbs dangled from their injuries to their bodies. Shields were strewn like cards across the floor, the few remaining guards dropped theirs and fled the area.

Scott quickly motioned for the others to follow him outside. He yelled, "Come on! Let's go! Hurry!" He stopped just outside the doorway, covering the front entrance. He saw nothing and stepped back inside as the others reached him. David was the first outside, he said wait, "hold up." Each of his partners cleared the doorway and when they were all outside, he laid his barrel securely holding the steel shot gun. Squarely in the crosshair he fired another grenade.

As they all ran down the steps they heard the blast. Scott fled down the steps passing everyone. Durbish was holding Sebastian who had not regained his strength. Sebastian was trying to sort out all the jumbled events going on around him. Melonie was running full tilt for the ambulance twenty feet away. When she tripped, the fall smashed her left shoulder into the sidewalk. The pain spread slowly at first, then she felt a bolt of pain run the length of her arm. She cried out, "Help!" David turned, gripped her right hand, and pulled her to her feet. She said, "I can't drive. My arm is either dislocated or broken. I'm not sure."

"I'll drive. Get in." He opened the door; she lunged into the front seat. The pain in her arm was excruciating.

The others scrambled into the back of the vehicle as Scott yelled, "Go!"

As the vehicle gathered speed, Scott slammed another grenade into the chamber and flung the rear door open. As he did, their speed was 40 miles per hour.

The silhouette of the guard in the last tower was barely visible. Scott gripped the roof ledge with one hand and placed his sights on the tower. He sent a grenade in its direction. As Scott fired, the guard's bullets were punching holes in the roof and windshield behind the ambulance. The windshield was shattered. Scott's grenade bounced off the tower into the road in front of them and never went off. He saw it spinning on the pavement and yelled, "David, get the hell out of here. There's a hot one on the road."

They all looked where Scott was pointing and held their breaths as David maneuvered around the unspent grenade.

Scott yelled, "Is everyone okay?"

They bounced over the last speed breaker as Sebastian said, "And why shouldn't we be?"

Durbish said, "What?"

"And why shouldn't we be all right? I've been in prison for weeks. I was beaten daily, I'm suffering from malnutrition, and some quack doctor half kills me and another idiot trying to save me is firing a grenade launcher at anything that moves--and you ask me if I'm all, right? You are damn right I am just dandy.

Durbish just looks at everybody and shakes his head and turns back to Sebastian and says, "I see prison life didn't change you much."

After Durbish made sure everyone was not seriously hurt, he told David, "Turn on the sirens."

One by one he flipped the switch, and the lights began flashing and blinking wildly as the siren wailed.

David asked, "Where's the map?"

Scott said, "I have it."

"Well then, where to boss?"

Scott said, "Cut those damn sirens off and I'll tell you."

After David flipped the switch, the sirens wound down to a purr and stopped.

Durbish said, "Well, this whole surprise--or should I say, so far, this escape plan for Sebastian has been a great success." His little speech was accompanied by a smattering of applause by the whole gang. "Now, you don't really believe we're anywhere close to getting out of this so easily, do you?"

While everyone thought about that Melonie said, "Someone needs to have a look at my arm." She had a cold, hard look on her face as her color paled.

David said, "Scott, you will have to drive," as he eased the ambulance over to the shoulder of the road.

Scott opened the rear doors, and David told him to help him get Melonie in the back. David and Scott gently lifted her out and carried her to the rear of the vehicle. David opened his medical bag and gave her a shot for the pain as Scott jumped from the vehicle and closed the rear doors. David gently laid Melonie's head on a cushion.

In the distance, Scott heard sirens wailing through the city streets. He ran and mounted the driver's seat as he said, "Big time trouble, guys. I assume they have mounted their efforts to find us."

As they were speeding off, Durbish said, "That can be expected. Turn left here. Two streets down we have a land rover parked inside a building. That's what I did this morning. You remember when I left?"

Scott said, "Yeah."

The ambulance wasn't very fast, but Scott pushed it to the limit of 63 miles per hour.

As the ambulance roared down the street, David probed along Melonie's shoulder and arm. She said, "It feels strange and hurts like hell. Is it broken?"

David said, "I don't think it is broken Melonie, in fact, it's more likely a torn muscle or a ligament. I'm going to have to wrap your shoulder, so take your blouse off."

David tried to help her. As she pulled her arm out, she screamed. She rolled to her other side and her blouse was off. David inspected her further. He said, "Your body is cold."

"Well, I'm half naked, David. What do you expect?"

David rubbed his hands over her, making certain no bones were broken. He said, "You seem to be okay. You never looked better. In fact, you look really good, Melonie."

"Give me my blouse, you pig." Everyone laughed, even Durbish. The stress from the last few hours was finally tapering off.

Durbish said, "Here--Turn here. This is where I left the land rover. There's an opening the entrance a garage door. Slow down, don't miss it, Scott."

Durbish watched his wife put on her blouse. He was also watching David who was gazing at her beautiful body. Durbish thought, "My God, he's not even trying to hide it. He's even flaunting it."

Scott slowed the ambulance to a crawl as the vehicle dipped in the road at the entrance of the building. The slight dip tossed Melonie over landing on David's shoulder. He gripped her like he had just saved her life. She looked at Durbish and shrugged her shoulder to show her dislike of the apparent come-on.

Durbish said, "Drive up two levels and to the left there is a ramp. We'll all be perfectly safe here." He did not speak again. Melonie noticed his coolness. She was aware of his jealous streak which was more prominent now than ever. As the ambulance came to a halt, she forgot about the whole thing.

Scott backed the ambulance next to the land rover and pulled up hard on the emergency brake. He glanced around the empty building and then shut the motor off. It sputtered as he killed the switch. He opened his door and let his feet dangle freely as he sat sideways in the driver's seat. He was relaxing, enjoying the view over the edge of the abandoned building. He commented, "From here you can see for miles."

David reached into his medical bag and handed Melonie a tube of ointment for her shoulder. He was animated as he suggested he could help her apply the ointment to her shoulder for her.

"David, you're way out of line. Is your intention to rub this goo all over me and expect it to turn me on?" She grabbed the ointment from David's hand as he lowered his head like a scolded child.

He mumbled, "Oh, yeah, you'd be perfect." He looked up a second too late. Melonie's slap could be heard throughout the building. David was shocked. She was mauling him. None of them had ever seen her so angry.

Scott grabbed her ankle and pried her free of David. She yelled, "I want to smash your damn face in." Scott held her firmly, but she started scratching him. David came back from the attack in the ambulance and hoped Scott could calm her down. Finally, Scott made her promise not to hurt David.

After he left her go, David wasn't sure if she'd keep her promise. He licked his lips and tasted blood. He hated that coopery taste. He spat on the concrete, noting that it wasn't bleeding badly. He decided to stay clear of the girl, hoping she'd calm down.

Melonie sat in the back of the vehicle glaring at the men. None of them dared say anything to her. It was obvious none of them wanted to find themselves in a scrap with this girl and she has a pistol stuck in her waistband. That made it that much easier to decide not to say a thing. With one hand, she tapped the butt of her pistol steadily to some unknown beat as if daring them.

Scott joined in, patting the side of his seat. After a few moments she cooled down and apologized to everyone but David. She said, "You are such a jerk."

Durbish said, "Look, he's uptight just like the rest of us so why don't we just cool down and forget it."

Sebastian asked Durbish, "What's your idea on how we get back to the States? I've about had it with these people and the way they've been kicking my ass lately. Frankly, I'm damn fed up with it and glad I won't be here to find out what else they had planned for me."

Durbish was tickled by Sebastian's outburst. He knew Sebastian was coming around. It was obvious that I was choked up and said, "Hold on." He looked him in the eyes and said, "I'm glad you survived, and it seems you are your old self again, but you'll find I've taken care of everything as usual. So, please, let's all get some much-needed rest. I have another truck coming." He glanced at his watch and continued, "We will depart in two hours. Wake me up in an hour and a half. All the others know the plan. I will fill you in when I wake up unless one of the others goes over it while I take a nap. Scott, what you need to do is take the ambulance out of here but first let's take out what we need and get some rest in the land rover."

Scott said, "It's a done deal."

Scott had completed the transfer and was jogging back toward the vehicle. Darkness had covered the city. As he kept a steady pace, his shoes made a loud crunching noise on the loose gravel in the street. The moonlight gave him a clear view of obstacles as he ran. He veered right and left to dodge an obstruction in his path. A girl stood outside a bar when he passed. She whistled, trying to gain his attention. Like a showman he turned his body and jogged backwards past her. The girl then eased her long dress upwards to show off her slender legs.

He turned and ran, placing one hand above his head as he waved goodbye. She cried out for him to stop. At the pace he ran, she knew this wasn't likely and cursed him in her foreign tongue. He had run two miles from where he had ditched the ambulance. They had agreed that it would be best if it were found and leaving it a few miles away gave them an advantage to slip out of the area. He was tired and slowed his pace as he neared the abandoned building. The others were dozing, but Sebastian awakened as he heard Scott's steady approach. Scott bumped into the side of the land rover and knelt beside it catching his breath.

Sebastian stepped out of the vehicle. The door ajar left the interior aglow. The light did not disturb anyone. Melonie was in a fetal position against the back left side. David was in the front passenger seat sleeping soundly as he leaned against the window. Durbish reclined in the driver's seat. Sebastian caught himself staring at them like he didn't recognize them any longer. As he eased the door closed the moonlight cast shadows of both men's figures across the floor. Sebastian said, "You look like Tarzan, all pumped up from working out."

"A man's got to stay fit."

"I suppose so. I try, but lately my strength has all but been gone."

"Yeah, well, you'll be all right," Scott said. "Is there any food in the truck?"

Sebastian laughed at Scott and said, "That's how I'll always remember you, eating or working out. Look cooler in the back. I'm not sure if there's any food in there but be quiet. The others are asleep. When you finish, come over here close to the wall and let's talk." Sebastian walked to the other side of the building.

Scott could be heard saying, "Is there anything to eat in here," as he rummaged through the back of the vehicle."

Pleasant memories flooded Sebastian's thoughts as a grin spread across his face. He swept the skies with his eyes. As he watched the stars blinking, it made him glad to be alive. The whole sky above him was fixed to his position. To regain the freedom to gaze into the heavens was something Sebastian had sorely missed while in prison. He spoke softly to the world he looked on, "I bet you thought I'd never be here.

It surprised me as well, but I'm very glad to see your magnificence again." He gently stepped forward, getting close to the ledge. He had a view through the open wall and sat next to the corner and just let himself release his fears and the immense sorrow he felt. He said, "Thank you God. As I sit beneath your domain, I suddenly feel your power again and that pleases me. Only hours ago, I was caught, and my life was in your hands, but even so my fear, Father, is for my friends' lives who brought me here. They will need your guidance, as I will, in the coming days. Do we stand a chance?" He sat there believing he had received an answer as he soaked in the wonders of the surroundings.

His mood suddenly turned defensive as beams of light flooded the street below him. A convoy of trucks had rounded the right corner of the building. He noticed two or three trucks full of soldiers, their lights sweeping from side to side and up the buildings as they slowly made their way down the street. Quizzically, he stared up and said, "Well, you didn't say it was going to be easy, did you?" The floodlight's beam reached his position. He flung himself backwards onto the floor and rolled clear of the searchlight. He thought he had moved quick enough.

Scott dropped his sandwich and froze instinctively at the sight of Sebastian sudden movements and the presence of the light. In the eerie darkness both men looked at each other, realizing their position was not secure.

With hope in his eyes, Sebastian told Scott quietly, "Wake Durbish." He went around to David's door and whispered, "Don't open the door, just tap on the window and keep everybody calm and quiet."

Scott leaned against the vehicle and furiously tapped. The constant tap, tap, tap caused Durbish to open his eyes. The sight of Scott so near the window momentarily startled him. Durbish's attention was quickly drawn by the sweep of the crisscrossing beams of light. The flashing lights flared up an old fear inside Durbish, reminding him of times he spent in the trenches. The flashing lights then were as real now and he knew they carried the same dreadful result if the lights found their mark. The loud rumbling of the trucks faded. The seconds had seemed like hours. Inside the vehicle everyone was petrified. None of them professed it. The fear was tossed onto everyone so fast it was impossible not to fear the intrusion. The large diesel engines shook the building as they nosily rolled past. A sense of triumph flood them as the thunderous roars faded. The gang all but cheered. The pitch black building was welcome relief.

After all of them surrounded the front of the vehicle, Durbish said, "That was quite a tumultuous event."

Scott said, "I don't know about to-mul-to-us, but it scared the hell out of me." Everyone laughed at his remark.

Durbish enunciating the word tumul-tu-ous, then said, "Scott, the word means chaotic, turbulent, frenzied and any of those can be scary."

"Well, then, why didn't you say scared. It makes better sense to me if you'd--ah, forget it, Durbish. My education is fine with me. You can keep your big words for all I care and mulch 'em. I was scared, not tu-mul-tu-fied!" All of them burst into laughter loud enough to wake the dead.

"All right, you guys, knock it off," Scott said. He politely asked Durbish, "Would cha mind speaking in plain English for my benefit?"

Durbish said, "Since earlier today, and even now, you've been so benevolent, I'll be certain to use small words for your benefit, Sir Scott."

"Ah, shit, Durbish, you're such an ass, but I'm most aware of your bombastic style and I'm not stigmatized by your behavior towards me." A roar of laughter from Durbish was heard down the streets. He loved what Scott said and so did all of them.

Melonie said, "Hey, Scott, that was really funny. Where did you learn to be so prudent?"

"Mel-on-nie--"

"Just--Jus'--Jus' kidding, Scott."

"Well, 'Jus' leave me alone, please."

"Hey," she said, "that was meant to be a compliment, if you didn't notice."

Scott turned to face her and looked down as if his feelings had been hurt.

Melonie approached him and said, "You're my friend. We don't always see things the same and I'm a bitch, at least that's how you've always treated me, but Scott, I'm not. You're not like I've envisioned you. You're more human than I thought and, well, I just want to thank you for saving my life today and I'm sure everyone else feels the same way."

Scott felt awkward and said, "Oh."

"Scott, what started the trouble upstairs?"

Scott said, "That Warden, whatever his name is, was acting real pissy, and he put Durbish in a bad spot. That kicked it off. The next thing I know, I'd blown a man's head half off."

"Did that bother you, Scott?"

"Well, not really, but yeah, it does. It was sudden like."

"Well, what about the others?"

"I had no choice," he said. "What about the guy in the booth, what'd he do?"

Everyone seated in the land rover waited for Melonie's answer. Melonie joked about Roy. "The buffoon!" and never answered Scott's question. She misdirected attempts by any of them to find out the reason she had done poor Roy in.

Durbish whispered, "It's apparent you're not going to give us any clear-cut reason."

She acted innocent at first and said, "Apparently, you've forgotten. You taught me that a long time ago."

"Taught you what?"

"How to avoid answering questions."

Melonie got angry by their probing and tried to avoid the whole business which had now been blown out of proportion.

Durbish said, "Just let it go, everyone. Whatever happened, we all know she must have had good cause." He apologized for trying to dig so far and said, "It's all right if you don't tell us."

Melonie laughed and rolled down her shirtsleeves, crossed her arms, stretched out against the back seat and instantly appeared to fall into a deep sleep.

Durbish said, "Scott, let's get out of this building. Those troops were too near. They may double back and search the building. We'll just have to forget about making the connection with the other truck."

The Warden had called the troops when they found the ambulance abandoned. Homes and offices were searched high and low in the surrounding area. The lieutenant scoured the city and was outraged that the group had vanished. All the evidence pointed to him that the group had outside help. The abandoned vehicle was full of bullet holes, had punctured tires and the windshield had been smashed. He said to the Warden, "I'm certain there were other people involved." An all out effort had begun to find the source of those unknown people. The lieutenant was angry at the Warden for being duped. The Warden's office was bombarded by phone calls.

The search was top priority throughout the country. All the surrounding countries were alerted. A curfew was effected immediately in Nigeria, beginning in the city of Abuja. The troops' task grew in constant scope in Abuja and the city was being literally torn apart.

Juliette saw light beams rapidly trace the sky out her bedroom window. She could think of only one reason for the light's rapid pace. She felt the name, "Sebastian," escape her lips, like someone else had spoken it. "Sebastian," she said out loud and wept in joy, realizing he was free.

Sebastian said, "Durbish, I know this road goes to the village. I'm telling you, it's about 30 miles from here."

"All right," Durbish said, "Scott, follow this road but be careful. It doesn't look like much of a road to me. David, what do you think?"

David responded, "Do we have any other choices? We're out of the city and Sebastian said he knows where we are. What else do you want?"

Sebastian reminded all of them how he had entered the city by saying, "I followed the two roads back there. One river road met the another. I crossed both waterways. Look on the map, David, one river goes south to Port Harcourt. It breaks out into several branches and dumps into the Gulf of Guinea."

"All right," David said, "I see it."

"Okay, then we're just above the Niger River."

"Okay, got it."

"But those were the main river roads. What we want is to follow the small area out there. He tapped on the map and sat back in his seat. Beside him, Melonie and Durbish were leaning in between the two front seats like kids. Scott drove slowly, following the river's course as it wound deeply into the jungle that Sebastian had walked through.

David asked, "Sebastian, how did you walk 100 miles in this terrain with no food except what you could shoot?"

"It took only three and a half days with a crudely drawn map."

David said, "I've gotta tell you, Sebastian, I'm very impressed that you could carry out such a mission."

"Do you mean you don't believe I did it, David?"

"Yes." he said. He didn't believe him, but he wouldn't say it. He thought it.

"Tomorrow, we'll all be on foot. Our easy traveling will be over. As untimely as it may be, it will be impossible to continue in the land rover."

Scott said, "Listen, as long as it's all right with all of you, I'm going to make a road somehow. Somebody is going to help me cut, push or drag this truck out of these woods because I'm not planning on walking period."

Sebastian said, "You're wrong, but if we can, that's what we'll do. Let me be the first one to tell all of you, these aren't woods. This is a jungle and to quote my old buddy, the pilot, who dropped me in this hell hole, 'Mister, this is the meanest jungle in the world.' I've spent much time cursing the man and the day he dropped me here."

"Forgive me now for warning you, but I have no doubts now. He was absolutely correct. Somehow I made it and I know the way out. We all know the roads in the city and airports are surely being watched. There is no way we can attempt to leave, but we can hide in here for a long time. We could also die in this jungle but my guess is, we won't. You see, I made friends with not only the people in the village of Kaduna, but with the jungle's creatures as well."

David said, "What the hell does that mean, Sebastian? Made friends with what creatures?"

"Oh, you'll meet them soon enough, David."

David said, "What happened to you while you were incarcerated?"

Scott said, "What'd you do in there? Did you go goo-goo crazy?"

"Hold it, one question at a time. If you really want to know, I'll tell you when we rest cause it's a long, long story. By the way, we're about to run out of road."

David said, "Real fine, messy place. Scott, pull over there."

"Wait a minute, Scott, let's check to make sure it's safe."

"Why?" David said, "It looks like a clear spot."

Sebastian was calm and replied, "If you'll check, you'll find out. It could be quicksand."

"Fine. This isn't funny, Durbish," David said. How did we end up in this God forsaken place. I thought we were going to Morocco. Suddenly, we're all in some damned jungle and the next thing you know we'll all be burned at the stake like we're in some old rerun movie."

Durbish said, "You're not kidding, are you Sebastian?"

"No, I'm not kidding. I'd check before you move. It's getting too dark to guess if it's just a sandy spot."

Brusquely, Durbish cut off Sebastian and said to David, "Check it out."

David said, "Why me."

Scott said, "Ah, hell, I'll do it. Let me go look at the spot."

David said, "Stop, Scott," then opened his door. Suddenly, the sounds from the jungle flooded their senses. Chattering lemurs, odd tones from exotic birds and far off roars and loud knocks filled the air.

Sebastian opened his door and hung his feet outside in the darkness of the jungle and said, "David, come on."

David stepped out and placed one foot on the ground carefully. Sebastian remembered the familiar ground, its softness and leaped out into the muck. David swung his body from the vehicle and sunk ankle deep instantly and began screaming bloody murder. By the time Sebastian placed his hand on David's shoulder, he was shaking terribly. Sebastian was trying to calm him as he begged, "Please save me from sinking."

"Calm down, David, you're in mud. The bottom is firm. Don't you feel it."

"Damn, I thought I was a goner."

As Sebastian helped him tug his feet loose from the mud, they heard a hyena laugh nearby. Durbish was suddenly aware of this noise, one of his least liked specimens in the wild. His fingers dug into the cushion of the seat. No one noticed how frightened he was of the carnivorous creatures.

Within the hour, the conspirators all voiced their opinion about how lucky they had been, making Sebastian's escape a reality. The unfortunate deaths caused by their improvising Plan B had been instrumental in freeing all of them along with Sebastian. The curfew throughout the city was widening. The search for the confederates had turned up nothing so far. It had been a wise decision by Durbish to forget about the second truck.

As the five compatriots sat around a roaring fire, the sparks trickled through the lower branches of the dense jungle. In the darkness that surrounded them, they all felt secure by the fire.

Sebastian knew when dawn came, the group's safety net would vanish. Slowly, they began to realize Sebastian was the only one who fully understood the danger of their surroundings. They all listened intently, waiting for Sebastian's plan of escape. They were fascinated with Sebastian's stories of his leap into the Kudana jungle and the recount of his prison experiences.

Sebastian thought it would be best to let his friends continue to believe they were perfectly safe. As he looked at their faces, one by one, he knew their awareness of the dangers were creeping in. He quickly thought of a distraction. He said, "David, Scott, help me get the tent out of the vehicle." As they busied themselves, the laborious chores burned nervous energy.

Sebastian sadly thought, "The morning's light would bring a host of problems." He did his best not to show his fears.

When they finished putting the tent up Scott said, "Let's get some sleep. I'm bushed."

"Okay, "Sebastian said, "I'll keep first watch. I've had all the rest I need for a while."

As Melonie joined the other three in the tent she said, "Durbish, do you know you've severely broken your rental contract on the truck?" Everyone laughed.

"They'll just have to bare with me. I'll call them in the morning. Sebastian can lead us to the nearest phone on the river."

Sebastian heard another blast of laughter as he settled down in a tree near the rushing waters of the river. He clearly understood the danger he could be in near the water, but the sounds from any animals or intruders could be observed best where he had situated himself. After his careful inspection of the area, he kept a sharp eye out for any signs of danger as the rest of the gang snuggled into their sleeping bags.

After a long, careful observation, Sebastian lowered himself quietly to the ground. He shivered as the moist air from the river pounded him. He made his way to the fire and sat down. He stirred the fire and the sparks flickered like fireflies and the ashes died quickly. Their bright glow just vanished, lost like all of them, in the jungle's darkness.

The tentmates squeezed together and found it suitable and cozy. They were tired and exhausted. As they settled down to sleep, Scott broke the silence, "Will someone call room service and order dinner?" Their laughter echoed throughout the tent.

Sebastian once again heard their laughter and knew it was better for them to be laughing rather than realizing the real danger they were in.

Melonie's distinct laugh trailed off and caused Sebastian to think of Juliette. He thought he should have told them of his wish to return for her. As soon as they made it back and his mission was complete, he'd tell them he was retiring. He'd say, "I'm selling everything. I'm cashing in my stocks so I can start a new life with Juliette."

Alone, by the fire, he tried to sort things out. The flames mesmerized him. He was lost in thought as the memories of Juliette flooded through him. He wanted to hold her again. He found it easy to imagine her profile. He could see her plainly, her lovely body next to his. He envisioned her sipping wine, the same wine they had shared so long ago. It seemed it never happened, yet it had. He knew she was thinking of him because the clothes she purchased for him while he was at the hotel were given to Melonie for him.

Juliette had sent all he had left behind. The shirt he now wore was the same shirt she had worn after they made love. He felt her closeness. His heart felt full of joy. The guarantee that he would always love her and come back for her was now stronger than ever. It was something to strive for, to return and take her away. As long ago as this seemed to him, he knew this dream would remain prominent in his mind until it became a reality. As he gazed up into the stars, he found the brightest star and silently swore to her that he would return. He knew that she would be safe with her uncle until his return.

Thoughts of the night he drove to the palace to shoot Andras kept resurfacing and he forced them out again and again. He only wanted to think of Juliette now and his love for her. Her blinding beauty and intelligence was wasted in her subservient life with her uncle. He relaxed and bathed in the absorbing pleasure that soon they would be together again. Entertaining himself with his new goals in life, he knew the 20 years of rejection and obsessive lust for his old love had fallen into a category of past stupidity. He began pushing his old memories out, filling the void with Juliette's love for him. Her love was complete. This knowledge overpowered the possession he once nurtured and with this came a renewed custody of his soul.

****

Unable to see beyond the firelight, Sebastian heard footsteps just firm enough to cause the slightest sound. He wasn't alarmed by the sound as he saw Melonie walk through the darkness towards the fire. The blazing fire cast an odd, but provocative lure on her. The reflecting firelight enhanced her figure and beauty. He noticed the stirring in his loins and casted it off as normal. Any man would find her attractive and desirable. He put down this arousal, knowing he had found his true love. Little above a whisper, he said, "Why aren't you sleeping Melonie?"

She sat down next to him. "I'm too keyed up. It's too exciting out here. The sounds of the water's passing and sudden noises from the wild animals is something I want to enjoy. I don't feel tired any longer."

He chuckled and said, "You'll be tired tomorrow and I understand what you mean by the sounds of the jungle. I suppose it is exciting if you look at it that way." He paid special attention to her, making sure she wasn't cold by throwing more sticks onto the fire.

"Sebastian, I've got something to tell you."

"Oh!"

"Well, Durbish and I--Well, we--"

"What?"

She blurted it out. "Durbish and I are married!"

"What? Why did--When did--Well, that's great."

"We've been married almost a year."

"Why haven't you told me? Who else knows?"

"Nobody," she said.

"Why not? Why the secrecy?" He suddenly felt angry for not being told. He listened to the fire crackle as the flame spewed and the moist wood made hissing sounds.

"Durbish didn't want anyone to know Sebastian. I'm sorry."

"Well, Melonie, isn't that a decision both of you would make. I just don't understand the reason for the secrecy, but congratulations."

"Wait, that's not all of it. It's not working. As soon as we get back to Washington, I'm filing for a divorce."

"My gosh, well, heck, I don't know what to say. I'm sorry it hasn't worked out. Does he have any idea?"

"No."

With a heavy sigh he stared at the tongues of fire, then turned to face Melonie. "In all fairness of your trust in me, I'll be frank here. I want to retire, which all of you know by now, and I've already done it. I have been wanting to retire, but this job was of a nature that it couldn't remain undone. This mission was my last. I plan to come back to Nigeria."

"Why? Are you crazy? What on earth for?"

"I've met a woman, and you know her. The young lady that gave you, my clothes."

"Anita, you mean?"

"Well, her name is Juliette and it's a long-complicated story, but Melonie we love each other."

"My God, Sebastian, she's awfully young, but very lucky. It's understandable that you love her. She's very beautiful and seems intelligent, but is that enough for you? I know how you are."

"Well, what do you mean, know how I am?"

"I know you. You haven't committed to anyone in years."

"Well, I guess you don't get it. I've finally found a woman that loves me and if you're trying to say I could never get over my obsession with Aneda the answer is yes, I have."

"I'm very happy for you--both of you." She leaned over into Sebastian's arms. He drew her near and held her in a warm, friendly embrace. When Sebastian released his hold, she held onto him more tightly. Sebastian sharply caught the look in her eyes. The firelight cast a sensual glow over her and was an unbearable sensation to him. Both had once been very attracted to each other. Melonie was full of life. Her breathing increased. "Sebastian, you know I've never stopped loving you."

Sebastian fought back his urges as she said, "You must have realized this. I've been so lonely. I've worried so much about you all month. I thought I would die if anything had happened to you." She dropped her head and gazed down into the fire. He could clearly see tears forming in the corners of her eyes as she shook her head and released her hold on him. She looked away and said, "All I wanted you to do is just kiss me one more time."

"Listen," he said as he knelt and poked at the fire. "The next time we're in a jungle--if we're in a jungle, remind me not to reveal any of my secrets to you." The burning wood created a loud pop that startled them both. Instinctively, she found safety back in Sebastian's arms. They found themselves falling onto the jungle's soft ground. This, planned or not, was more than both adults could cast aside. Their desires for each other, planted long ago, resurfaced. They had never gone beyond heavy petting, but both felt a need for each other.

Their friendship had been more important. Now, all their emotions were mixed up. Melonie was kissing Sebastian and in seconds the two of them were touching each other in frantic desperation. He, because his love was far away and, hers, a desperation for someone to hold her. Both stopped, but they knew this was something that should have happened a long time ago. Now it was too late. Taking no chances, Melonie smiled as she pulled him near and slid her hand across his chest. With her slender fingers she delicately unbuttoned his shirt. Not wanting to stop herself, she opened his shirt and ran her soft hands across his warm chest.

Sebastian knew this had to stop, yet he did not attempt breaking away. Her touch felt so nice he was willing to let this continue. Suddenly, he said, "I can't. Melonie, you can't. I can't help myself. No, Melonie--" His tone softened. "This isn't right. As much as I wish it were, it just shouldn't be."

Exasperated, she broke away from him and said, "You're right," as she rolled over and sat up with her legs crossed under her body. "Damn it, we've always had awful timing, huh, Sebastian?" She slung a stick into the fire.

"The worst timing. Let's give this a lot of time and space. You know I'm crazy about you Melonie. It just wouldn't be fair to Juliette."

"You're right, still I'm not giving you up that easily. I've known you a lot longer and Juliette is a long way from America."

"Yeah, but so are we." She gave him an impish grin over her shoulder as she quietly retreated into the tent.

He rebuttoned his shirt and thought all this reminded him of his responsibilities. He promised to keep his word to Juliette, to hold their love above all else. Relief spread over him as he realized his will had not been broken by Melonie. His stay in prison had made him miss the sensations of another's touch. This was obvious to him as he realized he had almost betrayed the greatest love of his life. He wondered then if Juliette would be so strong. He was sure she would try to be, but he knew what she had begun to enjoy had ended quickly. He had been careful not to push too far too fast. Her sexual awareness had quickly developed into a strong desire for lovemaking. He hoped he had been successful in his show of tenderness for her and that her promise to wait for him would be as strong has his.

As he stood alone in the jungle, he thought about what she was doing at that very moment. He looked at his watch and knew it was time for her to awaken to another busy day. He wished he could see her as this new day began to turn the skies brighter, a golden-greenish haze was prominently cast through the jungle's canopy.

What was taking place in the hotel across the city was that Juliette's uncle was being interrogated by the lieutenant as six of his soldiers stood guard. She cracked her bedroom door and nervously watched them. The lieutenant and her uncle were arguing. The front door of the hotel was hanging by one hinge.

She heard the lieutenant say, "Mr. Nannon, we have official papers, a warrant to search your Juliette knew she and her uncle had cleaned the hotel thoroughly in case this situation occurred.

"Before you begin, let me wake my guests. It is barely daylight, you will frighten them if your men just appear." He and the lieutenant argued.

The lieutenant said loudly, "Very well, but one of my men will go with you."

"Sure, that's fine, but what is all this about anyway? Why is it necessary to break my doors in?"

"Mr. Nannon, it is because your place of business is believed to have harbored a band of killers. This is not a routine search."

"What does that mean, not routine? I have done nothing."

"We also believe you housed the man that killed President Andras and gave his supporters help." "That's absurd!"

"Sir, only this morning they were seen here, and you were seen with them. This is very serious and if you are found guilty, you face severe punishment. If charges are brought against you, you will be prosecuted. Do not hold me up any longer! I've been most kind to you, my interest at this moment is only to capture these dangerous murderers. You will be questioned later."

"I have nothing to hide. Please, look for yourself. I have nothing to hide here." Mr. Nannon and the soldier stopped at Juliette's door first. Her uncle quietly opened her door so as not to frighten her. He calmly said, "Get out of bed, get dressed and meet me in the hall."

Juliette opened her eyes and saw the soldier standing next to her uncle. She was so afraid she could barely move from her bed.

They closed the door and made their way down the hall, waking their guests. The seven guests, unsure of what was taking place, followed the uncle's command. One by one they went down the stairs. The soldiers situated at the foot of the stairs guided them into the dining room.

The lieutenant looked at Juliette and said, "We have been up all night, we could use some coffee." As Juliette made her way to the kitchen, one of the soldiers followed her. The guests seated themselves at tables in the dining room, quietly observing.

Juliette tried to remain calm as the guard made crude remarks and sexual advances. She continued making the coffee and ignored his advances. He sarcastically said, "You live in a whorehouse and what do you expect." He reached out and caught her arm. The moment he touched her; she began to speak in his language. Her uncle could not hear clearly what was being said behind the closed doors, but caught a word or so of the conversation, just enough to know she was being accosted. He realized she was using her usual defense; the same line she had learned from him. She was frightened and it was a signal they had worked out years ago.

Mr. Nannon hastily sought out the lieutenant. He collided into him as he rounded the corner of the long corridor. "You have a job to do, and your position is being carelessly undermined by the soldier in my kitchen. I will personally bring charges against you if you do not take steps to correct this. My niece, the young lady in the kitchen, is being accosted this very second."

The lieutenant was angry and rushed alongside Mr. Nannon as he headed to the kitchen. The bat doors burst open. Both men rushed in, shoulder to shoulder. The lieutenant barked, "Attention!" The solitary word immobilized the soldier.

Juliette quickly passed both men and retreated to the dining room. The soldier stood erect as the lieutenant's anger grew. He walked rapidly to the soldier and hit him solidly across the face. The first blow sent the man backwards across the kitchen. The lieutenant's wrath was evident as he continued striking the soldier.

Finally, Mr. Nannon stepped in front of the lieutenant trying to gain control of the situation and stop the beating that was in progress. The soldier stood up facing the two men. Blood oozed from his nose and lips. His left eyelid cut so severely his eye had swollen shut.

The lieutenant said, "Mr. Nannon, I assume you are satisfied this worm has been punished sufficiently. If you don't think so, I'll have him shot!"

Mr. Nannon said, "He has been punished enough."

The lieutenant ordered the soldier, "Clean yourself up and the kitchen thoroughly," he added, as he passed through the doors exclaiming, "Now, we'll continue our search."

******

The sun was rising rapidly above the campsite. The struggle for life had begun anew. The lions, the water buffalo, the hippos and crocodiles ruled their domain. In the never-ending cycle of the jungle, they ended heartbeats in a matter of seconds. The daily routine of searching for food and water was their only means of survival for the beasts.

At daybreak Scott and David left the campsite to search the area. Sebastian shook his head in disbelief as Durbish said, "Kudana is a large, thriving metropolis." Durbish tried to convince him the city was nearby.

"If there's a city out here, why did you have me walk a hundred miles in this jungle to reach Abuja?"

"Sebastian, we've gone over this three times. It was the safest way at the time for you to enter Abuja by way of the river."

"Then why didn't the pilot or I ever see this city?"

"Well, Darford knows this land and I'm sure he stayed just beyond sight of it somehow. Sebastian, no one is disputing you about how dangerous these riverbanks are, but I'm sorry, this is just not the Congo out here. It's a wide strip of thick cover I found suitable to hide your entrance. I, myself, told Darford to drop you here."

Sebastian yelled, "Melonie." She was busy pushing things into the rear compartment of the vehicle. "Melonie," he yelled, what did you do with my old map?"

"I never saw a--oh, yes, yes, a map. We looked at it in the hotel. I remember. David had it."

"Where is it now? It's my only proof that what I'm saying is true. Durbish says this isn't the wild jungle I traversed 3 days, I say it is. And, he also says there's a large city out here somewhere."

Compassionately, she said, "We all had the map at the hotel. We all looked at it and compared it with ours. I even retraced the markings you had on the old map. You of all people Durbish are a master in deception."

"Yes, he is, but I visited no large city on my way to Abuja."

"Sebastian, on your map there was a village. It existed before the turn of the century. Now, it is a largely populated city."

Sebastian stormed off. He tried to stay calm as he passed Durbish. He made his way into the heavy brush, seeking a clear view of the water. He was mumbling all the way, "This is a dangerous jungle." He viciously stomped the reeds along the bank to the river's edge. He remembered the snakes and crocodiles he had seen, realizing they were not there. The river was flowing slowly, not rushing past as he recalled. Sebastian's mind was spinning. He decided none of this was making sense. He knew there was a village out here, but realized last night as they drove through the jungle, even that was different. He looked at the ground closely and observed it was sandy, not muck. "What the hell!" he kept thinking. "These waters were full of crocodiles, not just a few here and there, but full." Precariously, he stood amazed as he looked down at the riverbank and swore. His throat tightened as he thought, "What is going on?" He knew the boat was no dream and began to question even that. He mumbled, "How confused I am." He chose to let this iron itself out, figuring there had to be an explanation, knowing he couldn't have dreamed of all his predator friends.

"Friends?" he asked himself. "This whole thing just doesn't make sense. Who could make friends with wild beasts?" His attention was turned towards the sounds of someone making their way toward him. He continued to stare out over the water, refusing to admit this was not the infamous Kudana jungle he tamed himself, but only a heavily wooded area. He stood still as Durbish stepped beside him.

"Scott and David are back and we are ready to leave."

Still lost in thought, Sebastian said, "What?"

"We are ready to leave. They found the road and it's not far. Everyone is waiting for us." Durbish looked at Sebastian and could see the veins in his neck. He thought how pitifully thin he was.

"What do you think happened here? Did I have some kind of episode, you know, like my mind does sometime?"

"Whatever happened out here, I'm sure you have cause to believe it occurred. If things were always the way people see them, it would be a boring life indeed. Let's save that for now and run this gauntlet to get back home. When we reach Washington, I want you to stay for a few days before you return home. There is a lot you and I haven't discussed." "If you need a doctor we'll go to my friend, have him analyze what you've told us, but my opinion now is not fair to you. Considering all the stress you were under, I'm sure this played a large part in your perception of things.

A horn blared. The two men followed the sound, finding their way back through the woods. Before they reached the land rover, Sebastian said, "Thanks, Durbish, you're probably right. My nerves aren't as good as they once were and maybe this whole ordeal is something for me to remember in privacy, but it sure did seem real."

As they stepped out of the woods, the others stood waiting impatiently beside the land rover. They heard Sebastian say, "All I'm worried about is how to get us out safely."

"We'll find our way. The roads aren't safe, but we're going to make it on or off the road and, oh, yeah, I've got to find a damn phone to call the rental agency." They all burst into laughter and took their seats inside the vehicle.

After everyone settled in, Scott announced, "The road is washed out, but David and I decided it could be managed. It won't be smooth going, but it's a road.

"Let's do it," Sebastian said. This made everyone feel better. Sebastian was willing to forget about his experience and the gang had been pulled together once again as one. "Come on, Scott let's get out of here and back on the road." Sebastian, realizing he had never seen this area kept thinking the whole illusion or whatever it was he decided to keep to himself. He would sort it out later.

******

Juliette sat in the back room badly shaken from her experience. The lieutenant spoke with her and tried to reassure her nothing further would occur. One of the soldiers approached and Juliette stiffened. He reported to the lieutenant, "Our search has turned up nothing."

The lieutenant returned his attention to address the frightened young lady. Beside her in the chair, something caught his eye. He thought it looked like a map stuffed in the edge of the seat. *Beyond that he could not tell. He asked, "Would you mind getting up while I inspect your chair?"

She did not understand and was thrown off guard by the question. She rose as the lieutenant reached between the cushion and unfolded the piece of paper he found in the chair. He laid it on the table. This was the same map David had laid beside him as their crew was preparing to leave yesterday. Juliette was overtaken by a sick feeling as she saw the lieutenant's eyes brighten as he quickly refolded the map. He placed it in his pocket and as he left the room. He yelled, "Load up. We're leaving now!"

It all happened so fast. The trucks raced off. Juliette was beside her uncle with her hand wrapped under his arm. She began to cry uncontrollably as she became fully aware of what had just occurred. She told the story of the map's discovery to her uncle, and he realized why the trucks had vanished so suddenly.

He said, "I can't be certain this will help them, Juliette. By now, Sebastian and the others have a huge lead. It will be difficult for that blundering idiot to find them. Sebastian will be safe, don't worry. She said, "I love you uncle." as the tears streaked her face.

"Often," he said, "we overlook things, but my dear Juliette, my responsibility lies in caring for you and this has been nothing but a pleasure from the day you came to live with me. When I realized you fell in love with him, this troubled me for a while, but soon I could tell Sebastian was a good man and gave you his love in return.

I watched him intently and found it easy to see the hardship he placed upon himself. Yes, I know you know what I'm speaking of. His decision to kill Andras was a struggle. He did it for all of us and I respect him for his decision. Sebastian has fine qualities and gained my respect. Be proud, you have found a valiant man."

Her tears were dried by the old man's wrinkled hands as he spoke to her. They continued to talk a long time as he repaired the hotel door.

****

Two hours later the lieutenant and his troops splashed down the muddy trail. Their objective was clear. They were driving as fast as possible. The triangle Sebastian had drawn on the map led them dangerously close to the fleeing five fugitives.

The winch cable strained to its limit. The land rover, with Scott's steady hand at the wheel, was snaking the vehicle out of the mud. The road proved to be hazardous, full of ruts and huge mudholes. The group had walked ahead and waited. A brief shower had passed. It left the air smelling fresh but humid. Their urge to rest was not to be. Scott pulled up beside them in the truck. He stepped out and leaned against the door. David, Melonie and Sebastian were covered in mud. As they approached the vehicle Durbish was saying they were between Bida and a place called Minna. Scott came up with a different location. He was sure they had passed Minna and said, "The city of Kaduna is not far." He cursed as he told Durbish this over and over.

Sebastian urged the others, "Come on before this gets out of complete control." All of them agreed and took their seats.

The soldiers had made fast progress. The men were hungry for blood and were on their trail. The war was over, yet their urge to kill was still strong. The lieutenant kicked the ashes that had been left a short time ago and ordered the troops to restart the search.

Having no choice in the matter, the group had left a steady trail, easy enough for anyone to follow. Luckily, the showers hampered the troops, so both parties traveled slowly.

Sebastian reached over and nudged David. Melonie and the two men in the back seat quickly noticed what prompted the gesture. Off to the northwest the tall buildings inside the large city of Kudana stood majestically etching the skyline.

Durbish had not noticed. He was involved in watching Scott's driving. He turned in his seat to look in their face and noticed a change. The once gloomy and sad looks were now suddenly cheerful. Melonie said, "I'd bet money we're almost out of here."

Durbish informed her, "We are miles away from any city."

Melonie happily broke the news to him, loving every minute of it because he was never wrong. "The city is just over the next hill."

He looked upwards and caught sight of the city, right before the vehicle dipped down into a steep grade. "Well, I'll be damned," he said. "Scott, you were right. Kudana is just over the ridge. You'll see it in just a few more moments."

"Hot dog."

He floored the land rover, quickly gaining speed as he topped the hill. This sent mud flying, sending a rooster tail 15 feet in the air behind them.

The city was there but did little to change the group's circumstance. They were still sought after and knew if caught it would be the death of them all.

They had needs to fulfill in the city, there on the outskirts of the city, they agreed to enter at dusk. Sebastian stared at the city and said, "Well, this is the city of Kudana." He was puzzled. He did not see the village that he was familiar with. He had looked all day for familiar signs and found nothing.

In the failing light, the troops pursuit remained constant. The group had a four-hour lead that was dwindling as they watched the sun setting in the west.

As the sun set each of them talked about what they would be doing if they were home. Durbish broke up the senseless chatter like a father scolding his children, he raved on about the imminent danger they faced. He had a good point and each person promised to hold back any outburst of excitement they felt until they safely reached Morocco.

Durbish informed them, "When we reach Morocco, I will be happier than all of you, but until then I don't want to hear another word about home. Is that clear?"

He sat inside the land rover by himself, unsure of what caused him to snap at all of them. His sudden outburst had come about so harshly. Melonie made her way to the vehicle and stood outside next to the door. She spoke sweetly to him, saying, "None of us meant to upset you." Durbish confided in her, then asked, "Send David over. I want to talk with him."

Once she found David, she went to get Scott. Scott's eyes lit up instantly as he saw Melonie preparing food. He rushed to give her a hand and they finished preparing some quick sandwiches. Scott said, "I've been so busy all day, I completely forgot about eating. Frankly, now I'm starving."

As they finished eating, Durbish told them to hurry up and get ready to leave. He closed the three-ring binder he had been looking at while he ate his sandwich. He placed it under the dash. David noted it was the first time he had seen the binder taken out and made a mental note of its whereabouts. At least, he thought, Durbish had hidden the binder. He was aware of what a lethally dangerous book they held in their possession. Its mere existence was bad enough, he thought, yet to have it in their possession was unthinkably dangerous.

Durbish said, "Are you all ready to go?"

"Just jumping' for joy," David said.

Melonie added her bit, saying, "Well, my oh my, Durbish, I can't tell you how thrilled I am, sir, and I just don't believe that as a lady I can find the appropriate words for this feeling I'm having."

Scott said, "I'm ready." He was chewing, walking, talking, and swallowing all at the same time.

Sebastian said, "Just look at that, would you? I have seen it all now. I thought I'd go through life and find newly discovered feats."

Scott glared over his shoulder and tossed his plate into the trash bag. Sebastian grinned at Scott and said, "Why does everybody get mad when I goof around." Sebastian was talking to Scott, but everyone took the hint.

"Let's just go," Scott said as he cranked the land rover. David asked Scott if he would let him drive. Scott told him to buckle his seatbelt and then said, "No."

Twenty minutes later they were in the city limits of Kudana. A commercial airliner, coming in for a landing, crossed their path. Sebastian told Durbish as the jet plane's engine rumbled overhead. "I thought about your offer, me staying in Washington a few days sounds like a promising idea. Sebastian was looked on as a martyr in the people's eyes, but the conservatives who had supported Andras believed his style of killing had been unprecedented and they would accept nothing but his public execution. So far this had been the first choice of Andras' followers. Public execution in front of a firing squad.

This is in the wrong place! I must find where I traveled into this city!

The only story he found about Sebastian today was on page four. The caption read, "KILLER'S TRIAL STIRS MORE VOWS OF

VIOLENCE." The story was the first story to even mention the trial. Durbish read it feeling disgusted. The mention of Sebastian being the cause of more battles was all nonsense. He could be blamed for his killing of the President, not the aftereffects. It was an ongoing battle, one that escalated after the rebels felt a surge of victory had been gained. Of course, he had been blamed, but it was a clever political cover-up for what was really in progress throughout this country and in the streets of Abuja. The whole complexity of the story was a build-up to his upcoming trial. There had been a date disclosed, but no mention of where the trial would take place. The trial was set for one week from today, next Friday.

He was getting cabin fever, feeling caged in, caused by the building tension of the trial being so nearby. He sat in a chair and felt confined, even in his massive suite. He felt with all their combined efforts they could save Sebastian before the people brought him to trial. He knew Sebastian was guilty, but he felt the least they could do was try to save him. Durbish had only one real motivation, money. He had made millions from Sebastian's dirty work. Durbish had become corrupted after the years of cleverly planned methods devised to fight inadequacies in powerful men. The independence of his procedures left him in point blank range to monopolize on Sebastian's killings.

While Durbish thought about Sebastian, he was getting plenty of exercise and getting over his fear from the violent spray from the water hose. The aftermath from the water was excessive. He tipped his cot on end to release the water which had been funneled into his cell. The heat from the afternoon sun had caused the air to be heavy. The humid condition hindered his breathing. Gasping from the lack of oxygen, Sebastian stood on the edge of his bedframe to reach the fresh air entering his small window above the floor. It was impossible to see out the window, yet the fresh air drifting in was warm. It was a relief.

Durbish looked eagerly at his watch, wanting to go ahead and call his wife, Melonie, but she wouldn't be expecting his call for two more hours. He felt an urgency to call her sooner and picked up the phone. After his conversation, Durbish hung the phone back in its cradle. The only thing left now to be done was for him to pick all his friends up once their plane arrived in Zaire. Their time had also been cut short one day in advance. Durbish would have to return to personally warn Sebastian. The trial was making things very complicated. His dilemma was

how to get to see Sebastian again. To profess more NATO matters could cause problems and the risk were far too great. Durbish reviewed his options and gained nothing but contempt for having such a role in this mayhem. He had resources in America which were unlimited. He was well known for being tough while handling business. Perplexed forms of political niggling was his specialty. Durbish needed to devise a plausible plan of action to show David and Scott they would be safe. All the way out Sebastian would stay in a hornet's nest of the likelihood of recapture. The whole idea was a stupendous feat to attempt.

Durbish was paving a subtle course of destruction for all his associates. Sebastian was the reason he now put his goal into action. He and his friends were being led into a disaster.

Durbish was sitting on the bed in his hotel suite. It was unpleasantly hot and sweat dripped from his forehead onto the maps he prepared for his three confederates. Durbish left his work which was near completion. He had developed a well designed plan to clearly route each person's escape. He left the stuffy room to purchase his favorite newspaper. He carefully searched the headlines. What caught his attention was a story on page 6A about South Africa. The headline gave Durbish a great feeling and improved his outlook on the situation for the people. It read South Africa would adopt a new constitution. The planned occurrence would guarantee equal rights for all. This is what Durbish's group had strived to accomplish. The plan being proposed by the government would complete its official transformation from Apartheid to democracy.

As he stepped out into the street he sensed a renewal in the people's expressions. He noticed the hard edged looks on their faces had softened. The death of Andras had restored human rights. Sebastian's mission had been a success. Durbish knew all along death or, at least, his imprisonment was a given. He hoped his promise to rescue him was not a mistake.

His return into the hotel lobby was met by a surge of heat. Now his overall outlook gave him a new perspective. The vulgar conditions the people had been faced with had turned from rude violations of civil unrest to the surrendering of the government adopting a new constitution, the proposed agreements would eradicate the old laws, removing obstacles in their way to a free nation.

As he sat in his room, the plans seemed to glide onto the paper, making it less of a chore. His plans joined and fit together in reasonable working order. His plan seemed plausible. Not one of them would be left behind but would eventually succeed in reaching Morocco.

Durbish's nerves felt singed. South Africa would be affected by this new development.

He clipped the article about Africa's party leaders detailing the ratification in a promise, making statements of the protection of the people's rights. The new leader, President Nelson Mandella said in the newspaper, "Victory is sweet." Chairperson Cyril Ramphosa had been quoted by the press to have said, "Today, this is the day when South Africa is truly born." His work on the details of the plan had been completed only hours before the ratification ceremony began. The Constitutional Assembly had worked two years to draft the 150-page document. It had been overwhelmingly approved. After the vote, the delegates leapt to their feet. The Associated Press article further stated there were loud cheers from the delegates, accompanied by dancing and singing. This show of happiness took place in the same Parliament chamber where Apartheid laws were once passed. The pledge given by President Nelson Mandela was, "Never ever again shall the laws of our land render our people apart or legalize their oppression and repression." Other reports from Johannesburg, South Africa, crowned the transition from Apartheid to a Democracy.

The challenge facing the country is very complicated. Unless the government acts to boost the economy by the creation of jobs to spur growth, the constitution's promise of a miracle would truly make a slight difference to the ordinary people. The constitution being no better than the paper it is written on, although an especially important piece of paper, by itself, it could not change things unless the economic challenges are dealt with.

The years Roxmir Andras reined in office and his misuse of power had created a huge budget deficit and caused unprecedented inflation. Job creation is by far the biggest problem facing the newly elected president today. Durbish read the print enthusiastically. The threats of more violence were never versed in any of today's paper.

Considering reactions to the upcoming trial, Sebastian's future was the cause for violence by some radical groups. This fact was a gift and the influence he needed to feel less negative about his and the others' chances of successfully freeing Sebastian.

The President's effort to overcome what the National Party had imposed by Apartheid and rule for the past 46 years would take a massive effort, in view of the less than full withdrawal by the old party members. This gave some negative affect to the new constitutional glory. Speculation on the outcome in any short term rebound of the economy was poor. The members now installed knew the old Nationalists who still had influence and their reaction to the new constitution could spell trouble.

As Durbish continued reading, he was drawn into yet another story of a renewed clash in Monrovia, Liberia, in western Africa. It read the same of the war that was in regression throughout other southern African countries. Another battle involving millions of people was breaking out in the neighboring the Republic of Côte d'Ivoire, 300,000 Liberians had fled their country over the last six years of civil war. This upsurge in new fighting began on April 6th when the State Council had tried to arrest a Krahn fascist leader for murder.

Durbish finished the maps and his plan was complete. He hoped these were his last days to be there. In the morning the three would arrive in Zaire from the United States. Of the three people, his wife, Melonie, would lift his spirits the most. Of course, none of the others knew of their ten month marriage. This was just another one of Durbish's carefully planned arrangements. Melonie had been against their secretive joining, but with his steady persistence she caved into his wishes.

Now that ten months had passed, she found herself under constant stress from the arrangement. She thought her reasons to marry Durbish had been valid, but now as she reviewed them they looked awfully shallow. Her reason for going to Zaire was for Sebastian's benefit alone. Durbish would be surprised by the difference in the wife he left behind over one and a half months ago.

In his hotel suite, Durbish laid out routes and drew maps for the members of the party and Sebastian. Sebastian's escape route would be more complicated than the others in the group. He thought the route was almost foolproof. Sebastian would be on his own except Scott would shadow his friend in a effort to provide extra cover for him and send information to Melonie. Scott was familiar on how this would be done. Scott had helped in various other ways before with others Sebastian had shot. This varied now differently because of the increased danger and involved three other members, which put it on a larger scale.

Durbish placed Sebastian ahead of the rest of the group to form a checkerboard stratagem. As one man moved into an area the others would follow his lead. Sebastian's first and, worst, struggle was to escape Abuja. In the event this failed the game was over and he would be the loser. Melonie's expert hacking skills were paramount. She would have to access clearances when needed, making sure the men stayed out of areas unsafe. The plan called for none of them to leave together. If Sebastian were wounded, it would be up to him to reach his destination. If he were unable to meet this demand, Scott would be there following closely behind him. If there was a reason to surface it would be their fault. Durbish hoped that this would be avoided at all costs. The whole route Durbish had devised would be effectively carried out in a relay out of Africa. A three-way shuffle was the only safe way to ensure all of them escaped. He and Melonie would reach the last destination first. The other three men would have to reach this point safely before they could proceed with his plan. If they made it to Morocco Durbish knew all five of them would make it home.

Durbish had another plan developing in his mind, one that none of the four would survive. Durbish found that this was the perfect time to do what must eventually be done anyway. One day h e is life would be in danger if he did not eliminate Scott, David and Sebastian. On the event the three men survived, Melonie would reach home only to die on American soil along with the others.

The hopscotch across Africa developed by Durbish was a trap or death by hands other than his own. He envisioned their attempt to escape would not succeed. He was sure death awaited Sebastian. His usefulness was over. Scott would die along with Sebastian in a vain attempt to save his life. David, he thought, would be lucky enough to reach his final destination. He would end his life in America. Durbish had a simple plan for him in America.

He already knew two men willing to do his bidding and their desire to step up in the world made them eager to hear from Durbish. If the need arose, the two men would perform any killing for him. Of course, Durbish placed little hope for their future. He would send for them to kill, only to be later terminated by his own method, a lingering, agonizing death.

From his years of increasing wealth brought on by Sebastian killing for him, Durbish was thrilled with the thought of no ties remaining to his organization. He knew he would never have a better chance to eliminate Sebastian. It would never be the same, not now or ever. If Sebastian made it to Washington he would die, there. It was over.

The sweat rolled onto the sheets of paper before him. He made three different plans. It gave each of them a slim chance to accomplish their goal.

Melonie would fly with him to Morocco forming a vital component in his confederation. He hoped she would be successful in keeping all three men moving. If they were able to unite this would be serious. His hopes were to cause an illusion for the others and her, one he wished would not be obvious. He knew to give the men continual help would not be wise, but Melonie's wish would be to see them victorious. Durbish was in the virtual position of playing both ends. All the information would be fed to Melonie and under his supervision. He would misdirect her with false accounts of news and her chore would be to send the men where he wished. He would navigate the men into danger, and she would never know until their sudden death. Unknowingly, she would send her friends into danger, her prudence would be for naught.

Durbish gathered his belongings. It was time for him to be on his journey to Zaire. He had planned on leaving for the airport tomorrow but changed his mind. There were things in Abuja he must take care of for his future escape. Before all the others arrived, Durbish would set in motion the things that would hamper the others' escape. Those who helped Sebastian to escape would die.

He entered the streets of Abuja to fulfill his last transactions at the stock exchange. When he finished, there were preparations to attend to for the arrival of his three associates.

Across the city, Sebastian found himself being transported to a new location in the prison. His new location was a cleaner cell upstairs. He wondered why they had taken him there. He spotted a guard and tried to get his attention. Since he did not speak their language, this was not so easily done. The guard ignored him as he walked past his cell. His attempt to find out information failed all day and into the evening.

He lay on his cot confused and angry, waiting for something to occur.

In another part of the prison the Warden's private line rang. It was a call from Durbish wishing to introduce a doctor from America. The Warden granted his appointment and Durbish hung up the phone saying the doctor would be appreciative for an audience with the prisoner.

From here on out things would be hectic, a sheer scramble for their lives. Durbish hailed a cab as his plans were in motion throughout the city. His mind was filled with unforeseen problems. A sudden smile came across his face as he rode through the streets. The streets were quiet, and he saw no battles anywhere. This and the fact that all his plans would soon fall into place, gave him a sense of relief. Sebastian was the key to the others' deaths.

Durbish asked the driver where he could rent a vehicle. Quizzically, the driver seemed confused. Durbish explained he wanted to take the vehicle across Africa's wilderness, and he needed an exceptionally good form of transportation, like a big Land Rover. The cabbie sped by the old barricades as they set out on a new destination to find a rental vehicle.

Durbish looked forward to his trip away from Abuja. The return trip with the others sharing his problems would also be a nice diversion.

In his rented Land Rover, Durbish stopped to speak with the owner of the hotel. He was assured that by the time he returned the things he had requested would be ready. He chose to leave Abuja and drive all night into the Congo (DRC). Once he reached there Scott could drive on the return trip. This would give him time to prepare the others with his detailed plans.

Halfway to the airport, Wanda's suspicions had not been satisfactorily addressed by Scott and David. Their reasons for leaving had been vague. The two men continued babbling on about meaningless things, not giving her any better idea of where they were going or what they were doing. She thought the two men had planned all of this as an act so Scott could fly to Washington to meet Melonie. Scott tried to assure her there was nothing to be jealous of. It was strictly business. Dr. Weston agreed and completely ignored Wanda. By the time they reached the airport, Wanda was glad to leave the two men behind and just drive away.

Inside the airport, Scott and David had reformed the old bond between them. They thought the whole encroachment by Wanda was hilarious. Scott said he was not so sure she believed them, and he would pay dearly for his antics. He told David he really hated not being up front with her and causing her to be alarmed by his responses. He added, "She is a great woman."

David agreed she was as the two men ordered a drink at the bar. Scott ordered orange juice and in one hour he drank five glasses of it. David had two glasses of brandy. They were amazed at the different types of people and how crowded the airport was on a Sunday night.

Little did they know that once they converged with Melonie in Washington, it would be the start of a spiraling ring of mishaps. The two men boarded the plane with no unordinary delays. In the air, on their way to Washington, both men fell fast asleep.

Twenty-two hundred miles away Melonie was amusing herself with her beloved feline. She was tossing a small ball filled with catnip to the cat for its pleasure. It had taken only a brief time for her to prepare for the arrival of her two associates.

She kept her studio apartment to get away from Durbish so she could handle her business affairs with no distractions. On foot, she was only thirty minutes away from their home or six to eight minutes by car. If she tried to work in their home, Durbish constantly summoned her for some trivial matter. She had grown tired of their marriage. Durbish had fallen short of her expectations. She was glad she had been wise enough to retain her apartment. Before they had got married, she had taken a stand before she agreed to marry him.

The decor of the apartment was simple; unlike the home she shared with Durbish. His tastes were an excessive show of apparent wealth. Her apartment was arranged simply to meet her needs in a computer-oriented profession. For her luxury was fine to a point, but his tastes consumed not only him but the house as well. Durbish had acquired an abundance of both riches and material gains in the last fifteen years. Melonie disliked all the material wealth he displayed. It made her feel she also lived a repulsive life. She knew all Durbish had done was pillage these prize possessions from private sources or so-called respected dealers in arts and finery. She felt the ambience of his showcases of arcane dubiously purchased items compromised her.

Off the record, Durbish had priceless artifacts, some primitive collections from pristine eras. Every article he owned was a quality piece. The home they shared was an aggravation to her. She spent much of her time away, and away from Durbish. His tolerance of her actions were Un forbidding and even encouraged. The marriage was all but over. She had voiced her opinion to no avail.

She played a role sought for his pleasure, her submission to him was as repulsive to her as the house.

Once she returned from Africa with the others, she would resolve her situation. She knew a divorce wouldn't cause any harm to his reputation.

As for any of their friends, no one even knew the marriage had taken place. Everyone just thought the two lived together.

As her cat became tired from rumbling across the floor, Melonie prepared herself for her drive. They would be expecting her to meet them shortly.

She thought if Durbish cared for her there would be no sense in hiding their marriage. If this were the case, things might be different. The men arriving would be more comfortable in the home she shared with Durbish, but the pied-à-terre would have to remain a secret. Her small apartment would serve its duty to house the three of them. In less than twenty-four hours all three of them would leave from Washington to Zaire.

She was uncertain of what lay ahead of them. She could only guess how Sebastian's release would come about. Her love for Sebastian was deep. It was caused by his self-induced devotion into humanistic values. The two of them shared many of the same opinions. Of course, she did not support the fact he was a hit man, but his concise methodical style led her to trust in his concerted belief. This seduction in recantation was known by Durbish, his jealously was pitifully distasteful of their friendship.

Rojo pounced onto the counter and began to clean his fur as Melonie locked him in the utility room. She knew he would be content as she listened to him purr.

Melonie passed through the apartment to the front door, her bags were already packed and placed near the door for their departure tomorrow.

Durbish with no map to aid him, set out across the country maverick-style beginning his journey. His land rover was well suited for this type of travel. The tires hummed wickedly as he sped along on the desert roads. The high-pitched hum reminded him oddly of a hyena's cry. He thought this was another good reason to have such a good form of transportation in Africa. The hyena, a carnivorous creature, lurked in this area of the world. The animals' jaws are very powerful. Like most of the animals in Africa, an encounter would be an extremely dangerous situation.

With the distractions from the last hours spent in Abuja, his decision to leave a day earlier relaxed him. Driving alone, the environment was dominating. He watched the sun's rays ricocheting off the mountaintops ahead of him. As the sun set, his view of the surrounding area was surreal. He was absorbed by everything around him. This overabundance of beauty stimulated his mind.

The outcome for the others was for his own personal gratification which ensured he would be protected permanently. The brilliance of his plan possessed him as the sun fell out of view behind the mountaintops. Durbish knew all the dangerous wild beasts roamed freely in the mountains. Much the same in life he thought, how only the strong survived. He visualized great plumes of smoke rising from behind the mountains and on the ground below smoldering piles of bones. His thoughts retracing deep into recesses of all his disgusting life's past lessons. The bones shattered in huge flames as their sorrow grew from misfortune and sheer bad luck. He drove silently as darkened skies caught remnants of the retreating sun.

Melonie waited in the area provided for new arrivals. She ground her teeth to keep a steady smile on her face. Passengers swarmed through the entrance of the airport waiting area. Dr. Weston saw Melonie first and waved as he and Scott emerged from the dissecting portico. Her smile instantly changed into her glamorously genuine smile. She rushed to greet the two men.

It was forty-five minutes later before all of them left the airport. Stepping outside, a light misty fog blanketed the area. David asked Melonie the time as he set his watch and advised Scott to reset his watch as well. Scott restrained himself from exhibiting his normal characteristics and reset his watch. She announced the ride to her apartment would take about thirty minutes. Scott's concern was for food. Melonie assured him she had plenty of food at her apartment for his consumption.

In the vehicle the group courteously limited their conversation. If any of them were experiencing impulses to mention the upcoming events, they never expressed it. Melonie entered the freeway taking the closest route to their destination. The tension of the situation provided them ample time to reflect on their mission.

She shook a cigarette free from her pack in hopes to ease her anxiety. David detested smoking but politely allowed her to smoke as he rolled down his window. Twenty-three minutes later, she exited the freeway into her area of town.

Smoothly, she maneuvered her car through the streets. The streetlights displayed beautifully manicured lawns. Most of the estates were owned by prominent politicians. "A few of the craftier members of the community have fallen from grace through scandals recently. Their reputations have been damaged by false, malicious statements."

A few minutes later they reached their destination, and Melonie manipulated the car into her parking space. The men took only their carry-ons into her apartment for their convenience.

Scott asked, "What time does our plane leave tomorrow?"

Melonie said, "We will take off at 9:00 A.M. but we must arrive one hour earlier. By 7:30 we have to be ready to leave here."

Scott and David just looked at one another and Scott said, "Gee, Melonie, couldn't you have made a later flight? I'm beat."

She excused herself without further comment. She called out, "The couch folds out into a bed."

Both men stared at the couch, knowing very well one of them would be sleeping on the floor. Rojo leapt onto the couch as David unfolded it. The cat startled David as he saw a flash of red land on the sheets.

David disliked cats as much as cigarettes. He called Jennifer and in an exasperated tone said, "Please, would you mind removing your cat I'm not going to sleep a wink with your cat here, I'm allergic to cats."

"Sure, David. "You're not awfully fond of anything are you?"

"I said, please, Melonie. I'm allergic to cats. I'm sorry if I was rude."

Melonie scooped Rojo into her arms and the cat eyed David with suspicion.

"Melonie," David asked, "How much does your cat weigh?"

"Oh, David, everybody makes fun of my cat, but he is big, isn't he."

"Well, how much, Melonie," David quizzed her in a challenging tone.

"He weighs twenty-eight pounds, David."

"My God," Scott said in amazement. "That's the biggest cat I've ever seen in my life."

Melonie proudly announced that Rojo would sleep in her room. She told Scott she would be right back. She would bring the extra blankets for someone to use on the floor. Moments later Rojo was secured in her room, she picked up the blankets she had placed there for her guests.

As she handed the blankets to David, she said, "I'm sorry for the lack of beds."

"Who cares?" David said. "Just let me settle in a place and I'll find a new day."

"Okay, you guys, the bathroom is down the hall, first door on the right. As for myself, I'm turning in. Oh, Scott, there's food prepared in the refrigerator and in the cabinets, you'll find assorted snacks." She left the living room in their care, saying as she left, "I'll make breakfast before we leave."

"Goodnight," was all she heard as she closed her bedroom door. The illumination from her bedside clock read 12:17. Rojo curled beside the edge of her extra pillow was already asleep. David's invective attack about the size of Rojo had irritated her. Looking at the cat, she supposed he was big. She compared him to the pillow he laid on beside her, his outstretched body was as long as it was. At 12:21 Melonie turned off the lamp on her bedside table. She lay on her bed worried about the upcoming days. She fought to block these uncertainties out of her mind.

The controversy over Sebastian killing the President of Nigeria, as well as his entire entourage had had a negative effect on her. Some of the men he had killed had been exalted since young ages. They were raised for those specific positions in power, entrusted to no one's control but theirs. Seven men, all skilled and trained in exhibiting charm, their shrewd ingenuity had been cunningly crystalized to mollify the larger picture of debauchery.

By 12:30 Melonie was fast asleep, as her cat purred softly beside her. Thousands of miles to the east, Durbish bared down on his accelerator, happy to put a full day behind him. The decreasing miles before him gave way for his mind to unwind. His acceptance of the prevailing mission made him feel like a villain coming out of seclusion.

The challenges he faced couldn't be imagined yet. There were worries he would face dealing with Sebastian. It gave him a sick feeling that he understood Sebastian so well. As infrequently the two men's lives had crossed paths, the encroachment was now dangerously close to Durbish.

Graciously, the plan to release Sebastian was just a show of courtesy. He would be keeping his word. It would mean very little because the outcome would remain the same.

What Sebastian faced now made him draw the last remaining strength within himself to muster up courage and hope to see him through. The upcoming trial was off-handedly mentioned to another prisoner by an orderly as he mopped the floor. Sebastian did his best to ignore them as they made bets on how he would die. Instead, he tried to recall any words that may have been mistaken in his conversation with Durbish. After a while he realized that if he had missed something it wouldn't make any difference to the trial's outcome.

Sebastian knew he was not the beast as he was perceived. He deliberately took a deep look into his past. He had been imprisoned for over a month and had thought extraordinarily little of it. He sat on the edge of his cot and thought of his poor judgment in choices he had made in the past. The chain of events had only intensified his manic-depressive state of mind. From childhood he had always seemed to embroider situations out of kilter. His mind replayed his past life events in slow motion. Compared to his memories of childhood, his incarceration was a cake walk.

He was deep in his memory; he knew so long ago something valid must have caused him to be the way he was now. He whispered, "What?" A feeling arose within him, and he was taken back by an unfamiliar force as he shook in fear. "Why?" Sudden images flooded his mind's eye. Uniformly, he retraced his memory, this exploration was critical. He realized what he saw in his mind was acceptable, but what he was experiencing was hard to believe. It was an age when he was still innocent.

Trembling with terror, Sebastian considered the concept as he tried to find meaningful implications to what all of this meant. He squeezed his eyelids tightly closed, unfamiliar in this area of his mind he saw the inside of his baby crib. It was as if it were yesterday. He was in his grandmother's room against the wall.

His stomach pitched and rolled uncontrollably. As this amazing view surfaced, he felt slightly concerned and very disheartened. He was lying in his crib crying, he supposed he was two years old to three years of age.

All this suddenly became very important to him. He understood now for so many years he had felt fear to this very day. This recreational inspection of it implied outrageous behavior by his jealous grandmother. Forbidden touches and exploration were immediately sensed. This had been buried in his subconscious until now. This host of seduction was permissive. Instinctively, it was shameless, physical manipulation, albeit a seduction he felt sure he was made to endure. To sense he was in the room even as a baby sent Sebastian signals of alarm too deep for him to pass off as unique. His body became rigid as this vision continued. He vigorously sought answers. His essential search for trying to understand the truth was overwhelming to him. He was in dire need to balance his life. He searched for any explanation which would redeem him. This total experience shook him to the very core. Psychologically, he grasped a new awareness for his actions.

He had never felt so stricken, what *caused this revelation was so simple. His grandmother gave him no* supervision. Instead, she had left him alone to cry in total fear, terror administered by a ridiculous degree of hate. Coupled with the hate his own grandmother had for him and his mother Sebastian knew this was true and that it all made sense now, it fit well in the maze of his personal feelings and the feelings of his grandmother. She had deliberately set out to harm him and his mother through means she had access to.

Sebastian was left for her to protect while his mother worked. He realized he had been emotionally abused, he saw an empty room and, in his mind, knew this was the abuse, his vision was proof. Nobody ever appeared she dared not give in giving no aid to the baby in the crib crying.

Sadly, Sebastian knew it was true - what, who and why. Quizzically, he wondered if it was just the lack of affection that had caused so much pain in his life.

He sensed a real relief flood over him. It was continuous and pliable, an opportunity he thought very well could have been programmed at an early age for his degeneracy.

By accident, Sebastian had been so absorbed in his past, he had not heard breakfast being slid under his bars. Blocking out any reason to feel sorry for himself, he ate his cold meal in an equally cold place. Like the cell, the meal gave nothing in value.

As Sabastian ate his lunch the lieutenant appeared. Sabastian continued eating ignoring him. The lieutenant stroked his hand through his small goatee just staring at Sabastian. The lieutenant struggled to keep his composure suddenly stopped stroking his beard. This awareness of his hand in his beard must have annoyed him. Instead, the lieutenant pinched the tip of his goatee delicately between his fingertips as he began to speak.

He carefully chose his words asking Sabastian what gave him the right to kill the president and his loyal followers employed by his office? Sabastian's heart rate increased as the question was asked. The lieutenant deserved a conclusive answer, but the question threw him off guard. Unprepared for the question he tried to respond calmly but his breathing had rapidly increased. This caused him to temporarily lose his composure.

Sabastian's first instinct was to avoid the question. But he knew he had nothing to lose by giving an honest answer.

He said " Lieutenant if I tell you why I killed the president it will put me in a fiercely compromising position. If you want to discuss this matter, it's customary in my country to do so only in the presence of an attorney."

Why, sir, I see your point to wish for a representative of the law present here for you but, I suppose it is purely for my own curiosity I've asked this question. I agree the ramifications could cause you difficulty. My curiosity to hear your reason or excuse to kill those men got the best of me. Their memories are all that remain now.

Sabastian thought about his response and said lieutenant, against my better judgement I'll tell you something off the record if you agree to it. Honestly? Yes honestly. Well fine, to satisfy my curiosity I'll agree to it. Sabastian gave the lieutenant a list of reasons why the so called six prominent figures were cast into the same category with the president.

The association pertaining to the six men with the president was not easy for Sabastian to justify for the lieutenant. Sabastian hoped to clarify to it was not his intention initially to kill them all.

His constant explanation was providing enough reasons for the lieutenant. He exploded into a rage as Sabastian spoke. He shouted at Sabastian to shut up. Then calmly the lieutenant said. "You materialize form know where and the nature of your acts have sent seven men into their grave. As macabre in nature as it was, I find it hard to believe you had no intention of doing just what you did as you did it.

I furthermore don't think you did this without outside help. Sabastian understood how the man fought to make sense of his act and the reasons for the massacre of the whole assembly of men. He spoke without losing eye contact, I freehandedly choose to kill the six men lieutenant, much for the same reasons I killed the president, all of them were guilty of serious acts against the country as well the people living here.

Sabastian knew the man was convinced; his corroborating statements were commonly known facts throughout the nation. The lieutenant did not respond, Sabastian thought he gained some amount of commiseration from his explanation. The lieutenant spoke in a civil manner as Sabastian listened relaxing his posture. He felt better after he told the lieutenant his side of the story. The lieutenant looked wearily towards Sabastian, he said you are not a very good photographer. The pictures you shot were unclear, perhaps you were a better lawyer.

Sabastian wanted to be friends with this man for now, he asked the lieutenant how he learned to speak English so well. The lieutenant informed him of some facts by telling him he had spent time in America. The lieutenant said "I understand the customs of your country and you believe the composition of your reasons. If what you say is not gibberish under the circumstances I'm inclined to believe you in the matter. How you made your choice, I think to a certain degree I even commend your fortitude if this story is not all fabricated.

When he finished speaking, he left without another word, he disappeared down the corridor, his arrogance compromised by his show of understanding, Sabastian's story apparently satisfied whatever the man had been seeking. The lieutenant had not ridiculed him for his comments, this raised hope for Sabastian even though it would not change the outcome of his upcoming trial.

Sabastian wondered if he could be as convincing to give the details during his trial, if he could dissuade one member of the jury the truth behind his killings would be heard one day. Long after his death someone might examen the case and enter the facts correctly. In the history books he hoped one day would show conclusively he had been right in doing what he had done.

History had been made but the heading would remain the same, THE PRESIDENT WAS SHOT.

Sabastian knew his memory in history would remain as it was, he would be remembered as a murderer! Sabastian knew specialists at this moment would be involved in a huge cover up; the truth never would be known. Records that could prove the president was corrupt would all be destroyed, anyone who could gain access to those records could never form a conceive conclusion.

******

Sabastian wished there were a way to recover any records of the president's money laundering activities. If it was unlikely, he knew they would not survive exceptionally long. He tried to think ahead about what Durbish was planning. His voluntary discussion with the lieutenant might have been a mistake. His guess was the lieutenant was fishing for something more than he led onto.

The smiling orderly stood still after the guard watched him slide the tray full of food into Sabastian's cell. The tray was piled high with food. Sabastian was sure there had been a mistake; the tray of food needed side boards to hold it all. The orderly shifted his weight from foot to foot. In broken English he said, "the food was sent by order of the lieutenant." To Sabastian the message was clear the lieutenant undoubtedly had something to hide. He accepted the food from the orderly, before he shuffled away Sabastian handed him some of the fruit. The young, orderly smiled revealing a set of bright white teeth. He slid the fruit into his pockets then whirled around to rush off down the corridor to catch up with the guard. Sabastian could hear them make their way down the steps. His situation in custody for the moment had taken a turn for the better.

Unable to believe his luck Sabastian formed a large pile of assorted foods. He placed some of it in the corner of his cell so the temperature against the wall would serve well in keeping the food cool. For a start he chose a bunch of grapes and two bananas, his taste buds proved to be intact, the exquisite fruits pleased him and his deprived stomach. Silently he ate and wondered why he had been given such a feast, then the thought occurred this was his last satisfying meal before the trial. Depending on the outcome of the trial it also meant these were the last few days he'd spend alive.

Accustomed to his privacy in the cell, he supposed the lieutenant gave him the food to help him relax. If it were known in the prison that he had done this for the killer of the president, the lieutenant might draw attention from administrative members causing difficulties for himself. Sabastian would not say a thing to anyone about the food. If the opportunity arose Sabastian would thank the lieutenant.

Inwardly Sabastian braced himself for the coming events, if Durbish failed, the trail would go on without incident, at least a firing squad was a quick way die. He thought of the prevailing trial and his execution with no real idea of when these events were to take place, he began to feel uneasy. He knew the trail would be quick and things would soon come to a head, his life hung on a thread, for now all he could do was wait. Durbish was on the way to free him.

Durbish clearly pointed out that Dr. Weston would do fine, he stated that he had told Melanie to call him specifically. No one else had been considered. Dr. Weston grinned as these facts were revealed for the group to realize his importance in being there. He said with all the respect directed towards the group his responsibility was not the most perplexing part to him, the fact remained that once the four of them were inside the prison how were the five of them going to just walk off with the most hated person in Abuja?

With all respect, Durbish was not stretching the importance of David's part. The success and deception the doctor must perform was vital. He had to administer a drug to Sebastian that would cause his heart to fail. This was a dangerous procedure, and it had to be done quickly with no margin for error. If the delivery of the drug was an inkling too much, Sebastian would have a massive stroke. This was David's concern that Sebastian's incarceration would triple the complexities involved in estimating the dosage of drug used.

Melonie's participation was also significant. She had to be a decoy drawing any unwanted attention away from David and the situation. It was an intricate plan with many unforeseen possibilities for failure. Overall, the plan was not much better than an outright scam.

The group was now 80 miles outside of Abuja's city limits. All their concerns had been answered, and doubts had been covered. There were no problems remaining and each knew their role. Many questions were answered concerning flaws in the plan. The what ifs was everyone's main concern.

Durbish felt his nerves were shot. He finally closed the discussion, making it perfectly clear that in the event of any misunderstanding or disruption on a whole, each of us will do whatever is needed. "Scott is here for just that reason," Durbish said.

Scott said, "Don't worry, if the plan collapses, I won't let any of you down. You bet you, I'm the last person, besides Sebastian, these people wanna fool around with. If anything goes wrong, just hold your position and do not be in my line of fire. Durbish says the weapon that will be here for me can control any situation quickly."

Durbish had promised Scott an inline over and under 10-gauge shotgun with a grenade launcher. The lead fired from this weapon could tear a person's limbs off. The latitude of the grenades in such close quarters, if used, would have no limitations on the damage it would cause.

Melonie had seen Scott in action. She knew his willingness to use such a weapon. She also figured he hoped he would have that chance; Scott enjoyed these types of situations. She admitted to herself if any one man she had to choose, Scott would be her first choice for a backup. To look at him you would mistake him for a jock, easy-going on the surface, but beneath his outward appearance lay a highly trained operative. He was highly skilled with a level of expertise that was unconventional. He was the only one cognizant of his methods.

The Nazis and Russians have their elite groups. The United States have the Marines, the Navy with its Seals, the Army, and Air Force, then there is the CIA accounting for the world's best classified or unclassified organizations -- as Melonie thought of all these groups, Scott was a one-man enigma devoted to one thing, his pursuit of pleasure in gruesomeness.

Twenty-five minutes away from the hotel, he told Scott to follow a deserted road. He turned to his left onto a barely visible trail, if you were not looking for it the road would easily be missed. The vehicle descended atop a steep hill, bouncing viciously as the suspension bottomed out in a ravine. Scott's remedy for the trouble was applauded as he engaged the vehicle into four-wheel drive. The truck was in an unsafe angle, but with all four wheels engaged he easily maneuvered them out of the ravine.

Durbish looked out the side of the narrow rut filled road and spotted the reason they were there. On the driver's side of the road an ambulance was parked. It was perfectly marked and secure. He told Scott to hold up beside it and the whole group got out of the land rover to inspect the hidden vehicle.

Durbish said, "Everyone needs to hurry, before the sun sets, we all have to put on our uniforms." "None of them are perfect fits, but suitable."

David inspected his medical bag. It was a large bag containing some surgical equipment and medicine for emergencies.

The paramedics' outfits had been laid neatly on the front seat, along with identification papers for each of them.

Drubish said, "From here on out, until Sebastian is safe, we will remain in these roles. We will be considered officials for the U.N. Of course, Melanie, you're the nurse here to assist the doctor, Scott your role is the driver. Now, let's prepare to enter the city." Durbish rushed to get them moving as darkness blanketed them.

Each of them looked the part they had to play; it would serve their purpose to gain confidence of any curious observers. As they all piled into the ambulance, they could barely hear over the grinding starter as the motor made its final protest starting. As it cranked, smoke bellowed from the exhaust pipe. He revved the motor, cleared the carburetor and the smoking stopped.

Durbish was ahead of them in the Land Rover, making the incline, about to reach the main road. Scott gave an efficient amount of acceleration for the ambulance to make the grade. The ambulance and its occupants had no choice but to sway and growl as the vehicle negotiated the hill. Slowly, they made the top.

Durbish waited and waved them on to follow him. He turned on his headlights and they brilliantly lit the pitch-black surroundings. Once Scott gained full control of the ambulance on the road, he did the same thing. Melonie studied each set of IDs, then handed them to her partners to familiarize themselves with their fake names.

Melonie's new identity now became Cheryl Estes, a registered nurse from Birmingham, England. She was a volunteer aid to the U.N. Peace Corps. "Scott," David said, as he read the information to brief him of his new identity, "You are Randall Cope, a university graduate from the U.S. Marine Corps, a technical sergeant. You've been granted permission as a volunteer for a three- month tour for the U.N. peace effort." At last, David read his and exclaimed loudly, "Why, I'm Dr. David Weston!"

Scott asked, "Why would you be you and we are different?"

Melonie reminded both men, "Scott and I are different only for anyone who may be suspicious. If you recall, Dr. Weston is scheduled to visit the prison. And lastly, but no less important, we are in this scheme only as props. Until we get fully organized, we play out this scenario and David, being the physician, will remain under his real identity. It makes perfect sense to me," she said. "Besides, who we are makes very little difference in the overall plan anyway."

"The whole idea David reminded them of the purpose was just for an introduction into the hotel setting," He added Scott, "Remember your flexibility my friend, you will just be waiting for any signs of trouble outside while we're inside the prison with Sebastian. Once we're there, I'll have to make my assessment of the proper dosage to give Sabastian.

You'll be called in by a guard if everything goes well. Melonie will ask the guard to take her outside to get you Scott. As Melonie distracts him you take time finding escape routes inside. Be sure you bring your gun. Melonie will stay in the booth, making sure the guard is well hidden. Once I know you're coming I'll administer the shot to Sebastian. We will act as though we're finished before the drug takes full effect. It's underdetermined how long the drug will be effective. We won't make our way out until it's fully effective. That will leave us there alongside their staff, hopefully."

"David," Melonie asked, "do you think these plans will work or do you think we're all crazy to attempt this."

"Melonie," he said sternly, "This whole damn plan looks doubtful that we'll succeed, but I'm willing to do it for one reason. I owe it to Sebastian." Plus, the fact that the trial is just a formality and he's surely going to die, I'll be damned if I can just not try to help him escape."

"Melonie, you'll need to secure the guard and stay downstairs. Joke around with the guards and keep them busy. I'll have my hands full trying to persuade their doctors of the need to move Sebastian. If they don't buy my story, Scott--I mean Randall has the solution for that. If you hear any loud blasts, be sure to keep the prison operational by whatever means possible. Don't let security get organized enough to shut down the system. If they do, we'll all be trapped and separated.

When you see us coming--if you see us, begin to make your exit as we planned. You drive and Scott will cover our backs. As we leave, Scott, send a few grenades in the corridors to delay their pursuit. That's the worst-case scenario, what we don't want to happen is cause the plan to fall apart. "But" David sighed, "Melonie, if things go right, you'll be downstairs flirting with the guard as Scott and I rush out with our patient having a massive stroke. Overall, it's a simple plan and it's understandable that we'll have a legitimate emergency. Once we have permission for his release form the prison. Of course, you realize they may add a guard to send with us."

"What if that occurs David?" Melonie asked.

"Well, we'll have one guard in the ambulance already and two will just make it cozier." Scott said, "This is the craziest idea Durbish has ever come up with and I smell trouble, but I like it."

The group tailed closely behind Durbish as he pulled into a side street, parking next door to a rundown hotel. All that was said by any of them as they exited the vehicles was how glad they would be to get inside. Their conspiracy was in full progress, now it took a back seat until the group got a good night's sleep.

Durbish said, "We all need a good night's rest." Then quietly, said, "Once we enter the hotel keep quiet about any of this. Don't even speak of it in the privacy of your rooms. We are safe here, but we can't afford any foul-ups. Inside you'll find you can get anything you need. The man that owns this place is very efficient. Each of you will remain in your room until we are ready to depart in the morning. Now, let's go inside and be on your best behavior. A lot depends on it."

They all followed Durbish into the hotel. As the four of them entered, all eyes were instantly drawn to the doctor, nurse and paramedic. The rough interior of the hotel's lobby had not changed Melonie stared at the girls who willingly bared their voluptuous breasts in the bar. The men gathered in the bar were totally unrestrained, they cheered from their satisfaction of the dancers tending the men's tables.

Melonie looked at Durbish totally discussed by what was going on but held her attention on him. He raised his eyebrows as he noticed her dislike for the nude swirling dancers Durbish quickly pulled her alongside of him. Holding her gently, he led her up the stairway. Several minutes later Durbish returned downstairs after being ridiculed by Melonie for his obvious enjoyment of what was going on downstairs.

He joined Scott and Dr. Weston having a drink while a woman danced on their table. The girls who danced had been trained to negotiate their moves with sophistication. Their heels were planted firmly on the tabletops. The slowness in which they revealed their bodies could hypnotize anyone. Both David and Scott were mesmerized by the dancer and unaware that Durbish had taken a seat beside them. They stared blankly as the dancer's routine grew more flirtatious. She bared her breasts and brushed her nipples across each man's face.

Durbish saw Anita and her uncle out of the corner of his eye. He quietly left the table as her uncle led him into the back room. Anita was disturbed by her uncle's sudden disappearance.

She was filled with dread but hoped that Sebastian would return for her soon. She then quietly peeked through the doors to see what was taking place in the barroom. She searched the crowd and, quickly discarding the familiar faces, she saw what she was looking for. She found fresh faces in the crowded room she knew they were there for one purpose, to rescue Sabastian.

Her heartbeat increased as thoughts of Sebastian flooded her mind. She could visualize him vividly in her mind. She staggered as she backed out of the doorway and had to lean against the wall as her breathing was erratic. She tried to catch her breath; she imagined the two of them together again. Not a day or a moment had gone by since Sebastian left that she hadn't believed he would return for her. He had promised that his love for her was undying and that he would return. She knew he had meant those words. Now, with Durbish's arrival and the presence of the two men in the other room gave her some assurance that Sebastian would soon be free.

The timing was perfect. She had read the trial of the President's killer would begin in two days. For whatever reasons these men were here now, their plans must remain secret. She knew these people, whoever they were, would save Sebastian and lead him back to her.

She was unwilling to expose herself to them out of fear of getting killed. She had to purposely act as though nothing unusual was going on. She would do nothing to jeopardize the safety of her uncle. Deep down she just knew Sebastian was going to be saved.

Soon and he would return for her. Juliette's heart was soaring from the renewed hopes of Sebastian being saved. She had a burning desire for him, the flame of love was rekindled, the inferno inside her was entertaining her. Juliette's uncle entered the kitchen and brought her back to reality. When their eyes met, he smiled at her, amazed by the expression on her face. He had not seen her smile in weeks.

With no need for words, her uncle crossed the room and reached out for her hand. His comforting words relaxed her worried mind. Quietly, he told her what he knew. "What we don't know for sure is if their plan will work. Everything possible is being done to save Sebastian, Juliette, and you must be brave for him. The chances for this to be successful is uncertain. The rescue itself or any attempt such as this has never been made. To accomplish what these four people have come to do--"

"Four?" she asked. "I only saw Durbish and the two other men."

Her uncle said, "There is a girl upstairs she's about your age. As well as beautiful she is part of their group and quite talented with a computer. "What are you implying, Uncle. Is the girl more than just a friend?"

Her uncle quickly attempted to diffuse the fury Juliette hid and said, "No, Juliette, that wasn't what I meant. She is a friend, nothing more. You'll see. You know Sebastian much better than I do and surely you believe that he loves only you. Trust me." Juliette left the kitchen. She did not return for quite some time.

Melonie sat staring at the laptop Durbish had supplied for her to use. It had all the bells and whistles she wanted to keep it for her own personal use. This laptop would be destroyed before they fled Morocco. Her objective was to outsmart the heads of state, and other officials in each country the group would pass through. The government personnel involved in trying to recapture Andras' killer would be misinformed all along by her.

The laptop used to its capacity would be their only means to implement their plans. As she stared at the computer in front of her, she felt more now than ever part of the plan. The computer would become her friend and her task would be to use that friendship in a way friends would never use one another. Every one of these men will be depending on me. She now clearly understood it was up to her to gain control of her part in the mission.

As she opened the door, Durbish entered the room perturbed over a trivial matter. It seemed to her to be nothing, but Durbish carried on. "My room has no facilities installed."

Melonie held back her laughter, she listened to Durbish become more infuriated over his predicament. When she could no longer contain herself, she fell back onto her bed roaring with laughter.

As mad as this man was, the sight of his wife rolling on the bed instantly had a positive effect. Durbish joined her on the bed as both broke out laughing hysterically. The two of them were in tears and had to finally force themselves to regain control.

Juliette walked down the corridor and stopped beside the doorway. Since their arrival, Juliette had been quietly observing their every move, something she disliked but felt a need to do. She did not want to sabotage their mission's success. Her jealousy and fear of the other woman had caused her to snoop. All she could hear was giggles and soft whispers. The sounds she heard were Durbish adoringly making love to the woman inside the room. This was sufficient evidence to end her prying. She quietly continued down the hall to the stairs. This episode had set her mind at ease for now. With her doubts quenched Juliette retreated into her room.

In her room she stood naked in front of her mirror. She was inspecting her stomach and an unborn child barely noticeable even to her was growing. Sebastian would be a father; she would have his child regardless of the outcome. She knew her pregnancy could remain secret for just so long. The time was not right to tell her uncle. If Sebastian died, she thought this way his legacy would continue. His child would be revered throughout the city.

Fabulously beautiful as she was Juliette was aching inside for Sebastian. She gently pressed against her stomach, making her feel a part of him. Somehow from this motion a true sense of togetherness was found. She then lay naked on her bed. Comfortable with her own body's sensations, she dreamed it was Sebastian touching her. A faint glimpse of Sebastian's image warmed her senses. The emanation of her pleasure eased her mind. With her needs left unattended and worries binding on her, she was drained. All this vanished as Juliette did a natural act automatically. The pressure released within her satisfied her emotional and sexual desires.

As she lay nude the hotel's construction creaked with the occupancy of others walking upstairs. Few guests stayed over on a regular basis. A few kept companies with the girls downstairs and had for years. With four new people, it would be busier than usual in the morning. As Juliette began to fall asleep, she softly whispered encouraging words to her unborn child. As she stroked her belly, she whispered of how her father had saved thousands of lives and was the bravest man ever. She told the baby how its father let God be his guide in any important decisions.

* * *

Scott and David had two drinks each. They walked upstairs to retire into opposite rooms, down the hallway from Melonie where Durbish was asleep cradling his wife.

David stopped at Scott's door as he opened it both men experienced a surge of adrenaline when they saw the supplies neatly stacked against the wall. David said, "Scott close the door gently," Both men were aware of the smell from the guns. David's impression was that it was a significant display of weapons. "Impressive," Scott said. David said, "Yeah."

David sighed wearily and walked to his room. The moon lit David's side of the hotel. Stirring under the covers he escaped the light shining in the window. The hotel was quiet.

Scott could sleep anywhere; his snoring was heard throughout the second floor. David was turning in his bed unable to sleep. As the clock approached 11:15, Scott snored with less intensity. Determined to sleep David buried his head under the covers. Scott slept in a room filled with guns. There were camouflage tents, pistols, rucksacks lashed to sleeping bags. The weight each of them would carry was at least 70 pounds. The presence of the guns and ammo had not disturbed Scott's sleep. David hoped all his snoring would not set off any of the explosives in his room. Scott finally quit snoring, but daylight was already approaching as everyone got a few more minutes of sleep.

* * *

After a delectable breakfast, the group lounged in the back room enjoying the last minutes remaining before their rescue mission. Outside the hotel, two vehicles bared the weight of all their supplies, their suspensions strained under the load.

The morning had been full of activity. In the early hours, the four of them loaded their supplies. Everything was ready, all that remained to be done was the execution of the plan. The possibility of abandonment would not be considered beyond this point. They were bound now to be inflexible and to do it. Each, in full agreement, now became a united group not an easy conjoining considering their differences in character. They were psychologically prepared to save Sebastian from certain execution.

The volunteers, with all their skills combined sat spellbound, gathered their wits calming their nerves. Not a word had been whispered for over ten minutes.

Durbish broke the silence as he placed a call to the prison. He held the phone waiting patiently before a woman said, "Warden's office." In a matter of moments after speaking Durbish secured permission for David, a United Nations doctor, to enter the prison accompanied by him and his staff. Abruptly, Dr. David Weston heard his name clearly spoken by Durbish, giving the Warden pertinent information and an approximant arrival time.

Durbish advised the Warden, "A group of volunteers will accompany the doctor, a nurse and my assistant." As Durbish completed the call he slid the phone back into its cradle. As he spoke to the group, he consciously did so without any trembling in his voice. "Be sure all of your paperwork is in order, other than that our entrance is granted with the Wardens promise of his full cooperation."

In Juliette's private room her uncle appeared in the doorway. In his hands he held a three-ring binder. He opened the binder displaying its contents to Durbish. Durbish looked pleased and said "The group and significance of the binder's contents would be vital to their success. It listed friends of her uncles, people who would help them hide as they tried to escape the country.

Juliette cautiously holding a tray of drinks handed both men their favorite beverage. Durbish ushered her into the next room instantly Melonie's and Juliette's eyes met. She sat the empty tray on the table. Melonie and Juliette stood beside one another. Each woman introduced themselves. Melonie said her name was Sheryl Estes. Juliette said her name was Anita. Both women were the same height. Their features varied, but both were beautiful women. To gaze upon the two women was quite a sight. Their combined beauty could conjure up pleasingly naughty thoughts. The men in the room were all trying not to stare, dismissing the effects they had on them. Melonie standing beside Juliette could not help but notice her perfect figure, even though she envied her beauty. Juliette was astoundingly well built. Durbish announced, "We have one hour to wait I suggest you find a place to relax. I'll be back shortly."

Juliette and Melonie enjoyed a friendly conversation. Juliette said, "she was bored and had nothing to do". The two of them sat next to Scott, Melonie introduced Scott to Juliette, she called him Randall. As he sat close to Juliette, he found her a pleasure to listen to. Her voice was delicate, every word spoken he savored. He was not listening to the words she spoke, but the sound of her voice was mesmerizing.

Nothing the lovely young lady said registered, Melonie pointed out to Juliette, "Don't pay attention to Randall, he can't help losing what little sense of respect he has for himself, he's a typical male they think with their peniss not their brains."

Scott never flinched the two women could easily predict his intentions. Both ladies said nothing more about him, they were used to men lusting over them and giggled continuing their conversation.

Dr. Weston chose not to rest his nervousness, which was difficult to cope with. He was reading the morning paper as he dealt with his personal situation. He agonizingly forced himself not to dwell on the danger he and the others were about to embark upon.

He controlled his fear, not letting anything break his train of thought. If worrying helped, his tactics reading seemed a successful diversion. The information in the three-ring binder was bothering him as well. If the police arrested Durbish while in possession of the binder, all those listed would be in imminent danger.

The police could easily track them, five fugitives on the run were going to make it hard to blend into a foreign country. Also, the names of people and safe houses, the intricate underground network would instantly be in the hands of the police.

David knew that the information should not be in their possession. The mere existence of the list would ensure many arrests, including the people who helped them now. He could not fathom recording this information. He wondered why it was being entrusted to them. The binder had details and directions to safe houses. These properties were too valued to be so flagrantly displayed.

Durbish had left an hour ago securing their escape, the binder with all its ramifications if found, was just risky. Dr. Weston did not like his life depending on one person's care. Durbish had complete control over their lives and David knew his eyes would be on him just to be sure nothing was amiss. For now, he chose not to mention any of his thoughts to the group, but certain he would in the event of any major screw-up.